HER
LAST
TEAR

BOOKS BY STACY GREEN

HER LAST TEAR

STACY GREEN

bookouture

Published by Bookouture in 2023

An imprint of Storyfire Ltd.
Carmelite House
50 Victoria Embankment
London EC4Y 0DZ

www.bookouture.com

ISBN: 978-1-83790-041-1
eBook ISBN: 978-1-83790-040-4

For Dad
'Stormin' Norman Green

PROLOGUE

The woman moved slowly through the massive three-story home, careful to avoid any squeaky floorboards. She'd memorized every part of the small space that had been a prison cell to her for the past few years. Her lowly spot on the totem pole meant that her room was in the third-floor attic that had been divided into two rooms. She had the smaller room, but it was closest to *his*, since she'd become his latest conquest.

She stole downstairs, her heart pounding even though she knew the other adults in the house were too occupied in amorous activities in the basement to care about her moving throughout the house.

"My little Queen Bee, what are you buzzing about now?" Her mother's gentle, steady voice haunted her as she carefully retrieved the bag she'd packed and hidden weeks ago. Thinking about her mother's nickname for her only strengthened her resolve.

Her own mother had escaped on a night like this, when she was just twelve. She'd fled with her older sister and begged Bee to come with them. A whole world waited for them, she'd said. A world where you can be anything you want instead of a...

Chattel.

If she had truly understood what her mother meant back then, and what would lie ahead for all of them, she would have dropped everything and gone with them.

But she'd been too scared. She'd watched her mother leave and then picked up the phone to call her father at work to tell him what happened.

Mama had promised to come back for her, but that never happened. Her older sister returned days after Mama had left, changed forever, walking around in a dazed state most of the time, quoting scripture to the children and warning them they were all going to burn in hell if they didn't obey the law.

Not God's law. And not the law in the way most people thought of it, either.

His law, the only word that mattered.

ONE

Color exploded in the night sky. Every boom and spray of lights elicited louder cheers from the tipsy crowd. Britney raced through the throng, the smoke and noise from the fireworks barely a blip on her radar. She ducked beneath someone's raggedy-looking American flag, frantically scanning the seemingly endless amount of people settled along the river to watch the fireworks.

Where are my kids?

Thea and Abby had probably walked over to talk to some other kids, she told herself as she pushed her way toward the river. It wasn't like Thea to be irresponsible, but Britney couldn't fathom the other alternative.

She reached the Disney princess blanket the girls had been sitting on and felt her knees weaken. They'd left the snacks and coloring books.

They'd taken the doll and the bag.

Nine-year-old Thea had promised to watch over her six-year-old sister until Britney returned from the bathroom after waiting for what seemed like an eternity. Now her children appeared to have vanished.

Britney scanned the crowd, trying to spot her kids, but she only saw a blur of people. Her stomach twisted into a painful knot; her pulse raced. She couldn't keep her hands from trembling. Every boom from the firecrackers sent a fresh dose of panic through her.

"Thea!" she screamed. "Where are you?"

A few people glanced her way, but most were transfixed on the show and their own kids. "Please, has anyone seen two little girls? They're wearing matching outfits, pink shirts and jean shorts with pink jelly shoes."

"Watch your kids better, lady." A man wearing a shirt with the American flag emblazoned across the front looked down at her with glazed eyes. He reeked of body odor and cheap beer. "We ain't your babysitters."

His beer-drinking buddies laughed, but a couple of the women in the group looked mildly concerned. "We haven't seen them," one woman said. "You should ask security to help you look. I think they're at the back."

The older of the two shook her head in judgment, but Britney didn't have time to worry about her opinion. She ran through the riverfront area, past the music stage and the food vendors, dodging the man handing out enormous chunks of cotton candy.

"Thea," she yelled again. "Abby. Where are you?"

A little girl in a pink shirt, her blonde ponytail swinging from side to side, skipped along behind a group of older girls, oblivious to anything going on around her. Britney rushed forward and grabbed the little girl's shoulder. "Abigail Walker."

Frightened brown eyes stared up at her. Britney dropped the little girl's arm, fighting tears. "I'm so sorry, I thought you were my daughter, Abby."

The little girl whirled around and raced back to her parents. Britney continued pushing through the crowd, her panic rising. "Thea, Abby," she screamed again.

No one paid any attention to her calls. She'd reached the other side of Pioneer Park, where the crowd lining Second Street wasn't as dense. Britney stopped to catch her breath. Tears and sweat blurred her vision, and the panic felt like a noose tightening around her neck.

She whirled at the pressure on her shoulder, grateful that someone had finally paid attention.

"What the hell?"

One of the mime-artists looking to make a few extra bucks had sauntered up to her. His garish white face seemed to glow under the streetlights. He frowned and pretended to cry, pointing at her.

"Are you stupid?" Britney yelled. "You think this is a joke? My kids are gone."

She sank to her knees in the dirt, her hands in front of her face. "Please, God—"

The mime-artist tapped her shoulder and pointed toward the marina, where a Stillwater officer leaned against a parking meter, watching the fireworks. Since she was a little girl, Britney had been taught that outsiders were dangerous. Her grand-mother had regaled them with stories of police raids, drilling into the children that law enforcement must not be trusted. Britney knew now that none of that was true, but her childhood fears waited in the shadows, whispering that the police would only take her children if they managed to find them.

"No." Britney put her hands over her ears, trying to drown out the last booms of the fireworks and the shadow whisperers. She had to find the girls before it was too late.

Britney stood, dizzy with fear and heat. She ran across the closed street towards the officer, who didn't look much older than her. "Please, help me. Someone took my babies!"

TWO

Nikki leaned against Rory, watching the final blast of colors streak up into the sky. Atop his shoulders, Lacey squealed and clapped for each one, gnawing on the red licorice she wasn't supposed to have, courtesy of Rory's brother, Mark.

"Well, Lace, what did you think?" Mark helped his mother get up out of her camping chair. He and Rory had managed to grab parking spots just north of the main festival area, near the trailhead that led to Brown's Creek Trail that wrapped around Stillwater. If they moved fast enough, they would be able to beat a lot of the traffic already queuing to leave.

Lacey started to answer, but an enormous yawn came out instead. The six-year-old had been going at full speed since her feet hit the floor that morning, but she'd finally hit the wall. She gave Mark a thumbs up. Rory laughed and set her down so he could help Mark get their parents settled into their SUV.

"I'm spending the night with Grammy and Grandpa," Lacey reminded him.

"How could I forget?" Rory winked at Nikki. His parents thought of Lacey as their own, and she spent a lot of time with them, but she hadn't had a sleepover for a couple of weeks, and he and Nikki were both looking forward to having the house to themselves.

Across the street, some of the teenagers who'd come to be seen and heard instead of watching fireworks were having a mini photoshoot. One of the girls stopped in the middle of the street for her friend to take a photo of her. She looked pointedly away from the camera, making the end result look like a candid photo similar to celebrity paparazzi pictures.

Nikki hated to see how vapid social media had made girls, and she hated the way Lacey admired the girls' bare midriffs and their constant struggle for attention. Taking pictures was one thing, but to go to such elaborate lengths, in front of a crowd no less, was something Nikki would never relate to. How would this generation of kids ever figure out who they were as people when all they did was emulate trends set by some influencer who hadn't really done anything in her life other than talk on her YouTube channel and get followers? Talk about a get-rich-quick scheme.

"Watch out." One of the blonde girls sneered at a gangly boy walking by. "You're ruining my lighting."

The familiar boy with sharp cheekbones and shaggy hair slunk by the group, his hands in his pockets and his gaze focused on the street. He puffed on a Juul, a cloud of overly sweet, stinking air billowing behind him. One of the girls snickered behind the boy's back.

Nikki moved to say something to him, but Ruth grabbed her hand.

"Let him be," Rory's mother said. "His grandmother said Zach is having a tough summer."

Nikki knew Zach well. Eighteen months ago, he'd almost been killed. He'd survived, but he hadn't come out unscathed. Nikki knew what that was like, and she knew he'd been having trouble the last few months. Nikki had met his mother, Caitlin, when she returned to Stillwater more than a year ago. A veteran reporter, Caitlin had been putting together a documentary on Nikki and her past.

"Caitlin said the same thing," she told Ruth. "She found him a new trauma therapist, but he's still struggling. I just don't want him to get in trouble for something as stupid as vaping."

Ruth patted Nikki's hand. "You can't mother everyone, honey. It's okay to focus on you and yours every once in a while."

Nikki forced a smile. Ruth meant well, but her words could have been said as an insult. Since Lacey's dad had died, his parents had been accusing her of neglecting him, of prioritizing her new relationship with Rory over the man she should have been able to protect.

Lacey had already climbed into the Todds' big SUV and settled into her booster seat, struggling to keep her eyes open. Nikki kissed her daughter goodbye, but Lacey barely managed to reply. She would be sound asleep before the Todds left.

With the fireworks marking the end of the festival, the focus turned to getting out of downtown, which was the same idea thousands of other people currently had. Vehicles inched along, bumper to bumper, with the occasional blaring horn.

"I feel like this year's Lumberjack Days was a success," Rory said to Nikki as they waited in the truck for their turn to leave. "Still wish we'd won the derby, though."

He and Mark had spent two weeks building the derby car, stretching the rules as far as possible. Lacey had wanted to drive the car, but the route was steep and fast, so the city set the age limit at sixteen and older. Rory painted the car hot pink and let Lacey draw her signature bees and butterflies on the side, complete with her messy scrawl. Rory crossed the finish line second, much to Lacey's delight.

"We'll win it next year, Bug," he'd told Lacey. "This year was just a test run."

Lumberjack Days had been a part of Stillwater since the

1930s, when the local townspeople wanted to honor the few remaining real lumberjacks of Minnesota. Lumberjacks had been a crucial part of the state's development ever since Stillwater's founding in the early nineteenth century. The festival had been celebrated for the past seventy-five years, but the last two years of economic turmoil had forced the promoters to cancel the event. This year marked the return of the festival, and judging by the sheer size of the crowd, Lumberjack Days had once again been a massive success.

"Although I feel like there should be a weight class," Rory grumped as they waited to turn. "I mean, the girl who beat me was probably forty pounds lighter."

Nikki laughed. "It's supposed to be fun."

"It was fun," Rory said. "Woulda been more fun if we'd won, that's all."

"Well, Lacey and I had a great time. Thanks for working so hard to make it fun for her." The weekend had been full of food, heat and laughter, something that was in short supply for Nikki most days. She was sad to go back to reality tomorrow.

Rory followed his parents and brother out of the parking lot onto Laurel Street, which connected with the main artery through town, Highway 95, better known as the St. Croix Scenic Byway that stretched well into northern Minnesota. Nikki's hope for a quick escape didn't look possible now. Every open street was jammed with cars, and there were several ahead of them waiting to turn onto Highway 95.

"Turn right instead," Nikki suggested. "Taking the long way around will still be faster, I think." She watched the traffic inching along, with some drivers already blowing their horns.

"Wonder if there's an accident." Rory pointed to the harried-looking Stillwater police officer talking to someone in a red pickup truck. Nikki couldn't tell what the driver was doing, but the officer seemed more interested in the pickup's bed. He finally waved the man on, who promptly gave him the finger.

"What an asshole," Rory grumbled.

Nikki scanned the side streets and realized other police officers were talking to anyone driving a pickup or SUV, instead of directing traffic like they would normally do after a major event. Were they looking for drugs? Nikki quickly dismissed the idea. None of the officers' body language suggested their actions were routine. They moved with a frenetic energy that set Nikki on edge. She spotted a man with dark hair and sergeant's stripes on his uniform talking grimly into his walkie. "Something's going on."

The screeching alarm of an Amber Alert filled the truck. Nikki snatched her phone out of her backpack.

"Thea and Abby Walker, ages nine and six. Both have blonde hair and blue eyes. Wearing denim shorts and pink shirts. Last seen in Lowell Park by the marina during fireworks. Thea is type 1 diabetic. Anyone with information contact the Stillwater Police Department." Rory read the alert out loud, while Nikki hastily called Sheriff Miller. Nikki's stomach dropped.

"Assume you got the alert?" Miller's voice had a grimness that sent a rush of anxiety through Nikki. They had worked together on a few complex cases over the past year, and she'd learned to read him as well as she could her partner.

"Yeah," Nikki answered. "What happened?"

"Mom says she left them for a few minutes right before the fireworks started to use the restroom, came back and they were gone. No one seems to have a clue where they went, despite being in a crowd of people. Stillwater PD is talking to the people who are still at Lowell Park and so far, no one seems to have noticed a damn thing."

"Make sure they're asking people who were nearby if they have videos of the fireworks or the minutes leading up to it. They may have picked up something. Where exactly at Lowell?"

Stillwater's riverfront had been a major construction project over the last decade. The historic Lift Bridge had been converted into a nature trail, and the riverfront around the bridge, including Lowell Park, was one of the city's crown jewels.

"Close to the marina, north end of the park. We're pulling CCTV from P.D. Pappy's right now, along with nearby traffic cameras and the marina security cameras, which are sparse and spread out."

P.D. Pappy's Bar was located right across from the marina, with two outdoor patios that were always full on Saturday nights.

"We've got fire and EMS helping search," Miller said. "But we're at thirty minutes."

She and Miller both knew the drill. If the girls had wandered off, they couldn't have gotten that far. Thirty minutes was a long time for a child to go missing, and in a relatively contained area like downtown they should have been found by now.

"We've checked the port-a-potties, dumpsters, anywhere a little kid might hide."

"What about the water?" Nikki asked. All the marina lights had been turned off for the fireworks, and her ears still rang from the noise. The girls could have fallen in without anyone seeing or hearing a thing.

"We've checked all the docks," Miller said. "We're also trying to look in parked cars, but we can't stop anyone. We don't have enough information to suspect anyone and have the right to search a vehicle. We're setting up a command area over by the old Warden's House, and the Stillwater sergeant in charge, Chen, and his officers are trying to check as many cars as possible from the outside."

Nikki could tell by the tone of his voice he wasn't impressed. "What about the police chief?"

"She's with the mayor, reveling in the success of the festival," Miller said. "She's supposed to be on her way, but Sergeant Chen's in charge right now. He's a good man."

As Rory inched closer to the main highway, Nikki could see the historical Warden's House and Miller's tall form, along with a couple of deputies. She looked over at Rory. "I can't just go home now."

"I know." He sighed and pulled over. "Want me to stay and help search?"

Nikki shook her head. "This place is such a madhouse I don't know how they're going to organize a search." Chen and his officers were likely trying to focus on the vehicles closest to Lowell, but it wouldn't be hard to drive out of the area with the girls in a trunk without anyone noticing. "I'll get a ride home," Nikki said. "If it turns out they've just wandered off."

Rory leaned over and kissed her. "Keep me posted."

Nikki grabbed the backpack she'd brought along for the day and made sure she had her phone. She hopped out of the truck and checked to make sure the southbound lane was still stalled with traffic before jogging across the road.

The SPD and county sheriff had teamed up to promote mental health awareness over the weekend, and the Washington County Historical Society had allowed them to set up their booth in front of the weathered retaining wall at the front of the Warden's House. They'd cleared everything before the fireworks, and Nikki was surprised to see the museum's front lights on at this hour.

Miller paced the small front porch, talking animatedly on the phone. Miller had been chief deputy when Nikki first met him, but the former sheriff's misdeeds had earned him an early retirement. Kent Miller had been interim sheriff, and he'd won the special election by a landslide. The people respected him, and he was fair and easygoing. Being a hometown football star helped, too.

"She's here. I'll call you later." He ended the call as Nikki hurried up the steps. "That was fast."

"We were coming out of the trailhead parking," Nikki said. "Good timing, I guess." She wiped the dots of sweat off her forehead. "What do you need me to do?"

"Chen and I have all available officers searching downtown proper right now," Miller answered. "I was hoping you could talk to the mother. She's a mess, understandably. I'm having a hard time getting her to talk to me."

"She's probably in shock," Nikki said.

"Maybe." Miller wiped the sweat off his face with his forearm. "But it's more than that. I can't put my finger on it, but she doesn't seem to trust anyone, especially me. She wants us to find her children, but she's also very tight-lipped. And she didn't want to be alone with me or Chen. That's why I asked them to open the Warden's House. It was the closest, quietest spot to interview her."

"Is she inside now?"

Miller nodded. "Edie, the property manager, was kind enough to unlock the building and sit with Britney, that's the mother."

He opened a wrinkled Lumberjack Days map, which included a decent map of downtown Stillwater. Miller tapped the grassy area between Lowell Park and the marina. "They were sitting here, and the mom said she went to the public restroom across the street, by the brewing company. Less than one hundred feet away. She was gone less than ten minutes, comes back and they were gone, just the Disney princess blanket they were sitting on left on the ground. The people around just shrugged when she asked if they'd seen which direction the girls went in. Thea also has a homemade pink purse she carries everywhere."

The homemade purse could be an important identifier. "Have we asked if Britney has a picture of it?"

"I thought about that," Miller said. "All the officers searching know, but at this point, with enough time passing, we have to consider an abduction scenario. I'd like to keep Thea's bag off the media for now."

"Good point," Nikki said. "What should I know before I talk to the mom?"

"Her name is Britney Walker, she's twenty-eight years old, married to Doctor Shane Walker, who is on call at Regions Hospital. He got pulled into surgery, and she hasn't told him what's happened yet. She says she doesn't want to bother him."

"Even though his kids are missing?" Nikki asked, shocked.

"Told you, she won't say much to me. The volunteer officer she initially told called Chen and me. Since I was closest, I went to her, and Chen took on the search." He looked past Nikki and waved. "Come tell Agent Hunt what you told me."

A barrel-chested man wearing a Stillwater Fire Department cap joined them. Sweat soaked the color of his navy SFD shirt. "This is Bobby Merrill. He's a volunteer fire reserve and was standing by tonight. He's the one Britney initially asked for help. Merrill, Agent Nikki Hunt with the FBI."

Merrill took his cap off, revealing a sheen of sweat on his bald head. He looked at Miller in confusion. "You just want me to tell her what the mom said?"

Nikki answered him. "Just tell me what you remember. Which direction did she come from? What did she say? How did she act?"

"Uh, I was standing on the north end of Lowell Park in case something went wrong with the fireworks," Merrill said. "I honestly didn't notice her until she was right in front of me. She was white as a sheet, sweating and crying. She ran up to me insisting that someone took her daughters. I tried to calm her down, but she was real upset. She showed me where she'd left the girls. The blanket and snack bag were still there. No girls.

That's when I contacted my superior. Stillwater PD found us within a few minutes."

"Okay, good," Nikki said. "The fireworks were over when Britney approached?"

"Uh, let me think," Merrill said. "Pretty sure the big finale was still going off, because she was hard to hear."

"Fire marshal said the grand finale started at 10:09," Miller said. "Stillwater police reported they'd made contact with Britney at 10:21. They started searching immediately, including Merrill here."

"I was worried about the docks," Merrill said. "They're so close and it was so damn loud. I figured people might not have heard them. Once the police got to us, I walked along the entire dock looking for any sign of disturbance or the girls falling in. Didn't see anything."

"Did Britney tell you when she'd gone to the bathroom?" Nikki asked.

"Right after the fireworks started," Merrill said. "She talked real fast, but I think she figured the line would be shorter then. I got the impression she was gone longer than she intended. But not very long," he added. "I don't want to blame her."

"Of course not," Nikki said. "We just need to try to get our time window as tight as possible. Did she say anything else?"

"Not really." Merrill shrugged. "I got out of the way when the cops came and started searching."

"Thanks for your help," Miller told him. "Check in with the fire marshal. He's communicating with Chen and myself on the search. I'm sure he'll send you somewhere."

Merrill nodded and loped away.

"You coming in with me?" she asked Miller.

He shook his head. "You have your credentials by chance?"

Nikki smiled and unzipped her backpack outside pocket and retrieved her FBI badge. "I'm always carrying."

"Good. I need to meet up with Sergeant Chen," Miller said.

"If we don't turn something up soon, we're in real trouble."

Nikki unlocked her phone and texted Liam. "Caitlin lives in the luxury apartments a couple of blocks away," she told Miller. "Liam's over there tonight. I'll ask him to help search."

Inside the historic building, Nikki could see two women sitting together on an iron bench. The older of the two rubbed the other woman's back while she cried. The dissimilarity between the two women was jarring. Edie, the property manager, looked to be around retirement age and wore her silver hair in a trendy cut. Her pink toenails peeked out of her Keen sandals. Edie was dressed like everyone else today, in shorts and a tank top, revealing her summer tan, but Britney wore dark leggings and a three-quarter-sleeved blue shirt. Her blonde braid hung halfway down her back.

"Hello," Nikki said softly. She held up her badge for both women to see. "I'm Special Agent Nikki Hunt with the FBI. The sheriff asked me to talk with you."

"They called in the FBI?" the gray-haired woman said. "This quickly?"

"You must be Edie," Nikki said.

"Yes, and this poor thing is Britney Walker."

Nikki knelt on the floor in front of Britney. "My family and I were across the street watching the fireworks. The sheriff thought Britney might have an easier time speaking with me."

Britney finally raised her head. Tears stained her pale face. Nikki was surprised at how young she appeared. Nikki fanned herself with her shirt collar and wondered how the young woman wasn't passing out from the heat. "Britney, is there anyone we can call for you?"

Britney twisted the plain gold band on her ring finger. "My husband is an orthopedic surgeon, and he's in surgery. I can't bother him." Her voice was delicate, almost meek.

"You don't think he would understand?" Nikki prompted.

"He told me never to call during surgery," Britney said. "I left a message with the hospital for him to call me as soon as he's done."

Nikki couldn't imagine a father who wouldn't rush to his wife's side after his kids disappeared, but surgeons had to be able to compartmentalize, something Nikki could understand. She would reserve judgment until she met Shane Walker.

"How long have you been married?"

"Ten years. We got married in St. Paul, in a small ceremony."

"Okay. Can you tell me what happened tonight?"

Britney let out a shuddering sigh. "We were set up at the end of Lowell Park, by the marina. I decided to go to the bathroom before the fireworks started. I told Thea and Abby to stay on their blanket and I'd be right back."

"Thea is the older of the two?" Nikki clarified.

"She's nine. Abby is six."

Nikki struggled to hide her surprise. The girls were awfully young to leave them during the festival, especially at night, near the river. "Was the area crowded?"

"Everywhere was crowded today," Britney said. "That was the most open spot I could find, but there were people crowded all around us."

"How long do you think you were gone to the restroom?" Nikki asked.

"There was a line, so longer than I planned. But not more than ten minutes. I got back, and the blanket and snacks were still there, but no sign of the girls. I asked the people closest to us, and they didn't seem to care. No one did. Everyone was too busy drinking and watching fireworks. And smoking marijuana. I could smell it and the police did nothing."

"I know it was dark, but did anyone around you stand out, maybe strike you as odd or off-putting?"

"Everyone around was friendly and focused on their families," Britney said flatly. "Before I went to the restroom, everyone seemed to be in their own worlds. I heard some people start talking about politics, but the rest of their group told them to shut up. That was really the only thing I noticed. I'm not a social person."

Nikki found her small notebook in her bag and a pencil. "You don't mind if I take notes, do you?"

Britney shook her head. "I don't see how that helps you find my children, though."

"For some reason, writing things down on paper helps me remember things better." Nikki scribbled a few notes on a fresh page. "You said you aren't a very social person, which I totally get. What brought you out to Lumberjack Days?"

"The girls saw a commercial about the petting zoo," Britney said. "I really didn't want to come, but they were insistent. I finally gave in."

The petting zoo had closed down before the fireworks, but the children's activities in Lowell Park continued up until the start of the show, and some of the food and drink vendors had still been there after the show ended.

"Did the girls have any money with them? Could they have gone to one of the food or souvenir stands?"

"No." Britney shook her head.

"Okay," Nikki said. "Was there anything they wanted to do today but hadn't been able to? Something that was close by they might have seen?"

"No." Britney slapped the bench for emphasis. "I have told you people, my girls would not wander off. Someone took them. Why won't you listen to me?"

"I'm sorry." Nikki softened her approach. "I'm just trying to make sure we've covered all the details. Is there any other reason you think they were taken?"

Edie continued to rub Britney's back, but she was listening

intently, her eyes on the scared young woman. Nikki debated asking Edie to step out, but she didn't want to override Miller's decision to have her stay.

Britney pressed her lips into a tight line, fresh tears brimming in her eyes. "Because they're gone. Why is that so hard to understand?"

"Okay," Nikki said. "Do you have any enemies? Is there anyone you think would take the girls?"

"There were thousands of people here tonight," Britney shrilled. "Some evil man saw my sweet, blonde babies and decided to..." She pressed her fist against her lips and shook her head.

"We aren't ruling out that possibility," Nikki said. "But statistically, stranger abduction is far rarer than crime shows want you to believe."

"I don't care," Britney said emphatically. "Everybody keeps telling me that they wandered off. Well, Thea doesn't wander. She's diabetic... she knows better. That's why she has the pink purse. I made it for her so she could have emergency insulin. And Abby stays with her sister, no exceptions."

Nikki wasn't an expert on juvenile diabetes, but she knew time was of the essence. Thea would surely need insulin by morning. "Does she know what her insulin dosage is?"

"Yes," Britney said.

Nikki had a bout of gestational diabetes with Lacey, and she'd been so afraid her baby would end up diabetic. "Do you have any sort of system in place if you get separated? Do they know your cell phone number?"

"They know to go to a police officer if we are separated and ask them to call me. Thea would never do something like this. Abby follows her sister, always. She's just a quirky little girl who loves pineapple pizza and bugs, but she knows it's important they stay together."

Maybe not, but they were close to the long, steep stairway

that led up to Pioneer Park, which provided stunning views of
the river. A new playground had recently been installed, and
there were plenty of places on the big hill for the girls to
wander, but not enough for them to get lost, at least not for long.
Nikki hoped they hadn't tried to climb the historical stairs by
themselves, in the dark. A fall down more than a hundred steep
concrete steps could easily kill someone.

"Is there any place the girls might go if they were in trouble?" Nikki asked.

Britney shook her head. "No, other than where we parked.
Thea wouldn't just leave and start walking back to the car. She
probably doesn't even remember where I parked, we were so far
away. I told the black officer where we parked."

Nikki thought she detected a tone in Britney's voice, but she
didn't press it. Now wasn't the time to reprimand Britney or
question her ethics. Finding the girls trumped any bigotry.

"Then I'm sure Sheriff Miller's got people checking that
area as well," Nikki said, emphasizing the title. "He's very good
at his job." She took a copy of the Lumberjack Days brochure
out of her bag and opened it to the map of historic downtown
with the various events. She handed it to Britney. "Can you
show me exactly where you were on this map?"

Britney wiped her eyes and pointed to the grassy area
between the lumberjack stage and the marina. "Right here."

She'd pointed to the same area when she'd told Miller, and
her story didn't appear to have changed. "I'm sure we'll find
them," Nikki said. "They couldn't have gotten too far." Unless
they'd decided to go on the docks and had fallen into the water.

Earlier that evening, Nikki had noticed bright, smaller firecrackers being set off from boats just a few hundred yards
offshore. The girls could have decided to try to get closer while
their mother was in the restroom. The booms of gunpowder
would have masked the sound of someone falling into the river.

"Who would the girls feel comfortable leaving with?" Nikki

asked.

"I don't know," Britney snapped. "No one... because of the diabetes I don't leave Thea with anyone as long as I can help it."

"How many people know Thea is type 1?" Nikki pushed her.

"We don't advertise it," Britney said firmly. "I don't know what you're getting at, but Thea and Abby wouldn't leave with anyone. And they both know how dangerous strangers are."

"Attention, everyone." Miller's worried voice came through the PA system that had been set up for the event and through the screen door of the Warden's House. "We're looking for two girls, ages nine and six. Thea and Abby both have blonde hair, and Thea is carrying a homemade purse. Girls, your mom is waiting at the sheriff's booth, near the pavilion by the river. If you see a police officer or fireman, ask them to bring you to your mom."

"Is that it?" Britney demanded. "Isn't he going to stop people from leaving? He's just going to let people drive out of here when my babies are missing? Someone has them, I'm certain of it."

Telling the distraught mother that the police couldn't just stop cars and look without probable cause would only upset her further. "Sheriff Miller and Sergeant Chen have every possible body on this. Fire and Emergency Medical Services are helping search, too."

The front door creaked open. "Nikki, we're getting together for a briefing outside. Could you join us?"

Britney stood on wobbly legs. "Did you find them?" She looked past Miller, her gaze fixed on the wall.

"No, ma'am, but we're not going to stop looking. I'd like Agent Hunt to help us figure out our next steps, and then she'll come back to talk to you some more."

Britney sank back down onto the bench and put her head in her hands again and started to cry.

THREE

Nikki promised Britney she would be back if there was any new information and headed outside to meet Sheriff Miller. He stood in the middle of the sidewalk, surrounded by other emergency personnel and Liam, in baggy cargo shorts and a white Vikings shirt.

"This is Agent Nikki Hunt with the FBI," Miller said. "She was in the area tonight and we're lucky to have her help. As some of you may know, she's a decorated criminal profiler and has worked several major cases involving missing kids. Her expertise—and her team's—is invaluable. You've already met Agent Wilson."

"Miller just brought me up to speed," Liam said to Nikki. "How's the mother?"

"Still in some shock, I think." As Nikki walked down the old stone steps to join the group, she felt like she'd stepped back in time and had entered the FBI Academy all over again. The other men with Sheriff Miller watched her with trepidation, especially the short, stout man in a Stillwater police uniform. His stony expression radiated distrust. Miller nodded in the officer's direction.

"This is Sergeant Chen. He's in charge of Stillwater PD's investigative unit."

Chen's black hair was slicked back and sweat glistened on his forehead. He shook Nikki's hand with a sigh. "Agent. I'm so glad there are two of you here now."

She caught Liam's eye, waiting for Chen to say they didn't need her help, that the Stillwater Police Department was fully capable of finding the girls, but to his credit, he kept silent and focused on Miller.

"Doctor Shane Walker is the father?" Liam asked Miller. "Is that the same Shane Walker who's the team physician for the Vikings and the orthopedic consultant for the Timberwolves?" Miller nodded. "He's the one who operated on their star player's knee and oversaw his rehab. Sports media acts like he's some kind of God for saving the season."

"Yep," Miller answered. "So, if we don't find these two little girls, this is going to be about as high profile as it gets."

The outdoor lights at the Warden's House provided enough light for Nikki to see everyone's expression, and they all looked as grim as Sergeant Chen. Miller introduced her to the assistant fire chief and the EMS supervisor who'd joined them.

"Thea and Abby were last seen fifty-three minutes ago," Miller said. "Sergeant Chen's officers have searched all the port-a-potties and dumpsters in the area, along with the playground and nearby parks. They also spoke to the few people who were still in Lowell Park after the fireworks, and no one remembers seeing the girls. Everyone was paying attention to their own family."

"What about the stairs and Pioneer Park?" Nikki asked. "It's a climb but the girls were close by."

"We checked the area," Chen said. "The crowd on top of the hill was smaller and still hanging around when the fireworks were over. No one saw the girls."

"Thea is a type 1 diabetic," the EMS supervisor reminded

them. "She needs to be found before she's due for another dose of meds."

"She has emergency insulin," Nikki told the group. "She knows how to administer the dose, so we have some time, but that isn't my primary concern." Her gaze drifted to the St. Croix River. Roughly a hundred boats were anchored in the marina, and the docks were poorly lit. Three days of heavy rainfall last week had caused the river to rise. They were nowhere near flooding, but the current moved at a steady clip. The current had yet to slow to its normal rate. If the girls had fallen in, Nikki worried they would have little chance.

"We're getting closed-circuit video from P.D. Pappy's," Chen said. "Along with security video from the brewing company and the marina."

P.D. Pappy's was located across from the marina, and it was likely their best shot at catching the girls on film. The marina was woefully lacking on security cameras, although the police had just received a large grant to install several new ones. "We're trying to find people who remember seeing Britney to establish a timeline, too," Chen said.

Nikki caught his underlying message. He wasn't blaming the mother, but a lot of people didn't have a good sense of time on their best days, let alone during a trauma. She may have been gone longer than she realized.

"We need to start thinking about the water," Miller agreed. "I'm in contact with the dive team captain. Given the situation and proximity to the river, we both think that if the girls or some information about their whereabouts doesn't turn up in the next fifteen minutes, we need to get people in the water to look for them."

Everyone in the small circle looked somber. Enough time had passed that if the girls had fallen in, this would be a recovery mission, not a rescue. Drownings weren't uncommon, sadly, but they usually involved alcohol or a lack of respect for the water's power. Accidents still happened, but not on the riverfront, in full view of everyone. Even with the fireworks, how could no one have seen the girls?

"What about your people?" Chen asked Miller.

A handful of sheriff's deputies had worked the festival, with the bulk of them handling everything else in the county during Lumberjack Days. "I've sent the girls' photo and information to all of them. They'll check any vehicle stopped for a traffic violation, but we can't open a trunk without probable cause, nor can we set up checkpoints since they're illegal here. What did Britney tell you?" Miller asked Nikki.

"She's pretty shell-shocked," Nikki said. "Her husband is in surgery right now at Regions, and she's adamant that he isn't bothered until he's finished. I'm not sure how to take that right now. She insists that Thea is responsible and would never wander off so she's confident we're looking at a kidnapping."

In Nikki's experience, the kids who wandered off and came back had usually given their parents a scare before, and when a parent insisted their child was responsible and knew better, the parents usually turned out to be right. Enough time had passed that the odds of the girls getting distracted in the crowd were slim, especially given their ages and Thea's diabetes. Crowds like this were every cop's worst nightmare, and the late hour made the situation worse. Slipping away from the crowd, with most attention focused on the fireworks, would have taken some skill and a calm head.

"We need to get her out of the immediate area." Worry clouded Chen's soft baritone. "I'll have one of my officers take her back to the police station. Her husband can meet her there."

They all knew the meaning behind his words. No parent needed to witness their child being recovered from the river.

"If it's possible, I would suggest having a female officer escort her," Nikki said. "She seems to be more trusting of women."

"Edie offered to stay with her until the husband arrives," Miller said.

Chen nodded. He tapped the mic on his shoulder and directed one of his officers to pick the two women up at the Warden's House and take them back to the station. The Stillwater PD was small, but it was closer and less likely to be surrounded by traffic.

Nikki debated offering to go with the two women, but she wanted to remain at the scene to help search and deal with the media that would no doubt descend as soon as word of a dive team reached them.

"I'm also sending a deputy to the hospital," Miller said. "I want to make sure Shane Walker is interviewed as soon as possible."

Chen's phone trilled with a message. The color drained from his face as he read it. "One of my officers found a pink, fabric bag in Trinity Lutheran Church's parking lot two blocks over. It's one of the main parking lots for the festival, with a fairly easy exit. Mostly empty now, which means thousands of people have tramped through there to get to their cars on the way home, and if they were in a car that was parked up there, they're long gone."

Nikki grimaced. She went back inside with the female officer who'd just arrived.

"Britney, this is Officer Tidwell. She's going to take you and Edie over to the police station. It's more comfortable than these benches, and Shane can meet you there as soon as he's able. The sheriff is sending a deputy to make sure he arrives safely." She hoped her meaning was clear to Britney. Shane Walker needed to be informed that his daughters were missing.

Nikki hated thinking the worst, but more than an hour had passed since the girls disappeared. If the pink purse had been found near the marina, the gnawing feeling in Nikki's gut wouldn't be so strong. Thea had the purse when she was last seen, and she knew the importance of it. She obviously hadn't taken it near the water. She likely would have realized that she'd dropped it, and the lot was travelled enough that someone should have seen the two little girls. Nikki was sure the girls had been kidnapped.

Nikki left Britney under the watchful eye of Officer Tidwell and headed outside to catch up with Chen and Liam.

"Lucky your girlfriend lives so close," Chen commented. "She's a big-time reporter, right? Is she out here searching, too? Better make sure she doesn't overhear any sensitive conversations. The last thing these girls need is a reporter sharing sensitive information on television."

"She's not here," Liam answered. "Her son will be home in a little while. And you don't need to worry about conflict of interest, Sergeant." Liam's testy tone surprised her. He was usually the one pulling her temper back from the edge. "And the last thing she'd do is run a story that would put the girls in more danger."

Liam stalked ahead, his long strides impossible to match.

"Britney's headed to the police station." Nikki fell into step beside Chen as the three of them walked quickly, tension radiating between the two men. Given the dire situation, her tolerance for butt-hurt male egos was minimal.

"Look, Sergeant Chen, I get the sense you don't want us here," she said. "I have no interest in running the show or taking credit for finding the girls. We're here to help."

"Sheriff Miller made that clear," Chen replied sharply.

Nikki counted to ten before she snapped back, trying to find some common ground with Chen. "I'm sure you're under immense pressure with the festival. I know it's important to the city that it's a success, and the last thing any cop wants is for a child to disappear on their watch. You do your best, but sometimes things are out of our control. We aren't here to judge or question your abilities. We just want to help."

"This is the worst possible scenario," Chen said, his tone softening. "A child disappearing is bad enough, but in this situation, with so much traffic and so many possibilities... it's overwhelming."

"It is," Nikki said, hoping to smooth things over between them. "No matter how prepared you are, when something like this happens, it is overwhelming. The Bureau is here to help any way we can."

Chen grunted. "Yeah, well, like I said, Miller is in charge. The chief of police told me to let him run with it. We're just supposed to be on traffic duty, basically."

Nikki had yet to meet the newly elected female police chief, but she'd heard through the gossip channels that the woman was focused on the police department's image and funding, leaving her captains to make the investigative decisions. Nikki doubted that would remain the case if the girls didn't show up soon.

"Well, I assure you Miller won't push you out of the case," Nikki said. "He only cares about finding the girls. We need every capable officer on the streets."

Chen stopped walking and looked at her. He was only an inch or so taller than Nikki's five feet seven, and the lack of wrinkles around his eyes suggested he was closer to thirty than forty, which likely meant he was relatively inexperienced with situations like this one. "I really thought they must have gone into the river. Not at first, but when they didn't show up..." His voice trailed off and he started walking again.

"The purse being west of the river means the girls had to have gone in this direction." Liam spoke without turning around or slowing his pace. "Why would two little girls try to get through a crowd like that?"

"Britney may have been gone longer than she realized, and they went looking for her?" Nikki said, though she doubted it. "That's why I would ask the public who were in the area to go over their phone videos before and during the fireworks. It's a long shot, but we might catch the girls leaving on someone's video."

"So they decide to look for mom, and someone grabbed them and took them to their car," Chen theorized. "Thea accidentally dropped the purse—"

"I don't know," Nikki said. "Britney is pretty insistent that Thea knew how important the purse was if they were separated. Thea knows dropping it means that she could get really sick, really quickly. She knows her insulin dosage."

"Maybe she did it on purpose," Liam said. "To let her mom know someone took them."

"Maybe," Nikki said. "Or she was dragged into a car and the bag got lost in the shuffle. Still seems like someone would have seen something. Not everyone stayed for the fireworks. The area was busy. It just doesn't make sense."

Commercial businesses flanked both sides of the lot, and the area was well lit. If Nikki was going to kidnap a child, she wouldn't have parked in such a trafficked area. Maybe the kidnapping hadn't been planned, or the girls were taken past the lot and onto one of the darker side streets to a waiting car. Britney claimed the girls wouldn't have left with anyone else, so the girls wouldn't have gone willingly.

Nikki recognized the Stillwater Police Department's small evidence response van, fighting the urge to call in her own team. This was Chen and Miller's case. Both the SPD and sheriff's office had competent evidence response teams, but Miller often sent forensic evidence to the FBI's lab. She hoped Chen would do the same, without Miller having to step in and overrule him.

The mostly empty parking lot had been blocked off with police vehicles, and crime scene tape was being strung across three parking spaces that butted up to a manicured curb. Crime scene technicians appeared to be searching for signs of blood or other evidence.

The bright pink purse lay on the ground, the small strap half in the bush. Nikki could tell Britney had considerable skill as a sewer—the seams were finely stitched with white thread. Thea's name had been stitched on the side in a very pale pink, with a white daisy next to it.

The reality of the moment settled over her. Britney had made this bag for her daughter, who treasured it deeply. If she and Abby had gone off by themselves and gotten lost, Thea wouldn't have just dropped the bag. And Nikki highly doubted two small girls could have walked this far away from the festival without someone noticing.

"This doesn't make sense," Nikki said to Miller as the forensic technicians began their sweep of the area. He handed her a pair of latex gloves. Nikki snapped them on and knelt next to the bag; Chen did the same.

Liam stayed on the perimeter, hands in his pockets, his head swiveling back and forth as he scanned the area. Nikki didn't have an extra pair of gloves to offer, and considering Chen's worries, it was probably better if just one of them worked the scene.

Nikki gently unzipped the bag, praying the insulin wasn't there, that Thea had taken it with her when she'd inexplicably dropped the purse. "It's empty," she said. She looked at Chen and Miller. "Britney insists Thea knows how important this purse is; she knows how to administer the insulin. She wouldn't have dropped it and left it under normal circumstances. Sergeant Chen suggested Thea did it on purpose to leave a trace behind, which is plausible, but this area makes no sense. How were they not spotted?"

"Good question." Miller gestured to the short distance to the curb. "Do we believe Britney that there was no one they'd have left with willingly? If they were taken, chances are strong it was by someone they knew. If that's the case, the girls likely would have gone with them, and there may not have been any struggle to see." He pointed to the six-foot-tall hedge that bordered the northern end of the lot. "If the vehicle was backed in, they could have put the girls in the car and driven away with no one noticing."

"Maybe Thea knew they were in trouble and didn't want to make the situation worse," Liam said. "She took the insulin and dropped the bag."

"We need to bag the purse for prints," Miller said.

"That's felt," Chen said. "Tricky fingerprinting."

"I'll send it to the FBI lab," Miller said. "They'll get the prints."

Chen made a face but didn't argue. Nikki caught Liam's hostile glare at Chen and shook her head. They didn't have time for egos tonight.

"You're certain Shane Walker is in surgery?" Nikki asked.

Miller nodded. "Deputy confirmed he went in well before the fireworks. He should be finishing any minute. They'll bring him back to the Stillwater police station." He looked at Nikki. "You two want to handle that while Chen and I run things here?"

Stillwater PD worked out of City Hall, less than two blocks from the church's parking lot. "We need to contact Trinity Lutheran for their security videos. Tomorrow's Sunday, so the church will be staffed in the morning." Chen addressed the group. "We can actually see the church parking lot from the break room. Soon as someone arrives to unlock the door, we'll send an officer over."

"Sounds good." Nikki and Liam crossed the street, and she took stock of the businesses. "Post office, a bartending school, a furniture store—they should all have security cameras of some sort. If we can match the time-stamp, we may have an image of the kidnapper's vehicle as it left."

"I doubt it," Liam said. "The purse was found on the east side of the church, and the vehicle was probably hidden by the landscaping." He hooked his thumb over his shoulder in the direction of the church. "If the person parked where that purse was found, it's an easy out onto Third Street. Maybe we'll get lucky with CCTV, but don't count on it."

His wrinkled cargo shorts revealed his pale white legs, which were desperately in need of color. At least his shirt looked better than some of the T-shirts she'd seen him in when they were off duty. Liam was normally a stickler about how he dressed, but every once in a while, he surprised Nikki.

"You're blinding me with all that skin," she teased.

"Sorry." Liam flushed red. "I was at Caitlin's. Hadn't planned on spending the night but one thing led to another..."

Caitlin and Liam had been together for nearly a year now.

"How's Zach doing?" she asked, thinking of the skinny boy she'd seen vaping earlier. Caitlin had made sure Zach had all the mental health resources he needed after his ordeal, and for a while, he did better than anyone expected.

"Not great," Liam said. "He's been having the nightmares again." The nightmares had started a few days after Nikki rescued Zach, but after a few months of intense therapy, meds and a lot of love from family, they'd stopped.

"What happened?" she asked.

"He started having trouble in school second semester, mostly with math, and it's just gotten worse from there. He tells Caitlin and the therapist that nothing has changed except the dreams coming back..." Liam shook his head. "He did work at one of the food vendors today, so he's doing something this summer other than staying home."

Liam and Zach got along well, as long as they weren't alone. Zach still had trouble being alone with male authority figures. Like Nikki, her partner had worked with enough trauma victims to navigate the situation with Zach better than the average person, but she knew it was hard for Liam. He wanted to fix everything now, and life just didn't work that way.

"Things okay between you and Caitlin?" Nikki asked. Liam was usually the optimistic one, even-keeled and patient. His tense posture and sharp tone this early in a case wasn't like him.

"Yeah," he said. "We had an argument. It's fine. Just frustrating."

"I know the feeling," Nikki said. "It seems like the worst arguments are always over the stupid, petty stuff."

"Tell me about it."

Before they went inside the police station, Nikki called Courtney. "Dude, it's past midnight." Courtney's groggy voice came over the line. "Someone better be dead."

"Not yet," Nikki said grimly. "Two little girls disappeared during the fireworks."

"Hang on."

Nikki heard shuffling on the other line, followed by an unfamiliar woman's voice. "I take it the date went well."

Courtney laughed. "That it did. I'm glad I swore off men for a while. Anyway, tell me everything."

Nikki ran through the night's events. "They bagged some evidence from the parking lot, but it's such a heavily trafficked area. The pink purse is the priority. It's homemade, like a felt material. We're hoping you can work your magic and get the most perfect, shiny print."

The last part was a running joke between the team. Courtney was one of the best forensic investigators Nikki had worked with in her twenty-year career, and she had cracked some tough cases for them. If a perfect print was there, Courtney would find it.

"Felt?" Courtney said. "Who uses felt besides kindergarten teachers?"

"I can barely use a safety pin," Nikki said. "Don't ask me.

Listen, I'm sorry to push, but Miller's evidence guy is on his way to the lab with the purse."

The FBI building was closed to the public, but law enforcement officials with verified credentials were allowed to bring evidence to the lab at any time. Courtney normally didn't clock in until Monday morning, but this case couldn't wait that long.

"I'm up," Courtney said. "I'll be there in half an hour or so, but don't expect to hear from me until morning. Fingerprinting fabric takes a minute."

FOUR

Nikki entered the tiny conference room at the Stillwater Police Department. A dark brick building, it looked eerie at night, especially with only a couple of lights in the windows. The SPD was usually a hubbub of activity, but most officers were out searching already. Britney paced back and forth in the room, while Edie worried her fingernails to the quick.

"Did you find them?" Britney asked Nikki urgently, her hands shaking.

"Not yet." Nikki sat down at the conference table and motioned for Britney to do the same. For some reason, she'd been conditioned to make sure someone was sitting before bad news was delivered, as if that somehow made the news easier.

"Police found Thea's purse in a parking lot a few blocks west of the river," Nikki said, her gaze on Britney. "The insulin was gone."

"I told you," Britney said, her voice shaking. "I told you someone took them."

"It's a possibility." Nikki chose her words carefully. "Right now, we know they were in that area, so we can narrow down witnesses and find out if anyone who was parked there saw them."

Britney rocked back and forth in the chair. "I can't believe this is happening." She shivered. "Why did this happen to my babies? Why would anyone want to harm a child?"

"That's the million-dollar question, isn't it?" Nikki wished she'd brought a change of clothes. She felt sticky from the day's heat. "I've been doing this over twenty years, and I still don't have a definitive answer, I'm afraid." That wasn't entirely true, but Nikki wasn't about to pile onto the horrors already going through Britney's mind. She prayed they found the girls before the worst could happen. "I know we've asked this already, but is there anyone else they might have trusted enough to follow?"

"I told you, no."

"What about a babysitter? Someone they might have run into and been excited to see? An old teacher, maybe?"

"I homeschool." Britney seemed to be debating her next words. "We have a part-time tutor/babysitter. Alyssa came with us today, but she left for work hours ago."

"Alyssa?" Nikki asked. "You didn't mention her before."

"I didn't even think about her until you mentioned a babysitter."

"Where does she work?" Nikki had lost count of how many missing children's cases she'd worked, and it wasn't unusual for a parent to forget small details due to shock, so she reserved judgment on Britney's faulty memory, for now.

"At Kincaid's," Britney said. "It's a steakhouse. Fish, too, I think. I don't like eating out. Alyssa works there weekend nights and helps out with homeschooling the girls three days a week. She'll babysit on the weekends sometimes if Shane and I go out to eat or something."

"And what do you do?" Nikki asked, realizing that she'd assumed Britney was a wealthy surgeon's wife, but hadn't asked.

"I'm a homemaker." Britney sounded defensive. "Just

because I'm a stay-at-home mom doesn't mean I don't need help. Shane works long hours, and sometimes I need a break. I'm also taking a couple of online courses." She grabbed a tissue from the box on the table and wiped her eyes.

"You don't need to justify that to me," Nikki said. "It takes a village to raise a child. Do you know if Doctor Walker's out of surgery yet?"

"He's on his way," Britney answered. "I've never heard him so upset."

Nikki glanced at Edie, debating on how much she could ask in front of the woman. She didn't want to contribute to speculation, but Edie appeared to have a calming influence on Britney. "What about extended family? Grandparents, uncles and aunts?"

"We don't have any." Britney looked down at the table.

"You have any family at all? Either of you?"

Britney worried her lower lip, her gaze darting to Edie. "Um, I would feel more comfortable speaking privately about our families."

Edie looked relieved and stood. "I need to check in with my husband. Agent Hunt, did you need me to stay?"

Nikki debated the question. "I might. I'll come find you in the lobby when I'm through here."

"Thank you for staying with me," Britney said softly. "And for your prayers."

"I will continue to pray for your babies until they're home safe." Edie patted the woman's shoulder and slipped out of the room.

Nikki waited for Britney to begin. The young woman tapped her fingers on the table, her nervous energy radiating through the room. "Shane was an only child, and his parents have both passed. My family's more complicated." Britney picked the chapped skin on her lower lip. "My mother died when I wasn't much older than Thea. I was the black sheep of an extremely religious family. I escaped after I met Shane."

"You escaped?" Nikki echoed.

"Left," Britney said. "It felt like an escape."

"And you haven't spoken to any of your family since then?"

Britney shook her head. "And it's going to stay that way."

"Forgive me if this seems intrusive," Nikki said. "Why don't you speak to your family? Do they know where you and Shane live?"

"I'm excommunicated," she answered. "They don't speak to me. And no, they don't know where we live. I decided a long time ago that would be best."

Her matter-of-fact tone unnerved Nikki, but she understood Britney's need for control and compartmentalizing.

"Why did I bring them here?" Britney pushed her chair away from the table and drew her knees to her chest. "I never do stuff like this."

"You mean to the fireworks?"

"I mean leaving our neighborhood," Britney answered. "I don't like getting out around strangers, but I've been trying to do better. It's not fair to the girls for us to just sit at home all the time. I don't want them growing up being terrified of the outside world."

Nikki guessed there was more to Britney's reclusiveness than just not liking strangers. "Are you afraid of strangers? Or is it just big crowds with too many people?"

Britney didn't answer immediately, instead chewing on her fingernail. "Agent, I was taught since birth that anyone outside of my religion is going to hell and beneath me in every possible way. I've spent the last ten years trying to retrain my brain to look at the world differently, and I've made a lot of progress. But going to the fireworks was a big step, and now I know I shouldn't have taken it."

"It's okay," Nikki soothed. "What about parks and playgrounds? Do you have any favorites?"

"In our neighborhood," Britney said. "It's gated."

"Where do you live, exactly?"

"Eden Prairie," Britney said. "It's a perfect, quiet little neighborhood, with nice people who don't pry."

Located southwest of Minneapolis, Eden Prairie was one of the wealthier suburbs, with gated communities, good schools, and plenty of affluent people.

"You drove from Eden Prairie?" Nikki asked. "Not with Alyssa?"

Britney nodded. "She met us here. My Tahoe is still in the parking garage. I told the Stillwater police about it. They checked for the girls, right? It was a walk but Thea's smart and could have found it."

"They checked and have posted an officer there in case the girls show up by your vehicle," Nikki said. "What time did you arrive today?"

"Around one, after lunch," Britney said. "We met up with Alyssa and watched the downhill derby and then went to the children's things at the river. She had to leave, so the girls and I ate the sandwiches I'd brought, and they played until the fireworks started."

"Did you record any of the day?" Smart technology had saved two children from abduction in the past year, including the attempted abduction of a six-year-old in Ohio. The attempt had been captured on the family's Ring doorbell camera, likely saving her life.

"Why?"

"We'd want to look through any videos you may have taken today and see if there's anyone who shows up in more than one."

Britney reached into her pocket and unlocked her phone. She tapped the screen twice and then slid the phone across the table. "I took three videos, including one about an hour before the fireworks started." She opened to the first video. "This was a couple of hours before the fireworks. They wanted to play at Teddy Bear Park."

"Mom, you hold my bag." A gangly, blonde-haired girl with a gap between her front teeth shoved the bag at her mother and skipped off toward the jungle gym.

"Abby, be careful." Thea stood at the bottom of the gym, her hands on her hips. "You shouldn't climb up to the top so fast."

"I can too." A little girl with blonde hair and a determined voice sat on the top bar, her little feet swinging.

A familiar head of dark hair popped up next to her, giggling. Nikki felt dizzy as she watched Lacey talk to the missing girls. She and Abby perched on top of the bars, while Thea gingerly climbed towards them.

"Lacey, be careful." Ruth's voice came from somewhere beyond the camera.

Ruth had taken Lacey to the park while Nikki, Rory and Mark enjoyed a couple of beers from the brewery.

She tried to keep her expression neutral as Britney played the next video. She and her daughters had settled into their spot to watch the fireworks and eat ice cream. Britney asked her daughters if they'd had fun, and they both gushed about their day and their new friend from the park.

"I wanted her to watch the fireworks with us." Abby pouted. "Maybe she could have come to play."

"Honey, she may not even live around here," Britney answered.

"She said she did," Abby said indignantly. "Her stepdaddy makes houses."

Nikki was overcome with emotion for a few seconds. She and Rory had never asked her to refer to him as anything other than his name. Rory would probably choke up when she told him, but she couldn't think about that right now.

She didn't want to divulge any more information to Britney than she had to, and while Nikki had been the focus of more media attention than she could count since she'd returned to Stillwater, Lacey's picture had been kept out of the coverage, even when a deranged serial killer had kidnapped her to get to Nikki.

"The girls are around my daughter's age," Nikki said. "I've been through this myself, with my little girl. There's a lot more to it than that, but I just want you to remember this: we found my daughter, and we will do everything possible to find yours."

Nikki checked her watch. Nearly two hours had passed since Britney had realized the girls were gone. "I'm going to check in with Miller and the rest of the team. I'll be back in a few minutes."

Nikki slipped out of the room and walked down the hall to the lone window overlooking Fourth Street. Officers and volunteers gathered at the corner of Fourth Street, and Nikki could see Chen barking orders as they worked to establish a search grid. Miller would make sure the purse was sent to the FBI lab, but Courtney would need time to lift a successful print, assuming she could find any.

"Agent Hunt?"

Nikki hadn't noticed Edie coming down the hall. "Perfect timing. Thanks for staying with Britney. I wanted to check and make sure there isn't anything Britney might have mentioned to you that she forgot to tell me?"

"No, but she's real worried about what that husband is

going to think," Edie said. "I can't understand why that's her priority and not her kids."

"Sometimes it's easier to make up problems to worry about than face the real ones," Nikki said. "Did she give you the impression he's abusive?"

"I don't know," Edie said. "Controlling, for sure. I guess that's a form of abuse."

"It can be," Nikki said. "A victim's advocate from the sheriff's department should be here to relieve you shortly. Are you okay to stay with her until then? I don't think she should be alone very long."

"Of course," Edie said. "I'll stay when the husband comes, too."

"There won't be any need for that," Nikki said. "But please make sure we have your contact information in case we have more questions."

She found Liam in the small bullpen. "Traffic-cam footage on the south side of the church shows the parking lot almost empty as of about ten minutes before the purse was found, and there's no sign of the purse in any of the images. Since there's a big tree and shrubs, it's impossible to see how it got there. But the lot cleared out pretty quickly after the fireworks. Only a few cars remained, and they were opposite of where the purse was found."

"You don't think he parked there?" Nikki asked.

Liam shook his head. "Times don't add up."

Nikki ran through what they knew so far, which was damn little.

"I did a quick public records search and confirmed the basic information Britney gave police." He turned his laptop so she could see it. "Shane's forty-five years old," Liam said. "That's a seventeen-year age gap."

"Not necessarily uncommon these days," Nikki said. "Any red flags on his public record?"

"Nope," Liam said. "He got a speeding ticket a couple of years ago, but that's it. No major malpractice suits, either, so that's good. That's why he's the head team physician for the Vikings, too."

Nikki didn't doubt his facts. During Liam's recovery from a head injury last year, he'd thrown himself into all sorts of stats and trivia, hoping the exercises would help his brain recover faster.

"I called the hospital from the car to make sure he was en route," Liam said. "The charge nurse said the staff is really upset about the girls, and that everyone loves Doctor Walker. He knows the nurses run the hospital and treats them with respect. Great bedside manner with patients."

That didn't gel with the impression about Shane that Nikki had gotten from Britney, but people reacted to trauma in different ways. Nikki needed to find the balance between pushing the two about their missing daughters without making them feel like they were suspects.

"According to the Department of Transportation, the Walkers own two vehicles, and that's it. No boat registered," Liam said.

"Well, Shane's clearly accounted for," Nikki said. "Miller called Regions Hospital earlier and confirmed Doctor Walker came in this morning for two scheduled surgeries." She checked her text messages to make sure she had Miller's information straight. "Around noon, a victim from a motor vehicle accident came into the ER with an open leg fracture. Walker scrubbed in at 4:5 1, and he finished just before midnight."

"Meaning if he's involved, he didn't get his hands dirty. I'm surprised the team physician for the Vikings is stuck doing emergency surgery at a public hospital on a Saturday night, but he still does emergency rotations."

"Must not be home much." Nikki explained the strange way Britney spoke about her husband. "She's very worried about his feelings. That could be her way of controlling her grief, or because he's not very nice to her. Britney said they were married ten years ago in St. Paul, in a small ceremony. Did you find that in public records?"

"Nope," Liam said. "I've ran every search available, and there is no record of marriage. Nor are there records for Thea and Abby's births."

"Home births?" Nikki suggested.

"They should still have birth certificates and social security numbers, but they don't." Liam leaned back, his hands behind his head. "Did you ask Britney where the girls were born?"

"Not yet," Nikki said. "I wanted to get Shane's reaction and answers first."

Her phone dinged with a text from the deputy the sheriff had sent to escort Shane Walker to the police station.

"He's here. Let's see what he has to say."

Shane Walker still wore his green hospital scrubs. He was only an inch or two taller than Nikki's five feet seven, but he cut an imposing figure in the claustrophobic room. He reminded Nikki of a wrestler who'd stopped working out but still retained plenty of intimidating bulk, like her ex-husband. Shane, however, didn't give off the warm and fuzzy vibe like Tyler always had. He moved and spoke with the usual confidence of a skilled surgeon. As out of place as it might seem given the situation, Nikki had to stay away from snap judgments. Surgeons were made of a different ilk, and she firmly believed that arrogance was a key ingredient to a successful surgeon. Some could shut it off outside the hospital, and some couldn't. Nikki had to find a way to crack Shane's tough outer coating without offending him so much that he took his wife and walked out.

Nikki knocked on the open door. "Doctor Walker, I'm Agent Hunt with the FBI, and this is my partner, Agent

Wilson. Can we get you anything before we ask some questions?"

Shane shook his head. "Where is my wife?"

Nikki's immediate response was to ask him why he wasn't more concerned with his missing daughters, but she could already tell Shane Walker wasn't going to be intimidated by the situation and if she pushed him the wrong way, he'd lawyer up. Plus, he'd been in surgery for several hours, and they hadn't uncovered anything connecting him to their disappearance. Nikki had to stop making quick judgment calls before she made another mistake.

"She's in our interview room with a victim's advocate. I hoped we could talk privately first."

"I should be with Britney. She's... delicate."

Nikki sat down at the table and motioned for Shane and Liam to sit as well. Liam liked to stand against the wall in interviews, observing while Nikki did most of the talking. She didn't think Dr. Walker would appreciate the intimidation tactic. "How so?"

Liam sat, but Shane remained standing and gripped the back of the chair across from them. "She grew up extremely sheltered from the real world," Shane explained. "Bringing the girls to this festival was a big step for her. She's never going to forgive herself."

Nikki showed him the same map she'd shown Britney. "They were right here, with people all around. Thea's a pretty responsible kid, right?"

Shane briefly closed his eyes at the mention of his daughter, as though he'd suddenly realized how serious things were getting. "Yes, because she's type 1 diabetic and has had to grow up fast. She has insulin with her. They haven't found that, have they? She has to have it."

"We found the purse in a parking lot just west of the river. The insulin pen wasn't inside."

"Good," Shane said. "Maybe she left the purse and took the pen with her. But she wouldn't have left without Britney knowing where she was going. Thea's as easily spooked as Britney."

"What about Abby?" Nikki asked.

Shane half-smiled. "She's our firecracker, but she wouldn't have wandered off." He looked at the map again, his skin growing paler. "They were close to the river. Thea can't swim, and Abby isn't that much better. But someone would have noticed if they'd fallen in, right?"

"It was loud, and the marina is poorly lit, so it's possible for someone to fall in unnoticed, but right now, we think the girls walked away from the river," Liam said. "Your wife said the girls wouldn't go with anyone other than the two of you or her friend Alyssa. She said neither of you have family, but can you think of anyone else the girls might trust enough?"

"No," Shane said flatly.

"All right, then," Nikki said. "What about enemies? Is there a patient who might be upset with you and want to seek revenge?"

"I keep my personal life at home," he said. "They'd have to do some real digging. I'm not on social media."

Nikki glanced at Liam, hoping he caught her meaning. The hospital staff had painted Shane Walker as a popular, well-liked doctor. She'd assumed that meant he socialized with the staff to some extent. But his answer was interesting. He didn't think an angry patient would be able to find his family... so it's possible he'd made some enemies at work.

"We spoke with hospital staff before you arrived," Liam said. "They said everyone was really upset about the girls."

"Well, yes," Shane said. "They know I have kids, so they're pretty upset. I work with great people. That doesn't mean I share details of my home life with them."

Fair enough, Nikki thought. "You've never taken the girls to the hospital to see where you work or for a family event?"

He shook his head. "Like I said, Britney doesn't like to go to anything large and public. I encouraged her to take the girls today because they both wanted to come so badly, and they've been kind of making her nuts this summer. I never dreamed something like this would happen."

"No one does," Nikki said. "By the way, can you tell us where the girls were born? We just want to have their fingerprints on file in case they've wandered somewhere outside of town and need to be identified." Nikki had no idea if the Twin Cities hospitals still did actual fingerprints, but she wanted to know where the girls were born and why she hadn't been able to find a single record of them.

"We had a home midwife," Shane said.

"So, no fingerprints or footprints on file?" she pressed. "What about Thea's medical records in case she needs immediate intervention when she's found?"

"She sees the pediatric specialist at Lakeview Hospital to manage her insulin," Shane said. "I'd have to look up the name."

"That's fine," Nikki said. "We can do that." She recapped what Britney had told her earlier. "Britney hasn't had any contact with her family since she left, and you don't have any extended family nearby, is that right?"

"Both my parents are gone. And no, Britney doesn't speak to her family."

"Is there anyone else in your lives the girls would have trusted enough to leave their spot?"

"Absolutely not," Shane said. "Like I said, we keep a tight circle. I don't want my children's names known to the public. Fans aren't always happy with my medical decisions."

"Have you received threats?" Liam asked.

"A couple of years ago," Shane said. "Vikings running back suffered a season-ending injury that I was blamed for. My office did receive several nasty letters and a few threats. The police in Edina took care of it."

Another wealthy suburb, Edina was home to doctors and athletes and other powerful people. She made a mental note to call the Edina police about the threats.

"Britney said the two of you met not long after she escaped her overbearing, religious family." Nikki threw in the adjectives hoping Walker would see them as an invitation to talk.

Shane looked surprised. "She told you she escaped?"

"Is that not accurate?"

"Well, yes, it is," Shane said. "That's all she said?"

Nikki nodded. "Is there something she left out?"

Shane didn't answer immediately. Nikki got the sense Shane Walker wanted to say more, just as she was certain Britney hadn't told them the whole truth about her family. It might lead to nothing, but they couldn't leave anything on the table with two little girls missing.

The only sound in the room was Liam's foot tapping against the old tile. Nikki let the tension grow, the room feeling hotter by the second. Whatever Shane Walker didn't want to say wasn't going to be forced out. He had to come to that point on his own terms.

His feet moved up and down, as though he were pedaling. He wiped his forehead with the back of his hand and sighed. "I should have known."

"What?" Nikki asked.

"That her past life would catch up to us eventually."

FIVE

"What do you mean, her past life?" Nikki asked.

"She told you about growing up in the religious sect, but did she tell you that sect was part of the Fundamentalist Saints of Zion?"

"No," Nikki said. "I've heard the name before. Aren't they Mormon?"

"Yes, but these people aren't part of the regular Mormon faith, because they still believe multiple wives and children earn them a place in heaven. The Mormon church outlawed that a long time ago."

"Right," Nikki said. "But the sect you're talking about is in Utah, for the most part."

"FSZ is a break-off sect of members who were excommunicated from the Utah group or chose to leave."

"I don't understand," Liam said. "What does having multiple wives have to do with religion?"

"Celestial heaven, according to the FSZ doctrine, is only achieved when the man has at least three wives who've all produced children. The more wives and kids a man has, the better his heaven will be. Women and children are essentially counted as currency."

"And how do the women reach this heaven?" Nikki asked.

"They're taught from birth that their role is to wed men and birth babies. Do that and do it well, you'll be rewarded in heaven with a special place next to God."

"Isn't this the same religious group whose leader is in prison for raping minors?" Nikki asked. She remembered reading the stories about the scores of girls in Utah and Arizona who'd been wed to men old enough to be their grandfathers and fathers, some as young as twelve. All of them had been forced to consummate the sham marriage and start producing children.

"Not entirely," Shane said. "Britney's father left Utah when she was twelve and came here to start his own church. Others scattered and went further underground to practice their beliefs and avoid association with the church leaders who were now serving various terms in prison for sex crimes against children as young as twelve, among other things."

"You're kidding," Liam said.

"The more wives, the more power in heaven," Shane reminded him. "The former leader claimed he was told by God to do all of it, and he was so influential very few questioned him. Many men who were supposed to be pious and pillars of the community were happy to take girls as wives and many of them became pregnant within a year."

Nikki remembered reading the book about capturing the leader in Utah. The women who'd escaped his flock bravely testified against him about the sexual assaults and forced unions of underaged girls to men old enough to be their fathers. One of the most damning pieces of evidence was a recording of the leader having sex with a twelve-year-old girl he claimed God had chosen to be his new wife. "Was Britney one of those girls?"

"Almost," Shane said. "That's why her father left the group and came to Minnesota, along with a few allies."

Shane nodded. "Britney's father was strongly against the church elders' decision to marry off girls as young as twelve to men old enough to be their grandfathers."

"Good for him," Liam said.

"Don't give him too much credit. His reasoning was that girls that young weren't ready to be mothers, which is their duty to God. He thought fifteen was a much more reasonable age." Shane's voice dripped with sarcasm. "Britney's father also felt a single religious leader was too much, so they have a council of leaders. None of them claim to have the power to speak to God like the Utah leader. They claim they don't follow the prophet anymore, but I have my doubts. They still follow a lot of the fundamentalist doctrine the last I heard."

"Everything I've read about the FSZ says that contact with non-church members is forbidden. How did you and Britney meet?" Nikki asked.

"I was doing my surgical residency in Thief River Falls," he said. "I met her there when she'd come to visit a family member, and we got close. The father who'd claimed he wanted to protect her decided that she should get married when she was fifteen, to one of the men on the council who was much older than her." Shane's face darkened. "It's not my place to tell you what happened over the next few years, but her only solace was that her so-called husband had been rendered sterile after an accident some years ago, so she wouldn't have to bear his children. Unfortunately, that turned out not to be true, and Britney found herself pregnant. When she found out the baby was a girl, Britney knew she had to leave before her 'husband' found out."

"Her father was fine with her marrying someone his age?" Liam was incredulous.

"It's the FSZ way," Shane said bitterly. "It's all supposed to be God's will, but the truth is that it's a buddy system. Britney's father was allowed to marry a council member's granddaughter, who was already at the ripe old age of twenty."

"To clarify, are you telling us that Thea isn't your biological daughter?"

Shane shook his head, tears building in his eyes. "That doesn't matter to me. She's mine, just as Abby is."

Nikki believed him, and she'd read enough about the Utah sect to know that Britney's story was typical. "Were the two of you seeing each other when Britney decided to leave the church?"

"No," Shane admitted. "She found out I was moving here for work, and I knew her well enough then that when she asked me to help her, I didn't hesitate. We got married later."

"If she hasn't been in contact with her family and they didn't know she was pregnant when she left, do you believe the FSZ is responsible for Thea and Abby's disappearance?"

"The first year, she had a burner phone and tried to stay in touch with her older sister, Rachel. At first Rachel supported Britney's decision to leave, but their older brother Hyrum found out and took the phone from Rachel. He threatened he would find Britney and bring her back, no matter how long it took."

"Hyrum?" Liam made a face. "I didn't know that name still existed."

"It does in Utah," Shane said. "Hyrum Smith was the older brother of Joseph Smith, the Mormon church's founder. Britney's father is a descendent of Hyrum, which is why he named his oldest son after him." He sighed. "Thief River Falls is a small community, so it wasn't hard for Hyrum to find out who'd she left with, and within a couple of months of his finding the phone, the emails started coming in."

"Were they aware she was pregnant?"

"Rachel suspected, and told Hyrum. I told him it wasn't true, and even if it were, the church couldn't risk taking her to court, because they wouldn't be able to hide the fact she was a child bride. I finally took matters into my own hands and set up a meeting with her father, back in Thief River Falls." He dragged his hands over his face. "I offered the church ten thousand dollars to leave us alone. I knew they were in the process of acquiring more land and had a cash flow problem—"

"How did you know this?" Liam cut in.

"I still had friends in town, and one was a litigation attorney. He had various dealings with the FSZ because they liked to use child labor, but Minnesota didn't ignore it in the same way Utah did. He accepted and promised to keep control of Hyrum. I told him if we were bothered again, I would blow their entire lives apart. Her father wasn't stupid, and he knew I meant it."

"Britney knew about the arrangement with her father?"

Shane nodded. "I received word last week that her father passed, and her brother Hyrum took his seat on the council. I haven't had the courage to tell her. She's just starting to get out and do things with the girls without looking over her shoulder."

"Out of curiosity, why has it been so hard for Britney to assimilate after all these years?" Nikki asked.

"Assimilating was easy," Shane told them. "She reveled in getting rid of the bland clothes and too-small shoes. She cut ten inches off her hair the day we moved here. But you have to understand the brainwashing she experienced, especially during her early years in Utah. All outsiders were evil and bad, and only their group—the Fundamentalist Saints of Zion—were God's chosen people. Growing up, she and her siblings lived in fear of being discovered by the authorities, as Britney's mother was her father's fifth wife, I think. The state could have taken them at any time, but the church had a lot of control back then. You know the prophet preached that black people were unclean? And they were brought up not to question him, because he was God on Earth, and to question meant eternal damnation. She still has trouble trusting people of color because of that ridiculousness." He shook his head. "She's a great mom, but sometimes I think her emotional growth ended out there in the desert."

That must have been why Britney had been leery of talking to Miller. "Well, it's no different than any other childhood experience, especially the traumatic ones. That shaped how she saw the world, and I can't imagine the level of manipulation it took to control all of those people."

"She's come a long way," Shane said hastily. "I don't want you to get the wrong impression. Sometimes she's not aware of slipping back into that mindset, especially when she's stressed. I know the Washington County Sheriff is black. If she was rude—"

"She wasn't," Nikki said. "And even if she had been, it wouldn't faze Sheriff Miller. His sole focus is finding your daughters. If you think the FSZ might be behind this, why would they take the girls and not Britney? She's the one who left."

"Britney's lived as an apostate now. She left the religion and lived among gentiles. Even though she still struggles at times, she's learned a lot, and they wouldn't be able to control her the way good FSZ girls are supposed to be controlled. My girls are young enough the brainwashing will still be effective." Shane looked disgusted.

"I assume Thea and Abby have no idea about any of this?" Nikki asked.

"No," Shane said. "We'd planned on telling them, once they're old enough to understand and protect themselves..." Shane stopped talking, moisture building in his eyes. "We taught them not to talk to strangers, to scream for help and run," he said. "I know Thea would have done exactly that. How could no one hear her?"

"The fireworks were exceptionally loud," Nikki said gently. "But officers were able to speak with some of the people sitting in the area, and they never noticed the girls leave with anyone, which is why we thought they might have wandered off to look for their mother. But at this point, with such an exhaustive search of downtown, I'm not at all convinced that's what happened."

"What do you think happened?" Shane asked, a tremor in his voice.

"I'm not sure, but less than one percent of children are taken by strangers. The vast majority is by someone they know."

"No one in our lives would do that," Shane said. "That's part of the reason we keep our circle so close. It's those religious freaks that took her, it has to be."

Nikki had dealt with religious fanaticism before, and she knew that most religious cults kept tight control over food and money, thereby ensuring their people remained dependent. She understood Shane's point, but he wasn't able to look at things as objectively as she and Liam. "They're definitely on the list of possible suspects, but you just said that Thea would fight to keep from leaving with a stranger, and these church members would be just that, right?"

"Yes," Shane said. "But their circle's also small, so most people are strangers to them. That's why none of this makes sense."

"Agent Wilson, see what you can find out about this FSZ group from the state police in Thief River Falls, and make sure they have the girls' pictures and information." Nikki looked at Shane. "I remember reading that the women in Utah wore prairie dresses like the Amish. Is the group in western Minnesota the same?"

"No prairie dresses, but only skirts and tops, nothing revealing or flashy. Everything to the ankle and wrists except in the heat of summer. No shorts allowed, and the women and girls do still wear their hair in that old-fashioned, poufy braid."

"But they know how to blend in with people outside of the ranch, right?"

"Depends," Shane said. "The women are so restricted they don't know any better, and some of the young men are almost as controlled. Why?"

"I know it's been a busy festival, but if they dress differently, they would have stood out," Nikki said. "We can ask people who were in the area if they saw anyone who matched that description. Does Britney have photos of any family members?"

"No," Shane said. "But the church has a website. It's mostly full of lies, but they might have photos of the council and elders."

"What was Britney's maiden name?"

"Lowden," he said. "Her father was Reginald Lowden. Hatch's the only other name I know. That's the man she was sealed to—that's what they call it when the man is already legally married. She doesn't talk about the past very much."

"Which brings me to my last question," Nikki said. "If your initial reaction is that someone from her former life took the girls, then why didn't Britney mention that? She doesn't appear to see them as a threat."

"I told you, she thinks her father is alive, and she knows Hyrum would never defy him."

Nikki didn't question his decision not to tell Britney about her father's death, but Britney's lack of transparency about her background still bothered her.

"I can tell you're pissed that Britney didn't go into detail about her background," Shane said. "Try to understand, Britney was brought up not to trust gentiles, meaning non FSZ members. She was brought up to live in secrecy, taught that us gentiles are evil, they want to keep the chosen out of heaven, that sort of thing. Some of these people have never left the acreage where the compound was built. She was brainwashed long before her father escaped the heart of the cult, which is all they are to me. Her education was church doctrine. She didn't learn about the real world until she left, and right now, she thinks her father is still in charge out there."

"I understand," Nikki said. "But her children are missing. She's been out of the cult for a decade."

"I know, but there's a part of Britney that's still a young girl and desperately wants to believe that all she was taught growing up wasn't wrong. That clouds her judgment."

Nikki nodded, still trying to make sense of the story. "Doctor Walker, I'm going to take you to your wife shortly. I just need to speak privately with Agent Wilson for a few minutes." She motioned for Liam to follow her.

In the hall, Nikki rubbed the aching muscles in her neck. "What do you think?"

"I don't know," Liam said. "I watched the documentary about the original group out of Utah and Arizona while I was rehabbing. I didn't realize they'd come to Minnesota. Not the polygamists, anyway."

"Well, they aren't exactly advertising," Nikki said. "Since the Bureau closed the North Dakota field office for budget issues, our best contact in western Minnesota is the state patrol. Give the district office a call and see what they know about these fundamentalists. Have they caused issues? What do the locals think of them? Have there been reports of young girls going missing in the area, maybe if the cult is recruiting? Run a background check on Reginald Lowden and see if you can find anything about Britney under her maiden name, but don't forget she was sealed to Hatch, so check on that one as well. That one shouldn't be too hard to find."

"Background check on Shane Walker, too?" Liam asked.

"Yes," Nikki said. "He's an unlikely suspect at this point, but we need to cover all our bases. Find out when he left Thief River Falls and came here and see if it lines up with what he told us. Pull lists of local sex offenders as well, but make sure you coordinate with Miller and Chen from the Stillwater PD so you don't end up stepping on toes. You can set up in this room after I take Shane down to Britney."

She left Liam, retrieved Shane and led him down the hall. "The Stillwater Police Department is pretty small, and these rooms are designed for interrogation. Britney's in their conference room."

"Is she alone?"

"No, she's with the woman who runs the Warden's House Museum," Nikki said. "The Stillwater PD had set up there for the festival, and we wanted to keep Britney away from the chaos of searching."

They reached the room and Shane opened the door before Nikki could say anything. "Brit?"

Britney ran to him and sobbed into his chest. "I'm so sorry."

Shane smoothed her hair, glancing over his shoulder at Nikki. "It's not your fault, sweetheart."

Edie stood and wished the couple good luck before quietly slipping out the door. Nikki thanked her again and handed Edie her business card, in case she thought of anything Britney might have said that could help the investigation.

"Let's sit down," Shane said. He guided Britney back to the table and took the seat Edie had vacated. He wrapped his arms around her, and she leaned against his shoulder.

Nikki sat across from the two, watching the tension unfold and trying to get a read on the family situation. She opened her notebook and listened.

"Why didn't you tell her about FSZ?" Shane asked his wife.

Britney looked at him in surprise. "I told her the relevant information. They've got nothing to do with this." She glanced at Nikki. "I don't want that dredged up unnecessarily."

"How could you possibly know the FSZ isn't involved?" he demanded.

Britney gave him a look. "It makes no sense after all this time."

"You mentioned escaping from your family," Nikki said. "Is it possible they came looking for you?"

"No." Britney focused on her husband. "Why are you bringing up the past? It's got nothing to do with what's going on now."

A muscle in Shane's jaw flexed. "You and I both know females are a prized possession in your family. That's why you escaped with me, remember?"

Britney's jaw set. "I wouldn't say I escaped. I *left*." She emphasized the last word. "And my father would never allow Hyrum to do such a thing. Don't forget that."

Shane sighed. "Honey, I need to tell you something."

"Can't it wait?" Britney demanded.

Shane was undeterred by her tone. "No, I'm afraid it can't. Early last week, a former colleague still working in the Thief River Falls medical community told me that your father passed last month."

Britney stared at her husband for a moment, her hands clenching into fists, her jaw clenched as she fought back her emotions. "How could you not tell me?"

"You never want to talk about them," he said. "You were planning on bringing the girls here today, and I wanted you to be able to do that without constantly looking over your shoulder."

"And now look what's happened," Britney shouted at him, slamming her hands on the table. "Is Hyrum in charge? He always wanted to be, and he wanted to get rid of the council."

"I don't know," Shane admitted.

"This changes everything." Tears rolled down her cheeks.

"Britney, do you honestly think someone from your religious community could be behind your daughters' disappearance?" Nikki asked.

"Not 'somebody,'" Britney said. "My brother Hyrum and Silas Hatch. I was Silas's fourth wife—in the eyes of the council and God—and my leaving was an embarrassment for him."

Nikki offered her a tissue, but Britney seemed to have forgotten she was even in the room.

"I left so my daughter wouldn't be forced into the same life that I had been. If I'd known about Father, I never would have come here, much less let the girls out of my sight. Especially Abby. He won't care about her. Just Thea."

Shane sat between Nikki and his crying wife, fighting his own emotions.

"Doctor Walker told us he isn't Thea's biological father."

Britney flinched as though she'd been slapped. "Shane is Thea's father. But Silas... he was supposed to be sterile. He forced himself on me for three years and nothing happened. And then one day I started feeling nauseous. I wanted to die when I found out, because it meant I was trapped forever. I would have been without Shane."

"And since my name is well-known around here, it wouldn't be hard to find out we had children," Shane said. "As long as Hyrum and Silas can do math, they'd be able to figure out Thea probably wasn't mine."

Nikki's mind spun from the additional information. Even if Britney and Shane were right about Silas and Hyrum, she couldn't just put out an alert with his photo and description. At best, without evidence, she would have to rely on the state patrol to snoop around the FSZ's property. If they lived their lives off-grid, there would be no records for them anywhere, and getting alibis would be impossible if they didn't speak to authorities. If Nikki showed up there and they did have the girls, they'd be able to move them quickly and hide them where they'd never be found.

And what would be the point? If Silas and Hyrum had located Britney, then surely they knew she'd married a well-connected surgeon and had another child with him. The FSZ valued privacy above all else. Inviting such a powerful spotlight into their lives made no sense, especially a decade later.

"Did you ever notice anyone following you when you left the house?" Nikki asked.

"No," Britney said.

"We have cameras all around our property, including ones that face the street," Shane said. "I can look at the security footage and see if someone drove by often."

Nikki found a business card in her bag and handed it to him. "Can you email all the footage to me? I'll have our video guys take a look. They'll be able to work some magic and make the images clearer, and they have the manpower to work through hours of footage. In the meantime, I think you and Britney should go home and try to rest."

"While my babies are out there?" Britney's voice rose.

"You're welcome to search," Nikki said. "But we have a lot of officers on the ground. Someone should be at home in case the girls return, someone calls your house phone, or we need to contact you with any more questions. Home is the safest place for you to be right now. Staying here doubles your exhaustion and anxiety."

Nikki managed to convince them it was the best thing for Thea and Abby. Sitting in the cramped, cold police station wasn't going to help them stay strong for their daughters. Home was their best option.

"It'll be fine." Liam's voice drifted into the hallway. He was on the phone, frowning, talking in a whisper. "Stop worrying about it. I said I would, didn't I?"

Nikki pretended to cough before entering the small room. Between Liam's height and the confined space, he looked like a redheaded version of Buddy the Elf in Santa's workshop.

"I have to go," he said into the phone. "I'll check in when I can." He ended the call and tossed his phone onto the table. "Any news?" he asked Nikki.

"They have a babysitter who could be a suspect. And Shane isn't Thea's biological father. They're afraid the real one, Silas, has taken Thea. He's on the council in her old religious group." She fought back a yawn.

"Christ," Liam said. "The FSZ church and all the homes on their property are private. No way we get a judge to even consider a warrant to search." He stood and stretched before stepping out to the vending machine.

"I know," Nikki told him. "Any luck with the state police?"

"I talked to the night shift lieutenant at the state patrol in Thief River Falls." Liam studied the vending machine briefly before pulling a couple of ones out of his pocket. "I hope this gives me some wings," he said, picking up the Red Bull can. "I'm dragging ass."

Nikki leaned against the door frame. "What did the commander say?" she prodded.

"He's new to the job, so he had to do some digging. Since the group showed up in the mid 2000s, only one complaint has been filed against them." Liam squinted at his notes. His vision had worsened since his head injury, and he needed to accept this and wear reading glasses.

"Two years ago, a family who'd recently moved to the area said their teenaged daughter had been influenced by the church and taken as a prisoner, essentially," he said. "Trooper Emily James worked the case. The FSZ compound is called New Hope Ranch, and it looks like pretty much all of the members live on the property. Trooper James found the girl, who'd just turned eighteen. She appeared happy and said she was there voluntarily. But according to the file, the trooper wasn't sure she bought it. She's kept an eye on them ever since then. The night commander is tracking Trooper James down. I gave them my number and yours."

"Good," Nikki said, skimming through the cult's history on the FBI's internal website. As Shane had explained, women and children were the key to a man's kingdom in heaven, so they were an important commodity, and in the southwest in the early 2000s, dozens of boys and young men had been kicked out of the church for imagined infractions so the older men could add to their harem. The need for more wives had led to polygamous marriages with girls as young as twelve.

Nikki swallowed the bile in her throat. It was one thing to believe a man who claimed to speak with God and take a girl as so-called wife, but it was more than religious piety that caused so many of the men to rape their underaged wives. Many girls had two or three kids by the time they were eighteen.

"I haven't been able to find much about the Minnesota sect other than what's on their website," Liam said. "They're secluded and the community doesn't appear to have issue with them, save for the parents I told you about earlier."

"What about Britney's father, Reginal Lowden?"

"He died last month, aged eighty-nine. Big service for him. There's actually photos on the website."

Nikki unlocked her phone and typed in the church's name. The FSZ website featured an aerial view of the green fields and forests near the group's massive acreage. Lowden, the highest ranking elder, was mourned by "dozens of children and grand-children, along with those nearest him."

Nikki assumed that was code for polygamy. She clicked through the photos from Lowden's memorial service until she came to a photo of five men, one seated, the other four standing beside him. "Hyrum Lowden will succeed Supreme Elder Lowden on the council and governing body."

"Where do you see that?" Liam asked.

"Memorial service photos, last one."

Hyrum sat rigidly in the chair, unsmiling. His dark hair was slicked back, his hands flat on the table. "He looks like he's posing for a nineteenth-century photo."

"The gray-haired guy standing directly behind him is Silas Hatch. He's Thea's biological father."

"He's got to be in his seventies." Liam shuddered. "I'll run that name by the state patrol when they come back, but let's see what I can find out about him now."

His fingers moved quickly across his laptop, his mouth pinched in concentration. "Clean driving record, no tax liens, no citations for anything. Wait, hang on. There's a family tree that's damn near impossible to read."

Nikki moved so she could see over his shoulder. At the center of the tree was the former supreme elder, now in prison for raping children. Jagged line after jagged line connected him to dozens of wives and children.

Liam pointed to the name at the bottom right. "Silas Hatch. He's related to the former leader, I think. It's pretty convoluted, but that might give him a sense of superiority and from what I've read, the Feds and district attorney are pretty confident there's been a lot of money laundered through various businesses, but they've only managed to prove a couple of cases out in Utah. Point is, it's possible the Minnesota sect somehow benefits from that money, especially if Silas is related to the formal royal family, so to speak."

"Justin Nash is still working white collar, and his parents have connections all over the country. Give him a call and see if they know anything that might help us get a warrant if we need it." Instead of ignoring their connection to the Utah and Arizona sects, the church explained their decision to part from the "perverse imposters who used the fundamentalist Mormon beliefs to have intimate relations with underaged girls."

The reformed FSZ wanted to live as the fundamentalists did prior to the infiltration of "false prophets." The FSZ had a council of five bishops who ran the church and made the decisions regarding the church's properties and teachings, along with guiding the flock to "everlasting" marriage choices. In other words, the polygamy was likely still happening, but the new branch of the Mormon faith had made a concerted effort to ensure no one man made all the decisions.

Nikki could tell by the photos on the website that the group still practiced modesty, but instead of the plain, homemade prairie dresses enforced out west, women and girls could wear dresses and skirts of their choosing, provided they were mid-calf or longer. The only rule that seemed to have carried over from the western church was the homeschooling.

"I wonder what sort of education they actually receive." While the FSZ allowed the option of public school, it encouraged homeschooling, most likely to keep the barrier between the church members and the outside world. The outside world was full of evil and temptation, according to the FSZ doctrine. They still believed they were God's chosen people, and as Britney had mentioned, it was clear the FSZ believed they were, in fact, above everyone else.

"During the height of its power, the groups in Utah and Arizona controlled kids' education, and many didn't have much more than a sixth-grade education," Liam said. "They were indoctrinated in church law and taught the outside world was bad in just about every way. Those Mormons were as put off by the modernized world as any indigenous tribe. I'm guessing some of that is still going on here."

"Still doesn't make them kidnappers," Nikki said. "Not to mention that Thief River Falls is almost six hours west, on the other side of the state. And even if Silas did come looking for his child, how could he have known Britney was going to be at Lumberjack Days?"

Liam thought about her question for a moment before answering. "He could have had eyes on the house and had someone follow her."

"I suppose," Nikki said. "It just seems like the Walkers are trying to convince themselves it had to be the cult, because at least they're blood relatives. They aren't allowing themselves to consider any other options. That's fine for them, but we need to consider all angles. Let's find this babysitter, look into both parents, and pull registered sex offenders in the local area, starting with Level 3s with charges involving a pre-pubescent child."

In Minnesota, sex offenders were assigned a level based on the severity of the crime and likelihood to reoffend. As far as Nikki was concerned, they were all going to reoffend sometime, because they were driven by a biological fail, but categories were crucial in determining parole and living arrangements. Level 3s were the most serious offenders, which meant they weren't granted parole as much as Level 1s and 2s.

"Pull the 1s and 2s as well," she told him. "Local offenders are priority, but check the Thief River Falls area, too, just in case. If someone affiliated with the church is on the list, we might have more wiggle room if we need it."

The station was small enough that Nikki could see the bullpen from the doorway. A woman around her age had arrived, her credentials around her neck.

"New police chief is here. Keep me updated."

Chief Ryan wore black slacks and a white Stillwater PD polo shirt. Ryan had been elected in the wake of racial injustice in Minnesota. She'd come up through the ranks at the Minneapolis PD, earning a reputation as a tough but fair cop. She'd championed police reform during her campaign, but like a lot of politicians, had been hamstrung by the system. Some of the bureaucrats in Stillwater wanted racial equality without actually making an effort to change the system, and Ryan had been up against the wall from day one.

"Agent Hunt?"

Nikki shook the woman's outstretched hand. "Chief Ryan,

it's nice to meet you. How up to speed are you with everything?"

"I spoke with Chen and Sheriff Miller a few minutes ago," Ryan said. "I'm told the parents were interviewed and have been taken to wait at home with an officer."

"Correct." Nikki filled the chief in on what she'd just learned from the Walkers. "Until she heard that her father had passed, and that her brother Hyrum was now on the council, Britney insisted no one from her prior life would have done this. But she's scared of Silas and Hyrum."

"I see," Ryan said. "What do you think?"

"At this point, we have to look at every possibility. We're working with the state police out of Thief River Falls, and we're focusing on immediate family and local sex offenders, Level 3s first."

"Those people should never be released, but that's the way our criminal justice system is." Ryan sighed and shook her head in disgust. "Do you think her family could have done this?"

Nikki shrugged. "It doesn't make a lot of sense. Too many uncontrolled variables. But we can't rule them out. That's why the state police are heading to the FSZ ranch."

"Agreed," Ryan said. "I'm here to support the search efforts in whatever way I can. I already told Miller and Chen that we all work together on this, and that Sheriff Miller and you will be running things from this point on."

Nikki wasn't sure how to respond. In her experience, most officials either micromanaged a case or took a hands-off approach in an effort to make sure their office didn't get blamed for mistakes.

"I can see you're surprised," Ryan said dryly. "I didn't take this position to pad numbers or tell perfectly competent cops how to do their jobs. I took it to make real changes. It's been an uphill battle at this point, but I'm not interested in using this case to look like a hero. I just want the girls home, safe and sound."

"That's... unexpected." Nikki hoped the chief was as sincere as she sounded. "How do you feel about handling the media?"

"I can do that," Ryan said. "That was actually going to be my suggestion, along with anything else you need me to do. I can shelter you from the mayor, too. He's pretty up in arms. Lumberjack Days sold a record number of tickets this year. In his mind, the sooner the girls are home, the better for the city." Ryan's expression was unchanged, but Nikki could hear the eye-roll in the woman's voice.

"That's one of the many reasons I don't want to be the big boss. The headaches of politics and red tape would send me to an early grave," Nikki said. "I heard the mayor wants a task force."

Ryan nodded. "I know that can be a difficult thing to manage. I've spoken to Sheriff Miller about it, and he agreed that the government center had more room. Unless the girls are found tonight, he and I plan on an all-hands meeting at eight a.m. at the county government center. Conference room B. He said you'd know the place."

"I do." Nikki's team had worked multiple big cases from conference room B, because it was the largest room with the most technology. "It'll be just like old times."

SIX

Nikki peeled her eyes open at the smell of coffee. She'd fallen asleep in the break room while reading about the Fundamentalist Saints of Zion around four a.m., shortly after the thunderstorm started. She rolled her neck trying to work out the kink from sleeping at an odd angle. She'd wanted to join the search, but they already had a lot of boots on the ground, and she knew her skills would lie in refining their suspect list. She'd shared her theories with Miller and Chen before she'd left the office.

"Hey." Liam sniffed the coffee pot. "This is some strong brew. You'll need to load up on cream and sugar."

"Thanks for the heads-up." Nikki stood and stretched, trying to get her bearings. "Any news?"

Liam shook his head. "They paused the search when the storm rolled in. I can't believe you slept through the thunder. We lost power for a little while. I was coming in here to wake you up. Task force meeting in twenty minutes." He rolled his eyes. "It's at the government center. You have the Jeep?"

"Rory dropped me off at the Warden's House last night. You'll have to drive. And don't get hung up on the task force thing," she told him. "Miller can handle the politics." She made herself a coffee, pouring in the generic powdered creamer. "Storm was loud, but did we get rain? What about the river current?"

"They called in the dive team, and the captain's here to talk about that," Liam said.

Nikki peered through the blinds onto Fourth Street. Steam rose from the concrete, signaling more humidity. "So much for the storm breaking the heat." She gathered her things and stuffed them in her bag. "I'm going to try to freshen up before the meeting."

The women's bathroom had only two stalls, but Nikki didn't have a change of clothes with her. She splashed cold water on her face before retrieving the three essential toiletries she'd learned to always have on hand: deodorant, toothpaste, and toothbrush. She finished brushing her teeth and rubbed on the deodorant, followed by a dab of flowery perfume behind the ears.

"Good enough for now."

She found Liam in the lobby and followed him out to his Prius. The air felt like a wet blanket, the fishy smell of the river strong thanks to the rushing current. The Washington County Government Center was connected to the sheriff's department, on the southern side of downtown. Nikki kept her eyes peeled as they drove the nearly empty streets. Sunday morning, at this hour, was for sleeping in. Most of the church-goers weren't even out yet.

"I don't understand why we're doing this task force," Liam started. "We should be out looking—"

"We will be," Nikki said. "Think of it as a briefing, because that's all it really is. No way she got an official task force approved by the mayor on a Sunday."

Unlike the small Stillwater police station, the county government center stretched over two square blocks, with the county courthouse as the centerpiece. Several conference rooms were located on the top floors of the main building. They followed the sound of voices to conference room B.

"Here's the rest of our task force now." Chief Ryan nodded at Nikki and Liam, who sat down in the two open seats.

"First off, thank you to Sheriff Miller for offering the use of the government center." Chief Ryan nodded at Miller, who looked like he hadn't slept all night. "As I told Agent Hunt yesterday—or early this morning, rather—my primary role in this investigation is support. I'm happy to aid the task force in every way I can, including with the media."

Miller fought back a yawn. "We appreciate that, but I think we're all a little leery about the task force. You get too many cooks in the kitchen and things get lost in translation."

Ryan smiled so genuinely it was off-putting given the situation. "And I understand what you're saying. But the mayor believes this is the best way to handle the situation."

"The mayor knows jack about law enforcement," Miller said. "No disrespect to you, Chief, but Agents Hunt and Wilson, along with myself, have worked some very high-profile cases, including kidnapping. We need people manning tip lines and officers willing to follow those up, but we don't need an official task force. Setting the damn thing up is doing nothing but wasting time."

"I think what the sheriff is trying to say is that we are the task force," Nikki said, trying to ease the tension and get the group focused. "We've got police, sheriff, FBI, and the dive team captain. If a task force makes the mayor happy, that's fine. But this is it."

Ryan looked at her for a few moments and then nodded. "Fair enough. Sheriff Miller, since you're in charge of the ground search, I'll give you the floor."

Miller thanked her and used the remote to turn on the interactive whiteboard. A map of downtown Stillwater appeared, with the search grids marked. "We have covered every possible piece of downtown, including knocking on residential doors near the parking lot where Thea's purse was found. Chen has officers canvassing this morning to touch base with anyone we missed. As you know, the purse was found in the parking lot of Trinity Lutheran Church. I've spoken to both pastors, and they will be distributing flyers with the girls' information and photos, along with our tip line. We've been through their CCTV and found nothing; the footage is grainy and at an unhelpful angle. I have a couple of deputies strategically placed to keep an eye on people after the services. It's a long shot, but there's a chance the person who took the girls parked in the church lot because they're familiar with it."

"Not only that," Liam said, "but with all the information on the news this morning, the kidnapper may have decided to attend church and get a feel for what's going on, revisit the scene. If this is someone obsessive or compulsive, they'll be interested in following our investigation."

"Agreed," Miller said.

"We're certain this is someone like that? And definitely a kidnapping?" Ryan asked.

"Captain Gannon, what do you think about searching the river with sonar?" asked Miller.

"The current has been strong, and if they fell in, they could have been swept out," Gannon said.

"But the purse was found in the opposite direction," Chen said before the captain could respond. "Why are we still worried about the river?"

"We need to cover all our bases so we can start alibiing suspects and checking off areas. I want to know every boat that was docked," Nikki said. "And I want to talk to each owner and make sure they're accounted for during the fireworks. Let's definitely use the sonar."

Captain Gannon sipped her coffee. "I concur with that, but we can't go out on the water until the wind dies down.

According to the forecast, it's supposed to slow significantly in the next hour. We'll be ready to go the second it's safe."

"The main marina, where the girls sat closest to, is owned by the city," Chen said. "They open for rentals at ten a.m. The other two are privately owned, but they both open this morning. I'm going to speak to all three and ask for boat rental, slip rental, and security cameras. The city marina is lacking, but the two private ones have better security."

"No one answered my question," Ryan said. "Why have we decided this is a kidnapping? Do we have any witnesses? Did we get anything from people's videos of the fireworks? The family hasn't received any ransom calls. I'm aware the parents think someone from the Church of Fundamentalist Saints took the girls, but we don't have any actual evidence supporting that, do we?"

"No," Nikki admitted. "The state troopers over in Thief River Falls are going to talk to members of the church. We're waiting on a call back from a trooper familiar with them, and we're finding out if there's any probable cause for a warrant to search their homes, just in case we need to."

"Good plan," Ryan said.

"We haven't had any footage from phones that shows the girls," Miller added. "It's been less than twenty-four hours, so we'll keep the request running on the news and radio for the time being."

Nikki passed around printouts from the websites she'd been looking at. "You'll see the men dress more modern, but they're always in jeans or dress pants, no shorts. No T-shirts allowed, it seems, but polo shirts are okay. Men are allowed to show some skin, unlike the females. Have to keep their virtue intact."

She probably sounded insensitive, but Nikki didn't have the energy to pretend she wasn't appalled at some of the religious group's strict practices, even the supposedly toned-down version of the church in Thief River Falls.

"I assume you're all aware that Shane Walker is not only a well-respected orthopedist, he's a connected one," Ryan continued. "He's the primary orthopedist for the Vikings, and he consults with the city's other professional teams."

"We are," Liam said. "Do you think that makes the girls a target?"

"Possibly," Ryan said. "A few seasons ago, the Vikings were fighting for the wild card spot in the playoffs when their best receiver suffered a season-ending injury. I remember hearing that the entire medical staff and coaches received threats for not taking care of their player."

"Shane mentioned that, but he downplayed it," Nikki said.

"That may be," Ryan answered. "But it's possible someone else decided to enact their revenge."

"Over football?" Nikki asked, doubtful. "I could see if the person was directly affected, but if you're talking just a fan, that's a stretch."

Liam and Miller both stared at her. "Football fans operate on a whole other level. I wouldn't put it past fans from sending the threats," Miller said. "But someone associated with the team, especially if they suffered a financial loss? I wouldn't be surprised."

"Which deputy is at the Walker home right now?" Nikki asked.

"Reynolds." Miller's chief deputy was a reliable cop with a knack for talking to victims. "He's there this morning until we relieve him. I'll have him talk to Walker."

"Let's get a whole list of anyone involved with the team that year who was disgruntled or blamed Walker for the guy's knee blowing out," Ryan said. "Where are we with the media?"

"We've got the girls' photos and information going on the morning news and radio shows with the tip line number," Miller said. "Plenty are coming in, and I've got a couple of deputies following up on all of them. Plus, the Amber Alert from last night will go out again this morning, and all of the state agencies have photos of Thea and Abby, including the Wisconsin boys across the river."

"Great," Ryan said. "Agent Hunt, your team is checking out the fundamentalist church in Thief River Falls. What about registered sex offenders, especially the Level 3s?"

"Two have been released this year and are listed as living in Washington County," Liam answered. "One's south near Atkins and had a history of crimes involving young boys, but the other rents a room in Stillwater. I'm headed there as soon as the meeting is done. We have agents following up on the other sex offenders in the area."

"What's the plan for searching on foot this morning?" Nikki asked.

"Sergeant Chen feels confident his people covered all of downtown before the storm came in, but we've got two officers essentially recanvassing, checking the dumpsters and the like, and patrol officers are going to knock on doors in the area where the purse was found. They'll check every open business as well as residences, and we're working to secure additional CCTV west of the river, in case the girls did walk that way and for some reason kept walking after the purse was dropped."

"I need a ride out to my place so I can shower and change and get my Jeep," Nikki said, feeling self-conscious in the same cut-off shorts and tank top she'd worn to the festival yesterday. "Then I'll pay a visit to Walker's office in Woodbury, see what I can find out about any problems with patients or threats. And head over to see the babysitter."

Ryan nodded as though confirming her own thoughts. She gathered her papers and tapped them on the table until they were even. "Keep me posted on any new developments."

Nikki glanced at Miller, who shrugged and stood. "Any chance you could drop me off at home?" she asked him.

．　．　．

Nikki shielded her eyes from the morning sun as she and Miller headed to his SUV. Despite the moderate morning temperature, humidity hung in the air. By noon, the outdoors would feel like a sauna. "Chief Ryan seems nice." Nikki climbed into the passenger seat.

Miller grunted and started the engine. "Too nice, if you ask me. She's a politician instead of a police officer."

Nikki had read up on the chief's background. Unlike the previous police chief, Ryan had a master's degree in public administration. She'd gone into the police academy following college, and earned her master's degree while she was still a beat cop on the street. Ryan had never been married, never had children. She'd been career driven, working her way up the food chain in the Chicago Police Department. Ryan had spent four years in internal affairs in Chicago before coming to Stillwater.

"Wonder why she left Chicago," Nikki said.

Miller headed toward the interstate. "Chicago's a dangerous city and internal affairs cops are considered the enemy," Miller answered. "I suppose she was looking for a change of pace. I just don't know her well enough to trust her."

"You're afraid she'll throw the sheriff's department under the bus to save face for the Stillwater police?"

Miller glanced at her. "Wouldn't be the first time."

"True," Nikki said. "I'm hoping she's actually putting the victims first."

"Which is surprising," Miller said. "You're usually wary of any authority figures besides your Bureau chief."

"I'm trying to be a little more optimistic," Nikki told him. "The last year and a half have been a crazy mess, but I'm still here. Lacey's still here. We have Rory and his family. As hard as it's been, it could have been worse."

"I noticed you called Rory's place home. You put the place in Highland Park on the market yet?"

Nikki's house in the St. Paul suburb had been paid off

during her divorce settlement, so she didn't have to worry about a mortgage. Rory thought she needed to get the house on the market soon given the real estate trends, but Nikki hadn't been able to bring herself to call a realtor. She and her late ex-husband had bought the place together. She blamed her hesitancy on Lacey, but the truth was, she didn't want to think about the Herculean task of getting the house ready to sell. "I don't know. It's nice to know I can stay there instead of a hotel if I get stuck in the city. I'm just trying to take it a day at a time right now."

"Good for you," Miller said. "Letting go of the past is damn hard, but it's also hard to walk forward when you're carrying it."

"I just wish I felt as optimistic about this case," Nikki said. "Britney found an officer shortly after she left the girls. The search began immediately. If they were lost in the crowd or playing around, we would have found them. We're looking at an abduction, unless I'm wrong about the river. Sadly, at this point, that's our best-case scenario."

"I agree with you," Miller said grimly. "Let's just pray nothing shows up on the sonar when the dive team goes out."

Rory's truck wasn't in the driveway, but he'd parked Nikki's Jeep in the garage. With Lacey staying with the Todds and Rory at work, the house felt too quiet and still. Lacey had been begging them for a dog, but with their schedules, the dog would be neglected and lonely. Still, it would be nice to have a wagging tail to greet her when no one else was home.

She set her bag on the kitchen counter and went straight to her and Rory's bedroom, stripping her dirty clothes off along the way and dumping them in the laundry basket. Her sticky skin wanted a cool shower, but Nikki's sore neck muscles from sleeping at an odd angle last night won the battle.

Like a lot of builders, Rory's own home needed plenty of upgrades. After purchasing the house from his parents, Rory had turned the Jack and Jill bathroom between his and Mark's old rooms into a master bath that connected to Rory's room. All the framework and drywall had been done, so the room was technically finished, but the bathroom fixtures were distinctly nineties, and the laminate floor had several cracks in it. When she'd asked about the change, Rory had told her he didn't want to sleep in his parents' master bedroom, and his room had a prettier view. He'd lived as a bachelor and worked long hours so he barely noticed the things that needed updating.

The shower was at the top of the list. Whoever turned on the water had to finagle the hot and cold until they were somewhere in the middle, meaning it was nearly impossible to take a hot shower without scalding herself at least once.

Nikki showered quickly, making sure to put extra product in her wavy hair so the humidity didn't make her look like she'd gotten a perm, even though she'd be lucky if she made it an hour before putting it up due to the heat.

She finished in the bathroom, glad to get the cotton taste out of her mouth. Nikki slipped on a new bra and clean panties. She found a pair of light-blue linen shorts and a lightweight, sleeveless top. FBI agents usually weren't supposed to wear shorts on cases, but Nikki's boss always made an exception during the summer heat, especially if they weren't in the office, as long as the outfit was still business casual.

Her phone rang. Nikki grabbed it off the dresser where she'd plugged it in to charge.

"Agent Hunt," Nikki answered tersely, yanking her shorts over her hips.

"This is Trooper Emily James. I'm returning Agent Wilson's call, but he isn't answering his phone. He left this number as a backup."

Liam not answering a call he was waiting for was unusual, but Nikki had given him plenty of things to track down.

"I'm Special Agent Nikki Hunt," she said. "Agent Wilson's supervisor. Thank you for calling back."

"No problem," James said. "Did you find the little girls?"

"No," Nikki said. "Our working theory is an abduction, but we are still searching. Shane Walker thinks one of Britney's family members from the Fundamentalist Saints of Zion came and took them. Agent Wilson was told you were the person to speak with about the FSZ."

James sighed. "Unfortunately, although there isn't a lot to tell. They own five hundred acres of land northwest of Thief River Falls. The church and administration offices are on that property, along with the members' homes. The area is rich in farming, and they're exceptional at utilizing all of their resources, including children."

"What do you mean?"

"I can't prove it, because we don't have the manpower or resources to do a thorough investigation, but they've got two construction crews of teenaged boys and men who work long hours. They underbid everyone else, and the employees are barely given enough to live. The rest goes to the church. Same goes with their tech business. Another extreme faction in Utah did the same thing, on a much larger scale."

Nikki could understand why Trooper James hadn't been able to prove her theory. Various privacy laws likely protected the church, and the federal government had a better chance at uncovering any wrongdoing. Unfortunately, the government tended to ignore cults until the situation was dire, and in many cases, too late. "Your administration officer said a local girl had converted to the church and her parents believed she was being held on the ranch."

"I tracked their daughter down at the FSZ compound. I found her living with a large church family—there were nine kids at the time—and she claimed she was working as a nanny to help out the family. She was happy, healthy, and eighteen. I couldn't do much."

"But you suspected something else was going on?" Nikki asked.

"The cult is polygamous, as you know," Trooper James said. "Their additional wives are 'in Holy Spirit only,' as one of the elders explained to me. They know polygamy is against the law, and this is their way around it. Everything the girl said to me sounded rehearsed. She'd left home as an opinionated, fashion-minded eighteen-year-old and less than two months later, wore a long denim skirt, long-sleeved blouse and had her hair done in the same long braid as the rest of the women. My boss said I might be projecting since I'm such an independent female."

"Sounds like you need a new boss," Nikki said. "Always trust your gut reaction. It's our survival instinct, and it's almost always right."

"That's exactly what I told him," James said. "I figured it was only a matter of time before she had a kid of her own, and sure enough, eleven months later, she had a girl. There's no wedding or birth certificate on file, but she told her parents that she'd married the man she was living with and become a sister-wife. She cut off all contact with them as they were deemed unworthy of the church."

"When was the last time you spoke to this girl?" Nikki asked.

"Two years, maybe," James said. "After I came looking for her, the church installed a gate at the ranch, with two security guards. We think there are about fifteen families—I should say, family homes, because who knows how many sister-wives there are—on the ranch. Since I was last on the property, they've built a medical clinic, staffed by a nurse practitioner who's a member of the church. I've also heard rumors of certified midwives, and we know they're building new houses every year to accommo-date growing families, but their census information has barely changed since they first moved onto the property."

"Sounds like they know how to skirt around the law," Nikki

said. Polygamy was illegal, but the church had found a work-around. There was no law against having your mistress or girl-friend or whatever they called the extra wives as long as the women were legal age. "What about the kids on the ranch?"

"The younger ones appeared happy and adjusted to me," James said. "Most of them attend the public school, at least through fourth or fifth grade. Then they are homeschooled."

"Meaning their education is focused on the church and not real life," Nikki said.

"We don't know," James said. "But that's my guess."

"Is there any way the FSZ would allow you onto their prop-erty?" Nikki asked.

"Maybe, as long as I say we're looking for missing girls, say it's a statewide search. If I play it right, they might cooperate. The elder council doesn't want to be challenged in the same way the Utah faction was challenged, and they swear they don't allow underage marriages or unions. They pay taxes, donate to charity, sell their wares at the farmers' market. They're all kind of standoffish, but the council wants to keep a low profile. I should be able to use that to my advantage."

"What do you know about Silas Hatch?" Nikki asked.

"I think he's one of the elders, but I can't say I've heard the name very much."

"Make sure you talk to him face to face." Nikki didn't want to reveal her entire hand to a trooper she'd never worked with, but she needed eyes on Silas. "See if you can get a handle on his inner circle and find out about their comings and goings over the last few days."

"That's a tall order," James said. "You think they're somehow involved in the kidnapping?"

"The Walkers think so," Nikki said. "I need you to help me find out if they're right."

Her phone buzzed with another call. "I've got to take a call, but please let me know what you find out as soon as possible."

Nikki hit the green button on the Jeep's touch screen. "Any news?"

Miller cleared his throat, and Nikki's stomach sank to her toes. "Kent, what is it?"

Nikki's stomach dropped as he replied.

"Thea."

SEVEN

Abby shivered in the dark place. Where was Thea? She always took care of Abby. The little girl reached out blindly in the dark for her sister and started to cry when she felt only cold floor. The room smelled bad, like the bathrooms at the festival. She rubbed her left hand. The skin was still sore from the needle he'd used before he took Thea away.

It seemed like hours since the man had dumped her in this smelly room and told her to stay put. She'd done exactly as he asked, curling up in a little ball on the hard floor. She'd quietly cried herself to sleep, but now her stomach growled, and she was so thirsty.

Where was Thea?

Her heart began to pound. She didn't remember much about the night before, only that they'd been taken to watch the fireworks. Thea did it, so Abby followed. At first it had been exciting, watching the colors explode over the water. Then Abby remembered feeling dizzy. After that everything became hazy. She remembered feeling so hot, she couldn't breathe. But then she shivered uncontrollably, just like she did when Mommy said she had a fever.

Hot tears built in her eyes. Where was Mommy? Why hadn't she come to help them? Even though she didn't know where she was, Abby knew she shouldn't be loud or draw attention, so she covered her mouth when she couldn't control her tears anymore.

A beep sounded from somewhere in the dark, and then another, and another. Abby heard a loud click. She rubbed the tears from her eyes and peered at the doorway. He stood there, without Thea.

He walked slowly toward her. A mask like the kind sick people wore at the doctor's office hid most of his face. Maybe he'd come to help her now. Abby had just misunderstood what happened. Thea must have gotten sick, and the man had brought Abby here so he could get Thea to the doctor, or Mommy.

Lights came on as he got closer. Abby saw everything at once: the weird, soft-looking walls, a skinny dirty mattress a few feet away, and a tube that looked like something she and Thea had found in Mommy's nightstand when they were snooping.

"Where's my sister?" Abby's voice sounded tiny and frail.

"At peace."

"Why can't I be with her? I want to be with her and Mommy!"

He looked down at her, wrinkles forming between his eyes. Abby wished she could see the rest of his face. She didn't really remember what he looked like. She'd been too excited to watch the fireworks.

"Because you're mine now, sweetheart." His big, rough hand wrapped around her arm. "Let's get you cleaned up."

EIGHT

Nikki drove down the two-lane road, her fingers aching from her steely grip on the wheel. Conway's Apple Orchard was located on the western side of Washington County, less than ten minutes from the house Nikki had grown up in. She'd only been to the orchard a couple of times in the last few years, mostly for Lacey's benefit, since the orchard always had fun kid events during apple picking season. The same family had run the orchard since it first opened thirty years ago.

A cheerful red barn greeted visitors, nestled beneath a towering maple. A large sign next to the circular drive announced the orchard was closed until apple picking season in August. At least Nikki didn't have to worry about the prying eyes of customers while they worked the scene, but it was only a matter of time before word got out to the media that a child's body had been found at the orchard.

A woman in running shoes and a Twins cap paced in front of the barn. Nikki parked next to Miller's SUV and grabbed her credentials.

"Agent Nikki Hunt, FBI." Nikki held her badge up for the

woman. Lean and fit, the woman appeared to be around Nikki's age.

"Rita Conway. I'm the owner. I found her. The sheriff said to send you around back."

"How big is your orchard?" Nikki asked.

"Two hundred acres," Rita said. "She's just a few rows back. You won't miss it."

"When did you find her?"

"This morning, I came to check on the trees. I was worried the high winds overnight might have caused damage." Rita's hands shook, her fair skin covered in a sheen of sweat.

"Is the barn your storefront?" Nikki asked. "And is it air conditioned?"

"Yes to both," Rita said. "Why?"

"You look overheated, and the stress of finding the body isn't helping." Nikki fired off a text to Miller, asking him to send the responding deputy around to stay with Rita so Nikki could walk the crime scene. She texted Liam and asked him to get a list of the Vikings fans who'd threatened Dr. Walker, and to track down the babysitter.

Seconds later, Chief Deputy Reynolds rounded the side of the barn, pale and sweating. She'd worked a few cases with him, and like everyone, he was deeply affected when the victim was a child.

"Get some water," Nikki told the deputy. "Rita, I'm going to take a look and check in with Miller. Reynolds, if the medical examiner shows up, send her around."

Nikki walked slowly around the barn, her chest tight. The hot afternoon sun glinted off the rows of apple trees, and the gentle northern breeze would have been welcome if the air hadn't been saturated with the stink of decay. Just as Rita had said, no one would have missed Thea's body.

Did her killer know that, or had this been a place of convenience?

Miller crouched next to the yellow crime scene tape, dry heaving. A deputy Nikki had never met handed the sheriff a bottle of water. He drank it too fast, spitting half of it out.

"Kent, are you all right?" The smell grew worse with every step Nikki took toward Miller. It was bad, but Nikki had dealt with worse, and she knew that Miller had, too.

"She never had a chance," Miller sputtered.

Nikki saw the small body lying on her stomach underneath one of the apple trees. Thea's hands and feet had been tied with zip ties, her blonde hair limp against her back. Flies buzzed around her. Nikki slipped on the protective booties and latex gloves she'd brought from the Jeep and ducked under the tape. Her heart pounded in her chest as she approached the body, and for a moment, all she could see was Lacey face down and dumped like garbage.

Nikki fought tears as she knelt down next to the little girl. Duct tape covered her mouth and part of her nose, along with her eyes. Her skin had a blue-purple tinge that usually accompanied suffocation.

Angry red streaks on Thea's wrists and ankles made it clear she'd struggled to free herself. It was definitely her.

"Is Blanchard on her way?" Nikki choked out. "Courtney will be here in about thirty minutes. Liam's chasing a lead."

"Soon, I hope." Miller got to his feet and ducked under the tape. "You talk to Rita?"

Nikki nodded. "She's pretty shaken up. Reynolds is with her inside the barn. No security cameras in the orchard?"

"Just one, up front," Miller said. "Cornfields behind the orchard, but I'm thinking the killer parked on the road on the east side of the property and came in, using the trees as cover. They're all pretty established and full."

"Check for any sign of tire tracks on the roadside?"

"Reynolds did, but there aren't any that look fresh. It rained enough we'd be able to see the imprint."

Meaning the killer had probably parked somewhere and walked onto the property. Nikki shaded her eyes from the glowing sun. The orchard was definitely rural, tucked in a pocket of maple trees and towering hedges. It wasn't visible from the main highway, and without the signs directing her to turn, Nikki would have missed the aptly named Conway Drive, which looped around alongside the orchard. "I'd say whoever did this had some knowledge about this place." Conway Orchard was one of two large, popular orchards in the metro area. Nikki could probably throw a stick and hit someone who'd been to the place at least once. "They have any seasonal employees?"

Miller nodded. "They like to hire high school and college-aged kids during the summer. It's closed in the winter, so the family takes care of the maintenance. Rita's daughter and her boyfriend usually come over and do whatever needs doing, like plowing so the snow doesn't pile up in the winter."

"Rita give you their names?"

"Not yet. I told her we'd come sit down and talk once the medical examiner took over." Miller looked at Thea, fighting back emotion. "I can't leave her here alone, Nikki."

Nikki rubbed her friend's shoulder. "I know, and I'm sure her family will be grateful. You want me to go to the Walkers'? We need to let them know before word gets out and they hear it on the news."

"Chen wanted to make the notification," Miller answered. "He's on his way now."

She heard the crunch of tires on gravel, followed by the sound of a door shutting. Within seconds, Blanchard rounded the corner carrying her clipboard and camera. Nikki was grateful the medical examiner hadn't sent a death investigator, which was the usual routine, but in the back of her mind, she wondered what Britney would say about Blanchard's dark skin.

Blanchard was one of the best MEs Nikki had worked with in her two-decade career, and little Thea would be treated with respect and love.

"Miller told me it was the little girl," Blanchard said. She stood on one leg to put on paper booties before snapping on latex gloves. "Is that how she looked when she was found?"

"I haven't touched her," Miller said. "Reynolds got here first and put up the tape. We have to get this one right."

Blanchard grunted as she ducked beneath the tape and started taking photos. "I always get it right. Where's Courtney and Big Red?"

Nikki couldn't help but snort at the nickname Blanchard and Courtney had bestowed on Liam, mostly because she knew it grated on him. "She'll be here any minute. He's going through the sex offender list."

"Good place to start, although I won't know if she was assaulted until we get her back to the lab." Blanchard crouched next to Thea and gently brushed her blonde hair aside. "No bruises on the neck so far." She pushed Thea's damp shirt-sleeves up to her shoulders. A deep bruise, complete with what appeared to be fingermarks, wrapped around her arm. "How good is Courtney?"

"The best I've ever worked with, but getting fingerprints off skin is a specialty that takes more than skill. Timing, the shirt-sleeve, the rain—less chance of those fingerprints not being washed away." Courtney's alma mater, the University of Tennessee, home of the famed "body farm" for studying cadavers in real world conditions, had recently released a study showing that prints could be lifted off skin in the lab and in the field, but it was tricky at best. "We have a better chance of her getting prints off Thea's purse. But she'll consider it a challenge for sure."

"Did she suffocate on the duct tape?" Miller asked.

Blanchard turned Thea over, cradling her head like an infant's. "Poor sweet baby. It's possible."

Miller put his head down, and Nikki willed herself to breathe after seeing Thea's face. Bits of dried vomit stuck to her chin and shirt. "Is that a rash?" She pointed to Thea's arm.

"Diffuse petechiae," Blanchard said. "Tiny spots of bleeding under the skin. Lots of times caused by hard coughing and other very strenuous activity. We also see it with heat stroke, especially in children. We also see thermal burns though, usually second or third degree, and she doesn't have any."

Nikki glanced at Miller. "It was still over eighty degrees at ten p.m. If the kidnapper stashed them in a car, especially if he put them in a trunk, it wouldn't take long for heat stroke to set in."

"No, it wouldn't," Blanchard agreed. "She's in rigor, but it's already passed through her facial muscles. Depending on the environment, facial rigor passes six to eight hours after death. What time was she found?"

"Around eight a.m.," Miller answered. "Less than an hour ago."

Blanchard tested Thea's fingers, which often came out of rigor before larger muscles like the legs. "Heat always speeds it up. Humidity makes it worse, and the dew point is already over sixty, but it's unlikely she was alive ten hours ago."

"She died within the first hour he took her?" Nikki felt like weeping. Thea really hadn't stood a chance. Nikki prayed that meant the kidnapper hadn't had time to assault Thea.

"It's very possible," Blanchard said. "Children can die in less than an hour from being trapped in the heat. And to answer the sheriff's question, yes, it's very possible she suffocated, at least to the point of losing consciousness. The tip of her nose looks like the skin got raw while she struggled to get it down under her nose. But I need to do a full exam to make that official."

"Hey, I found the party." Courtney and one of her lab assistants appeared at the front of the orchard, already in protective gear.

"Is that a dolly?" Miller pointed at the neatly stacked equipment her assistant had wheeled into the orchard.

"It's called a hand truck," Courtney said. "Brits call it a sack truck." She gave Nikki a pointed look. "Recently met a British forensic artist who told me that."

For once, Courtney was seeing someone in her own field, going against her established rule of never dating anyone who knew as much about death—or more—than Courtney.

"My back is messed up from lugging equipment around the last few years," Courtney said. "This is just easier."

If Liam were here, he would have pointed out the dolly being taller than Courtney, who barely crossed five feet.

Courtney wiped sweat off her face and joined them on the other side of the tape. "We're still working on trying to get prints off her purse, but it's going to take a while with that fabric."

"Can you rush it?" Nikki asked.

"Yes, but remember the state crime lab has such a backlog of forensic testing that they've asked us to help them catch up. We're all juggling at least ten cases at once right now." Courtney looked at the motionless little girl on the ground. "I hate people."

"Me, too," Blanchard said. "Child killers deserve their own special ring of hell."

"We need to find out if she was in a car or some other enclosed space," Nikki said. "Get as many fibers as you can to test. I'm going to check on Rita."

"Send Reynolds back here," Miller said.

Nikki retraced her steps back to the barn. Sweat rolled down her neck and settled into the groove of her collarbone, but she barely noticed. She'd wanted to echo Courtney's sentiments about people, but that line of thinking wouldn't help her find Abby before she met the same fate as her sister.

"Miller wanted me to send you his way," Nikki told Reynolds, looking past him to the young woman now sitting with Rita. "Hi, I'm Agent Hunt. Are you Rita's daughter?" Rita had a more athletic build and narrow face, but the resemblance between the two women was undeniable.

"Joy." She adjusted the brim of her baseball hat and looked up at Nikki, twisting a lock of dirty blonde hair around her index finger. "I can't believe this happened. It's one of the little girls on the news. Thea, right?"

Nikki nodded. "And her younger sister is still missing, so any information the two of you can give us is crucial."

Joy blanched. "I'm not sure what we can contribute. Mom said she already explained the security cameras and checked the footage with the sheriff. I've been telling her to invest in more cameras around the property, but she hadn't had the chance." She wiped her nose with a crumpled tissue in her hand. "Who leaves a dead body in an apple orchard?"

"That's a very good question," Nikki said. "We can't rule out the killer choosing this place for convenience, but it's very possible that they chose this place because they were familiar with it and the summer routine—the fact that you'd walk past there in the morning."

"To make sure someone found her?" Rita finally spoke.

"Maybe," Nikki said. "Have you had any customers yet this year that were unsettling in some way, noticed anyone wandering around the perimeter?"

"Strawberry-picking season just finished," Joy said. "We've been slammed the last two weeks. Mom and I are usually in here, working the registers. Dad usually tends to the plants and trees, but he's recovering from back surgery, so we've hired a couple of college students to do the heavy lifting. I can give you their information, but they're both good boys."

"Thank you, that is helpful," Nikki said. "Your mom mentioned your boyfriend helping to snowplow in the winter. How often is he around to help out?" She kept her tone light, careful not to sound accusatory.

Joy looked out the large back window at the trees. "We broke up last month."

"I'm sorry to hear that," Nikki said. "Would you mind giving me his information?"

"What for?" Joy asked.

"We want to talk to anyone with extended access to this place," Nikki said. "He might have noticed something weird and ignored it, that sort of thing."

Joy shook her head. "He wasn't here much this summer. We were having problems."

Rita stepped in. "Tell her what you told me this morning. Don't protect that bastard."

"Mom, it was a rumor; that's not why we broke up," Joy snapped.

Rita rolled her eyes. "Like I was born yesterday. Joy, a child is dead and another missing." Rita looked at Nikki. "Joy found out that her boyfriend Rod was accused of inappropriately touching his second cousin when she was seven. He's twenty-two now. Nothing came out of it, but it was the last straw for Joy."

"That doesn't mean he was guilty," Joy said. "The cousin had made up stories before."

"I understand," Nikki said, "but as your mother mentioned, one little girl is dead and the other still missing. I need his information. Either you give it to me, or I get it myself. Time is slipping away for Abby."

Joy sighed. "Rodney Adam. He lives downtown at the Riverview Commons."

Rita looked sharply at her daughter. "That's assisted living. I thought he lived in a house with roommates?"

"He moved in to help with his grandmother last month," Joy said. "Right after we broke up."

"When was the last time you spoke with him?"

"Not since we broke up." Joy hugged herself. "You're wasting your time if you think Rod did this. He'll be so hurt that I talked to you."

Sounded like Joy wasn't over Rodney to Nikki. "I don't know who did this, but Abby may still be alive, so I don't have time to worry about anyone's feelings."

"We need to get an officer downtown right away," Nikki told Miller. "The daughter's ex-boyfriend was accused of molesting his cousin when she was seven. She recanted the story, but he lives at the Riverview Commons with his grandmother. Rita's daughter clearly still has feelings for him, so I'm sure she's going to give him a heads-up."

"That's less than a five-minute walk to Lowell Park." Miller swiped his phone open. "Christ. I'll see if Chen can get some officers to keep an eye on the exits until you get there. My buddy's mom lives there, and it's pretty well lit and security is tight, including CCTV. I'll call the main office and let them know you'd like to look at security videos."

"I hope they cooperate," Nikki said. "Those places can get funny about privacy." Nikki understood the need to protect the patients, but CCTV also protected them from mistreatment and wandering off, among other things.

Miller snorted. "They will. My buddy's the head of security."

He and Nikki had gone to high school together, and while the last two years of Nikki's time at Stillwater High was marked by grief and hazy memories, Miller's time earned him several records as a running back and a college scholarship. He'd known everyone in high school, and that personality trait served him well as county sheriff.

"You have a picture of this guy?" Miller asked. "A friend of mine and her sister heard about the girls on the news and called me directly. They parked at Trinity Lutheran. Around 10:30, they saw a teenaged boy wearing a white Minnesota Timberwolves shirt standing in the church parking lot with the purse. He dropped it into the bushes where we found it. They got a good look and said they'd come to the sheriff's office to sit for a sketch."

Nikki clicked on the text she'd had Joy send her. "His name's Rodney Adam, aged twenty-two, works at the 3M factory in New Ulm. He's due to go into work at noon, so we need to move fast."

"That's a thirty-minute drive from downtown at least," Miller said. "Is taking care of grandma the only reason he moved? Did he have a falling out with the roommates?"

"She didn't say, but she did give me the old address." Nikki rattled it off to Miller and used her key fob to remote start the Jeep, as though a minute or two of air conditioning would make any difference in a closed vehicle in this heat. "It's only ten minutes from the 3M factory. I'll see if Liam can track down one of the roommates after we've talked to Rodney. He may not be our guy, but we have to move on this in case he is and Abby's still alive."

"Chen also called while you were talking to Rita and her daughter," Miller told her. "The Walkers took it about as good as you'd expect. Britney's asking for you, by the way. Chief Ryan has Chen hanging around their house in case the kidnapper calls. I don't know why she thinks that's going to happen, but whatever. I want eyes on Shane and Britney anyway."

"His alibi's pretty strong," Nikki reminded him.

"I know, but I still want an eye kept on the guy."

"All right, let Chen know I'll head there after I talk to Rodney. I don't want to give him time to get wind of my visit." Nikki got into her Jeep and called Liam, but the call went to voicemail, so she fired off a text asking him to meet her downtown at Rodney's building. Liam had the unenviable task of tracking down registered sex offenders in Stillwater proper, so he'd probably wind up beating her to the building.

NINE

Riverview Commons overlooked Main Street and the St. Croix River, barely more than a stone's throw away from the festival area where Thea and Abby had last been seen. Nikki scanned the street for Liam's silver Prius. If he hadn't found a spot on the street, he was probably in the parking lot. She quickly drove through, but there was still no sign of his car. She double-checked her phone to see if he'd texted her back, but her message remained on delivered.

Nikki was used to missing persons cases moving at break-neck speed. They only had a few days to look for Abby before the chances of finding her became almost nothing. But this case, and her suspect list, was getting more complex by the day. She wondered if the babysitter had been found, or if they'd found anyone holding a grudge against Shane Walker.

Chief Ryan had sent Chen to deliver the news to the Walkers, and even though she felt selfish, Nikki was glad she hadn't been the one to tell them. She needed to focus her attention on finding Abby.

"He better have some damn good information," Nikki grumbled, spotting a Stillwater police car parked a block down from the building. Nikki found a space behind him and tapped on the unmarked car's window.

"Any sign of him?"

"No," the young officer said excitedly. "We have another car around back, and he can see the fire escape and back doors. No sign of the guy. Ran his information like the sheriff asked; he owns an older Jeep Liberty. It's parked in the back, backed into a space near the exit onto the street. Thing is, Riverview is assisted living for elders and people with disabilities. Why's this young guy living here?"

"Good question."

Nikki checked her texts, but still nothing from Liam. It wasn't like him to not respond. "He better have a damn good reason," she grumbled.

"I'm sorry?" the officer said. "I didn't catch—"

"Talking to myself." Nikki checked to make sure her gun was loaded and ready before slipping it into its holster. "What's your name?"

"Jackson," he said.

"Well, Jackson, let's go talk to Rodney."

The building's head of security greeted them in the lobby. His straight posture and mannerisms, along with his cropped haircut, made Nikki think he was former military. "Chuck Randall. Kent told me you were coming and briefed me on the situation. We're pulling the CCTV from nine p.m. last night to an hour ago. You want to come look?"

"After I talk to Rodney," Nikki said. "I want to check the apartment out for myself."

"Fair enough," Chuck said.

Officer Jackson bounced up and down on his heels, clearly ready to break down some doors. Nikki had to handle this situation with finesse, and if Rodney was guilty, she didn't need an inexperienced cop mucking it up. "Officer Jackson, would you mind looking through the footage while I talk to Rodney? You're young and sharp, and I'm terrible at catching things on grainy black and white security film," Nikki lied, trying to make the kid feel important and not dismissed.

He looked disappointed but nodded.

"His grandma lives on the third floor, apartment 3B."

"Rodney just moved in to help his grandmother last month," Nikki said. "You ever met him?"

"Oh yeah," Chuck said. "Polite, friendly to the residents. No noise complaints, which is what these guys always worry about when someone's younger family member comes to stay."

"Do you know if his grandma actually needed him, or is she helping him out?" Nikki asked.

"I don't know," Chuck said. "I never had occasion to ask."

Nikki got on the elevator while Chuck and Officer Jackson headed back to the security office. She checked her messages on the short ride. Liam had finally texted, saying he'd had his phone on silent while he was chasing down leads. He'd never done that before, but even though he'd recovered from the severe head injury he'd sustained in the spring during a triple homicide investigation, Liam sometimes had trouble with constant noise, something he'd never had issue with before the attack. She responded, telling him to stay put and she'd brief him when she was finished.

The elevator dinged open, and Nikki stepped into the bleak, gray corridor. Riverview Commons was an income-based facility, which meant the funds were spent on necessities instead of décor. But the hall smelled like fresh laundry, and the few motel-type paintings hanging on the wall didn't have any major dust buildup.

Nikki stopped at apartment 3B and knocked on the door. She held her breath and leaned close to the prefab wood, listening for any sound of distress. Footsteps clunked toward her, so Nikki moved back, her right hand close to the gun holstered to her hip.

Rodney answered the door, freshly showered and smelling of cologne. "Agent Nikki Hunt, right?"

She managed to stop the scowl starting to spread across her face. Nikki had expected Joy to warn Rodney they were coming, but it still pissed her off. "I see you're all prepared for me," she retorted, showing her FBI badge.

Rodney flushed. "No disrespect meant."

"It's fine. Can I come in?"

"Just stay in the kitchen with me, please. Gran's sleeping."

Exhaustion and frustration were starting to get the best of Nikki. "Look, I know you know why I'm here. I want to look in every room and closet. I can be quiet, but I want to look. You don't have to let me," she added. "But I don't have to tell you what it looks like if you refuse. I can come back with a warrant if you want. I'm trying to find a missing child. I can't worry about your grandma's nap."

She normally didn't lead a person of interest, but the ticking clock hanging in the kitchenette taunted Nikki. She had to find Abby alive.

Rodney flushed. "I've got nothing to do with whatever's happened... those girls... the child at the orchard," he said. "Look around all you want. I'll deal with Gran if she wakes up."

Technically, if the grandmother was the tenant on file, Nikki needed her permission to search, but she decided to take the risk and plow ahead.

The kitchenette was smaller than Lacey's bedroom at Rory's. The subway-tile countertop was cleaned, and a couple of dishes were in the sink.

A fat, black cat leapt onto the countertop and looked at Nikki with sleepy eyes.

"Get down, Amos."

The cat ignored him.

"Sorry." Rodney grabbed the cat and put him on the floor.

"He's a pain. Gran wants me to re-home him. She doesn't like cats, or the litter box."

Nikki smiled tersely. "Can I look in the cabinets?"

"Uh, yeah."

She opened the three lower-level cabinets. She thought of Abby and how small she was. She'd found kids in tighter places.

Rodney stared at her. "I can't believe you actually think I took those kids."

"I don't," Nikki said. "But I know you were accused of inappropriate behavior with a seven-year-old."

The living room wasn't much bigger than the kitchen. A recliner and an old bean bag faced a modest-sized flat screen. A couple of magazines and board games sat on the end table next to the recliner, but the room was tidy, with no sign of anything out of place.

"Two bedrooms?"

"Sort of," Rodney said, hooking his thumb over his shoulder. "Bedroom and a den, which is just big enough to put an air mattress in."

"Can I take a look?"

He gestured for her to go ahead. "My room's on the right."

He hadn't been lying when he said the den was barely large enough for an air mattress. It looked more like a small walk-in closet with a cot. Plastic bins had been stacked next to the mattress, which had been wedged into the right corner. Rodney had enough room to stand up and move a couple of feet, but that was about it.

Rodney knocked on his grandmother's door. "Gram, you awake?"

A muffled female voice on the other side of the wall said something Nikki couldn't understand, and then Rodney inched the door open.

"Gram, remember I said that little girl was found in that

orchard my ex's family owns? Well, the cop is here and wants to search our apartment."

"Search for what?"

Rodney shrugged. "The other kid, I guess. Just doing her job."

"Well she don't need to be in my damn room."

Nikki remained behind Rodney, careful not to infringe on the woman's privacy any more. "I'm Agent Nikki Hunt with the FBI, ma'am. Because your grandson has a connection to both the last place the girls were seen and where the body was found today, we need to make sure he's ruled out as a suspect."

"You can't do shit without a warrant," came the defiant reply. "I have my medical card."

Nikki realized she hadn't seen any sign of marijuana in Rodney's room, but the odor since he opened his grandmother's door made her think she'd been smoking instead of following the legal use law. Minnesota's medical marijuana rules were pretty strict, and most of the time was dispensed in pill form. If the odor were any indication, Gram was growing her own in her room.

"Ma'am, I'm not concerned about anything other than finding a missing six-year-old girl," Nikki said.

The floorboards creaked, followed by the sound of a closet door opening and then closing. "Move, Rodney."

He moved out of his grandmother's way, and Nikki came face to face with a shrunken, white-haired lady wielding a cane and a case of red eye. "Don't act like I'm too senile to understand. You're here because that damn niece of mine put her little daughter up to saying Rod had touched her. She took the story back. My grandson is no creep."

"I understand your frustration," Nikki said. "But I just saw the body of a nine-year-old who had her life snuffed out for no reason, and her baby sister is still out there, alone with a predator. I have to cross your grandson off the suspect list so I can find the real killer."

Grandma's face softened. "Fine, but this place is small. Everything is packed full."

"I'll only be a minute."

Nikki peeked under the full-sized bed. Four clear plastic storage boxes had been lined up neatly underneath. The little closet was more of the same, and Nikki assumed the bit of green leaf peeking out from under a sweater on the closet shelf was the contraband Grandma was worried about.

As expected, there was no sign of Abby in the apartment. Grandma and Rodney sat at the kitchen table, watching her warily.

"Thank you for cooperating," Nikki said. "Rodney, did you go to Lumberjack Days over the weekend?"

He nodded. "I worked the beer tent across from the river. I had to help shut down. We were there past midnight."

"Do you remember if you took any breaks?"

"Other than the bathroom? Not really. We were slammed all night."

Nikki found the photos of the girls Britney had texted, including one with Britney herself. "You don't remember seeing them last night?"

Rodney shook his head. "I didn't see that, but I did see the girls standing in the beer line with their mom. Looked like they were nagging her about something, 'cause she finally shoved the big bag she was carrying at them and yelled something. The girls ran off and she stayed in line to wait."

Nikki had been close enough to Britney that night that she would have smelled beer on her breath. "You remember what the mom ordered?"

"Vodka lemonade," Rodney answered. "She asked me to pour it into her water bottle, but that's not allowed. Didn't see her after that."

Nikki left Rodney with her card and instructions to call if he remembered anything else. She headed downstairs and found the security office.

"Anything?" Nikki asked.

"He got home around one a.m.," Jackson said. "Alone. There's no video of him leaving the building since then."

Rodney was likely innocent, unless more than one person had been involved. "Report back to Chen and let him know this is a dead end. I'll let the sheriff know."

Nikki stopped at the Washington County Sheriff's to pick Liam up. He paced outside, phone cradled on his shoulder, talking animatedly. Nikki honked and drove up alongside him.

Liam opened the door and got into the passenger seat. "I've got to go. I'll talk to you later." He ended the call, roughly shoving the phone in his pocket.

"Everything okay?" Nikki asked, threading her way through the full parking lot.

"Yeah, just Caitlin being Caitlin. We didn't talk about the case, by the way."

"I trust you." Nikki merged onto the road. "Trooper James called me. She said you didn't answer your phone."

"Shit," he said. "I had it on vibrate. What'd she say?"

"The FSZ keeps to themselves. No reports of trouble, save for the parents who reported about their daughter being held there. It sounds like they're trying to right some of the wrongs from the Utah sect, at least on the surface. But they also have church-run homeschool starting with middle school. If it's anything like previous sects, kids—girls in particular—are taught little to nothing about sex or contraception, STDs. Many in the Utah sect barely even had an elementary education. Doesn't sound like it's as bad at the ranch, but things aren't always as they appear. Anyway, James is headed there to see what she can find out. Also a tip came through directly to Miller through a friend. She and her sister parked at Trinity Lutheran Saturday. They saw a young white male toss the purse into the hedges by the church. Thin, baggy jeans and a white Minnesota Timber-wolves T-shirt."

Liam's head shot up from his notes. "What time was this?"

"Around 10:30," Nikki said. "Witness remembered seeing the time on her car's touch screen and then seeing the teenager."

"She saw him that well?" Liam asked.

"Trinity Lutheran's lot is well lit, and he was only a couple of feet away. Miller's got both women coming to the sheriff's office to sit with a sketch artist."

"Didn't expect that one," Liam said. "A teenage boy?"

"I know," Nikki agreed. "But we've seen kids do some horrible things. Very little surprises me anymore, you know?" She'd seen the photos of Silas Hatch and Hyrum, Britney's brother. Neither one of them could have been mistaken for a teenaged boy, even in the worst light.

Liam nodded, his eyes on his notebook. "A witness called into the tip line about half an hour ago. A couple of guys were hanging out at the beer garden, across from Lowell. They talked to a woman matching Britney's description for almost thirty minutes leading up to the fireworks. They offered to buy her a beer, but she declined, saying she had her own and holding up her water bottle. Fireworks started, she kind of freaked out and took off."

"Great. Any idea if she was drinking water or something else?"

"They thought she was tipsy."

Nikki remembered the empty coffee cup sitting next to Britney at the Warden's House. "I didn't smell alcohol on her, but vodka doesn't smell. She ordered vodka lemonade before the fireworks, and she asked Rodney to pour it into her bottle, but he refused."

"He's the one with the connection to the orchard? Is it possible he's actually the person the two women saw?"

"I don't think so," she said. "Rodney's over six feet, thick and tattooed. The women were very clear on the person they saw being a teenager."

Trooper James's number flashed on the Jeep's screen. Nikki put the call on Bluetooth. "Agent Wilson is with me as well. We're heading over to the parents' house now. Any luck with the FSZ?"

"Actually, yes." The trooper's voice blasted through the speakers. Nikki turned the volume down.

"My supervisor and I drove out to the compound, and they didn't hesitate to let us in the front gate. We spoke with the entire council, including Silas Hatch, and showed the photos of the girls to as many people as possible. They allowed us to walk through the school and other buildings."

"You showed the photo to Silas?" Nikki hadn't told James that Silas was Thea's father, and she hoped he hadn't caught any family resemblance or bothered to do the math. "You didn't reveal the Walkers' names, did you?"

"No," James said. "I just told them that the daughters of a former member were missing and we were helping the FBI in the search. They were totally compliant, and as much as I hate to admit it—because I'd love to catch them breaking the law—the council and other church members we spoke to didn't give us the impression they were hiding anything."

They wouldn't have been allowed to go into any of the private homes, which meant Abby could still be hidden at the western Minnesota compound, but the logistics made it unlikely. If anyone involved with the church was involved, the kidnapper probably hadn't made it back to Thief River Falls.

"My supervisor also gave me some interesting information,"

James continued. "Shane Walker's first wife was ten years older than him and died under suspicious circumstances about a year before he left town. They rented a townhouse in one of the newer areas of town, near one of our more difficult hiking trails. She was found at the bottom of a steep hill, not far from the main path. Consensus was that she must have gone off trail to look at something and slipped, hitting her head on a rock at the bottom. But there were external abrasions not consistent with that sort of fall. Bridget Hyland had a million-dollar life insurance policy. Bridget's former husband and daughter, who was around ten, insisted Shane killed her for the money."

"You said her name was Hyland?" Nikki asked. "Why does that name sound familiar?"

"Hyland Industrial Supply," James answered. "They make fasteners and other construction products. They're one of the leading employers in western Minnesota."

That explained why the name sounded familiar. Rory owned a successful construction business, and he was always complaining about various suppliers like Hyland. "Does Shane still own a stake in the company?"

"No, after Bridget's father died, she sold the company to Fastenal and liquidated her assets. Fortunately, most of her money went to her ex-husband and daughter instead of Shane. But he was the only beneficiary of her life insurance policy."

"Can you track down the daughter and first husband?" Nikki asked.

"Working on that now."

Nikki thanked James for her help and ended the call. Liam furiously flipped through his notes. "Here we go," he said. "I remember seeing that Shane's loans had been paid off for a long time and was surprised given his specialty and the amount of schooling he's had. He paid the majority of it off ten years ago, which would have been around the time he received the dead wife's life insurance check."

"Was there a life insurance policy on Thea or Abby?" Nikki asked.

"Not that I could find during the review of their financials."

Nikki turned in to the gated community the Walkers lived in and showed her badge to security. "We need to find a way to bring up the ex-wife without sounding accusatory. He'll likely lawyer up fast if we give him the impression we're looking into the former wife's death."

"Are we?" Liam asked.

"Not officially," Nikki answered. "Unofficially, everyone's a suspect."

TEN

The Walkers lived in Eden Prairie, a small suburb west of Stillwater. The price per capita was among the highest in the state, with the most expensive places located on the peninsula at White Bear Lake. Despite the close proximity of the neighbors, the lush landscape of trees and well-maintained shrubs offered a sense of seclusion and privacy. Nikki parked behind the black Range Rover in the bricked driveway.

"This must be Shane's car. Britney drives a Chevy Tahoe." She pointed to the older model Mustang convertible parked on the other side of the drive. "Let's hope whoever drives that car has some information that will help us find Abby alive."

Sergeant Chen met them at the front door. He still wore the same uniform he'd been in the day before, and lack of sleep made his eyes appear red, although Nikki suspected some of the redness came from tears, as Chen pressed a handkerchief to his face and motioned for them to go inside.

He led them through the spacious great room into the kitchen. Shane Walker sat on a barstool, staring into space. He wore cargo shorts and a faded Led Zeppelin shirt roughly the same color as the circles beneath his eyes. "Britney's upstairs with Alyssa in the girls' room."

"I'm truly sorry for your loss," Nikki said before introducing Liam. "We're doing everything we can to find Abby—"

"You said the same thing last night, and now Thea's gone." Shane's voice shook at the sound of Thea's name. Without a life insurance policy for Thea, she didn't have any concrete reason to believe Shane was involved, despite what they'd learned about Shane's late ex-wife. Nikki had been a cop long enough to know that just because a grieving family pointed fingers at someone didn't mean they were guilty. Shane's former step-daughter had only been around ten at the time, and it was entirely possible her opinions were influenced by her father.

"I'm sorry," Nikki repeated. "The state police have been to the FSZ compound in Thief River Falls. There's no sign of Abby, and they spoke to dozens of people. Everyone was very cooperative."

Shane snorted. "I'm sure. Greasing people is what they do."

"We'll keep an eye on the FSZ, but right now, it appears they likely didn't have anything to do with the kidnapping."

"What did Silas say when they told him about Britney and the baby?"

"They didn't name any names," Nikki said. "Just showed photos of the girls."

"Thankfully Thea looks more like Britney." Shane stared down at the countertop. "Are you going to tell us how she died?"

"We're waiting to hear back from the medical examiner," Liam said.

"It was the insulin, wasn't it? She went too long without it?"

Nikki glanced at Chen, who stood off to the side, clenching his jaw in what looked like a Herculean effort not to lose his composure. "The medical examiner will be able to get a better idea from the bloodwork." Nikki needed to steer Shane in another direction. "Are you familiar with the apple orchard where she was found?"

Shane shook his head. "Not the sort of thing I have time to do. Britney said she'd never taken the girls there, either."

Nikki heard footsteps upstairs. "Before Britney comes down, I wanted to ask about your ex-wife."

"Ah," Shane said. "I think of Bridget as my former wife, not ex. I didn't choose to lose her. I suppose the state troopers told you that her ex-husband accused me of killing her for the life insurance. Didn't seem to matter that I was working brutal hours back then and did nothing but work and sleep."

"What about your former stepdaughter?" Nikki asked. "She also believed something wasn't right with her mom's death."

"Susie was ten years old," Shane said. "Her father liked to tell her all sorts of stories about Bridget and me, even before she died."

"Do you still stay in touch with her?" Liam asked.

"I tried for a while," Shane said. "But her dad didn't want me to communicate with her, and I figured it was better for her if I listened to him. Bridget and I were only together for sixteen months, married for less time. I never really got the opportunity to know her daughter that well."

"Does Britney know?" Nikki asked.

"Of course. We have no secrets. I'm not going to pretend that our marriage is completely conventional. But we love each other."

"What are you doing here?" Britney's sharp voice came from the kitchen entryway. "You said my babies would be found. You promised me."

Nikki was certain she hadn't made such a promise, but before she could respond, she realized Britney's anger was focused on Sergeant Chen.

"That's it?" she demanded. "You don't have anything to say to me?"

Chen cleared his throat. "I never should have made that promise. I am truly sorry."

Nikki stepped in before she could direct any more ire at Chen. "I can't imagine what you're going through, but we still have a chance to find Abby. We can't give up hope now." Her gaze slid to the tall, willowy young woman standing next to Britney. Nikki assumed she must be the babysitter who'd been with Britney yesterday. "You must be Alyssa?"

Alyssa nodded. "What are you doing to find out who did this?"

"Can we all sit down at the table?" Nikki asked. "We need to go over some things."

Britney looked like she wanted to argue, but Shane ushered her to the kitchen table. Alyssa sat dutifully at Britney's other side. Chen shook his head and remained standing near the large bay window overlooking the back deck, which wrapped around an in-ground pool. A lump formed in Nikki's throat at the idea of Thea never getting to play in it again. But she wasn't going to give up on finding her little sister.

"You haven't answered my question," Alyssa said.

Liam already had his notebook out. "What's your name again?"

"Alyssa Winters."

"And how did you meet Britney and the girls?"

"I answered an ad for a part-time babysitter six months ago," Alyssa said.

"I assume you take the girls to the park and other places?" Nikki said. "Did you ever notice anyone paying too much attention to them?"

"No," Alyssa said. "Nothing like that's ever happened."

Nikki had been trying to think of a way to bring up what Rodney the bartender had told her without making Britney feel like she was being accused of negligence. "Britney, can you think of anything else you might have done last night before going to the restroom?"

"No."

"And the girls never waited with you, correct? They stayed on the blanket you had set up?"

Britney stared at her. "Why are you asking me that?"

Nikki decided not to waste any more time beating around the bush. "Because we know that you were in line at the beer tent with both of the girls before the fireworks started. One of the workers said the girls kept asking you something, and you finally sent them off back towards the park." Nikki left out the part about the vodka lemonade Britney had purchased, at least for now.

Britney's mouth trembled, the cords in her neck straining from the effort not to cry. Alyssa patted her back. "It's okay."

"No, it isn't," Britney burst out. "They were driving me nuts and I told them to leave me alone. Those were the last words I said to them. Oh God, Thea. I left everything for her, and now she's gone."

"They're going to find Abby alive," Shane said. "I feel it."

"You're delusional," Britney snapped. "Did you talk to the church?"

"We did," Nikki answered. "There's no sign of Abby at the FSZ ranch, and no one recognized the girls. And frankly, if Silas or someone from your church was involved, killing Thea seems counterproductive. But the state troopers will continue to investigate." She looked at Britney. "I want to make this as clear as I can. We aren't blaming you, nor are we judging you. Parents have done the same thing to their kids thousands of times, and nothing happened. That sounds harsh and unfair, but it's the truth, and it's better than you beating yourself up. Okay?"

Britney rubbed her eyes. "Doesn't bring Thea back." She stood on shaky legs. "I'm going back to bed. Shane, will you come up and sit with me?"

Shane glanced at Nikki and Liam. "Unless you have more questions?"

"Go ahead," Nikki said, leaving a couple of cards on the table. "If you or your wife or Alyssa remembers anything, no matter how inconsequential it may be, call me."

"I'll walk them out, Doctor Walker," Alyssa said softly.

"Thanks." He smiled warmly at her before gently taking Britney's elbow. She leaned against her husband, and he wrapped his arm around her for support. Nikki waited until they had left the room before turning to Alyssa.

"Thanks for walking us out. We actually have some questions for you, if you don't mind."

"Of course, anything I can do to help."

"Can you think of anything Doctor Walker or Britney might have forgotten in terms of a problematic case at the hospital or any other stressor?"

Alyssa thought about it for a minute. "Well, you know Doctor Walker got death threats when the quarterback blew out his knee. I think those were all investigated, and that's been a couple of years. Other than that, I can't remember anything specific."

"What about the Walkers' relationship?" Liam asked. "Were there any problems before this?"

"Like what?" Alyssa said. "I mean, they bickered, but Doctor Walker works *a lot*."

"Your tone of voice doesn't really match the words." Chen had followed them down the hallway.

Alyssa sighed. "I don't want to cause trouble. Doctor Walker is a good father."

"Doesn't matter," Nikki said. "What did you really want to say? I won't tell the Walkers, if that's what you're worried about."

"You know Britney comes from a religion that follows polygamy, right?"

Nikki nodded.

"I guess that's why she doesn't care about Doctor Walker's... you know."

"No, I don't," Nikki said. "Doctor Walker didn't come from the same background as Britney."

"No, but she was raised to believe women are only put on earth for men. She's come a long way, but she doesn't seem to care if Doctor Walker has a girlfriend, or several."

"Britney told you this?"

Alyssa nodded. "I overheard him talking on the phone in his office, saying some truly disgusting things. I knew he wasn't talking to Britney, but I didn't want to say anything. She could tell something was bothering me, though, so I finally told her what I'd overheard. She just laughed this really soft, delicate laugh and said that sometimes meeting your husband's needs means allowing him to be with other women physically. She didn't seem to care as long as he came home to her." Alyssa looked between the three of them. "I'm not sure I should have said anything. It's their private business. Please don't tell Doctor Walker I told you. I need this job."

"You're right, but we're trying to find Doctor Walker's daughter." Nikki debated going back inside and putting Shane on the spot in front of his wife, but she didn't want to get Alyssa in trouble. But Abby was in mortal danger—if she was still alive. "Did you happen to get the woman's name?"

"I think it was Carly. Or maybe Carol." Alyssa looked between the three of them. "He said something about Regions Hospital during the call, too. Please don't tell him you heard that from me."

"You have my word." Nikki thanked her again for her time as she and Liam headed outside into the miserable heat. "We'll be in touch if we have more questions."

Alyssa nodded, closing the door behind them.

Nikki and Liam walked down the sidewalk, with Chen

trailing behind. "A disgruntled girlfriend... or jilted lover. Maybe she wants Shane to herself and getting rid of the girls was the only way," he said.

"It's possible," Nikki said. She'd been touched by Shane's affection toward Britney. She felt certain his love for her was genuine, but that didn't always help a man keep it in his pants. "I wanted to talk with the orthopedic director at Regions Hospital anyway to get a better understanding of why Shane continued to take patients at Regions. He came from Thief River Falls to Regions. If we're lucky, I might be able to dig up some information on his late wife. Hopefully the director checks her voicemail on the weekends."

"A nurse named Carly." Liam swore under his breath. "She won't be hard to find at all."

"Sergeant Chen, where are you headed?" Nikki asked.

"Chief Ryan wants me back at the station to brief her," he answered. "I don't know what she expects me to tell her that she doesn't already know."

Nikki sensed something else was bothering the Stillwater police sergeant, but she didn't know him well enough to press the issue. "We'll see you at the afternoon briefing, then."

She hoped the derision in her voice wasn't too strong. They needed to stay on Chief Ryan's good side.

Chen nodded and walked down the street toward his black and white.

Inside the Jeep, Nikki turned the air conditioning on high. "Chen's taking Thea's death hard."

"Yeah," Liam agreed. "Never make a promise like that. Hard lesson to learn, but he won't forget it." He took a long gulp of water from the insulated bottle he'd brought along. "Doctor Walker's got his own private practice, too, right? That's where the athletes go for surgery."

"I assume so," Nikki said. "It's interesting how thin Doctor Walker has stretched himself. He's making great money at his own practice, and he's got two young girls. Why does he still take shifts at Regions?"

"Good question," Liam answered.

"We should find out whether he was a suspect in his ex-wife's death," Nikki continued. "Was it ever investigated? Does Britney's drinking have anything to do with his infidelity? Who is this Carly or Carol? This family is getting more complicated by the minute. Plus, we still need to find the two boys who were working in the apple orchard. They could fit the description of our teenager with the bag. I also want to go talk to the police in Edina about the threats Shane Walker received."

"Can you drop me at the office before you head out to Edina? I'm going to touch base with Kendall and Jim on the sex offenders. I've also got them searching for similar crimes in Wisconsin in case this is someone who crossed the river to do his dirty work." Stranger abductions in children were far rarer than crime dramas and documentaries made it seem—less than one percent of missing children were taken by strangers. They were also the toughest to solve, even when law enforcement had been quick to act as they'd done when Thea and Abby had been reported missing. But they needed to consider that it wasn't the family.

"How are you going to get back to Washington County?" Nikki asked. "Your car's at the sheriff's."

"Caitlin's in Minneapolis working on a story. She can give me a ride back."

Nikki merged onto the interstate and headed toward Brooklyn Park, the picturesque suburb that housed the FBI offices. "This is getting murkier by the minute." Just speaking the words out loud made her feel nauseous.

ELEVEN

Edina's zip code consistently ranked as one of the state's wealthiest, and the police stood as a shining example of that wealth. Located in City Hall, a large modern brick building complex with solar panels, the Edina Police Department enjoyed a stunning view of the golf course on the other side of the street. The window shades were pulled low enough to block out the sun reflecting off the water at the 14th hole.

Police Chief Roger Shultz offered Nikki coffee, which she refused. Her stomach was turning with too much caffeine and not enough real food. She followed Shultz into his office, which had another stunning view of the golf course. Edina crime rates were low compared to the rest of the metro area, but like everything else in the world, the city's wealth meant top-notch accommodations for their officers. As an FBI agent, Nikki couldn't complain. The Bureau prided itself on having better facilities than just about everyone else, but as a cop, it was frustrating to know that resources weren't allocated fairly. The most overwhelmed precincts in both Minneapolis and St. Paul had the least amount of funding and equipment, making their jobs ten times more difficult. Coupled with the rumors that Edina police made more money for less crime, it was no wonder why so many city cops were growing even more disillusioned with their jobs.

"Please, Agent Hunt, have a seat." Chief Shultz gestured to the comfy-looking chair in front of his desk. Nikki sat, pretending to admire the various accolades on the chief's wall. Shultz took his time, shuffling papers on his desk.

"Thank you for coming in on a Sunday."

"Of course," the chief said. "Normally, I'd have you speak with the officer who investigated the threats against Doctor Walker, but in this case, that's me." He smiled. "I was lieutenant, and the Walker case is probably one of the reasons I was promoted to chief." Schultz's smile faded. "How are he and Mrs. Walker doing?"

"They're holding up all right," Nikki said. "With Thea's body found, we're working hard to find Abby while we still have time." The discovery of Thea's body was all over the news, and more volunteers had showed up at the police station to help search for Abby. She ran through the small amount of information they'd managed to find. "We're racing to find the other little girl before it's too late, and we're still searching for a motive. There hasn't been any communication from the kidnapper, but given the prior death threats against Doctor Walker, I wanted to speak with you as soon as possible."

Schultz's eyebrows furrowed together. "I understand they were very close to the river."

"Stillwater PD and the sheriff's department are working together on that," Nikki said.

"Well, I pulled the file on our investigation into the threats against Doctor Walker." He reached into his desk drawer, withdrawing an expanding file. "These are copies for you."

"Thank you." Nikki took the file from his outstretched hand. "It's all here, then? You didn't feel the need to redact anything?"

"No," Schultz answered. "It's all pretty straightforward. As I'm sure you know, threats aren't new to someone in Doctor Walker's position. We were able to disregard most of them as harmless pretty easily, as most of them were made online, several by younger fans not thinking about the consequences of their actions. There were a handful of threats sent by mail that we were able to investigate and clear, with the exception of a couple. The first guy threatened to ruin Doctor Walker's life like he'd ruined the entire team's." Schultz sighed. "Dave Hartley picketed outside of Doctor Walker's offices here in Edina and tried to confront Walker and other physicians who worked for him. After Hartley's second arrest for harassment, Walker got a restraining order and threatened legal action. Scared the guy, and he backed off. Second guy's a compulsive gambler who lost twenty thousand when the quarterback went down that year. Name's Jack Buck. He tried to confront Doctor Walker in his office and also followed him on at least one occasion."

Nikki found the information on Jack Buck in the file he'd given her. "He wanted Doctor Walker to pay off his bookie." She pulled a photocopy of a handwritten letter from Buck to Walker. "Plus ten grand for pain and suffering?"

"That letter was slipped under Doctor Walker's door at his orthopedic facility. Buck posed as a janitor and got in. Doctor Walker also observed Buck sitting in the parking lot, taking photos with a telescopic lens, although we're not sure what he was trying to get photos of at the office." Schultz shrugged. "He was sentenced to sixty days for trespassing and threats, but Doctor Walker convinced the court to allow him to receive inpatient psychiatric care. Buck was released eleven months ago and hasn't tried to contact Doctor Walker since then."

Nikki studied the photograph of Jack Buck. He looked like an average, slightly overweight middle-aged businessman. "The woman next to him—is that his wife?"

"Ex. She filed for divorce while he was in jail, and it was finalized a few months after he got out. Last I heard, she got the house and pretty much everything else. I assume she still lives in it."

"What about Buck? Any idea if this is his current address?" Nikki asked, referring to the one in the file. "North St. Paul?"

Shultz nodded. "Double-checked it before you got here. I also ran a records check on Buck. He's kept his nose clean since serving time, but his wife filed for divorce six months ago."

"Any idea if his threats to Walker were part of the reason?"

Shultz shook his head. "Buck was a financial consultant for one of the major firms in Minneapolis. After news about his gambling and threats came out, he lost his job at the firm. Best I can tell, he works at a factory not far from his apartment."

Nikki thanked the chief for his thoroughness. He waved her off. "One little girl is already dead. We'll help in any way we can."

"I appreciate it." She slipped the file into her bag. "Cop to cop, what was your gut feeling on Buck? You think he's capable of something like this?"

"I don't know," Schultz confessed. "I'd like to say no, but the guy lost his job and his wife. If he blames Doctor Walker for that, too, then maybe."

Nikki called Courtney during the drive back to Stillwater. "Are you still at the scene?"

"Yeah," Courtney answered. "I've collected several fibers from Thea's hands and body, including a few from her mouth. Once I get the results, I should be able to give you a better idea of where she was before she died."

Due to recent court cases and newer research, Nikki was a little leery about fiber evidence, but she had complete faith in Courtney. "Can you dumb that down for me a little bit?"

"Well, different vehicles use different fabrics, with different backing and different glues. I won't be able to tell a lot until I get them under the mass-spec and start running tests, but I'm hoping we'll at least be able to rule some locations out."

"How long will that take?"

"A couple of days at least," Courtney said. "I've got to get the fibers tested, and then start comparing. It's not a quick process, but I'm making it top priority."

"Thanks," Nikki said. "What about prints?"

"We're not sure yet. I'll print her clothes back at the lab and see if the prints from them match the one from the purse—once it's fully analyzed. Shane Walker's prints are already in AFIS because he's a medical doctor, but I'll need Britney's to rule hers out. Miller sent Chen back to the Walkers' with a kit to get her prints."

"Good." Nikki took the exit for Stillwater. "Call me as soon as you get any results."

TWELVE

Nikki hurried into conference room B where the rest of Ryan's task force had already started, minus Miller, who'd refocused his search for Abby around the apple orchard where Thea's body had been found. An additional group of volunteers had arrived, including retired members of the county search and rescue team, hunters with knowledge of the area, and a few college kids on summer break. Miller had instructed them all to leave their phones at the check-in area, unwilling to risk some attention seeker getting a photo of Abby's dead body and putting it online. The family was going through enough.

"Agent Hunt, we were just ready to start." Ryan smiled as though they weren't discussing a child kidnapping and murder. Ryan looked at Liam and nodded. "Agent Wilson, the Level 3 sex offenders?"

"Accounted for," Liam said. "Both have solid alibis, and so do the lower-level offenders in the area. The apple orchard employees have strong alibis as well."

"Chen, what have you found out from the marinas?"

Chen looked at his yellow legal pad. "Since it's Sunday, the marina offices are closed, but I finally reached the owner, and he's meeting me at Stillwater marina right after this meeting. He's pretty old-fashioned, so I'm not sure what sort of records he's going to have. But we'll find out if anyone saw the girls there."

Ryan turned her attention to Nikki. "I hope I saved the best for last. Agent Hunt, what do you have for us?"

Nikki started with Chief Shultz. "He gave me a copy of the case files investigating the threats made to Doctor Walker. We may have a person of interest." She told them about Jack Buck's harassment. "He's living in North St. Paul right now, working at the local UPS warehouse. I called and pretended to be a friend —he's off today but will be in tomorrow morning. Told his boss he was going up to the north woods to fish this weekend."

"Meaning he may have an alibi," Ryan said.

"Maybe," Nikki agreed. "But given the magnitude of his threats and Jack Buck's time in the system, he may have found some accomplices."

"You think he could have had the girls taken out of revenge for getting locked up?"

"I don't know," Nikki said. "Shane actually spoke at his sentencing and asked for a mental health facility in lieu of a conviction. In the end, Buck spent three months in county detention and the rest of the time at a halfway house. He had weekly check-ins with his parole officer and never missed one. He also attends regular therapy, conditional with his release. Chief Schultz gave me the parole officer's contact information. I've got a call into him."

"You don't sound convinced he's a good suspect," Liam said.

"I'm not. It's certainly plausible, but Walker went out of his way to get the guy help, and he's out and working a decent job at UPS. Why take such a huge risk that could lead to his winding up in prison for the rest of his life?"

"Revenge is a powerful motive," Ryan said. "What about the orthopedic director at Regions Hospital?"

"She emailed me right before I got here." Nikki unlocked her phone and opened the message. "She offered to meet with me at 7:30 a.m. tomorrow. I'm going to speak with her first and then follow up with Jack Buck. Hopefully Blanchard has the autopsy results tomorrow morning as well. We also spoke to the babysitter who told us she's certain Shane has a girlfriend, a mistress—someone called Carly or Carol. We've had reports that Britney was drinking at the fireworks, so we have to take all of her testimony with a pinch of salt. And we've also been told that Shane's ex-wife died in suspicious circumstances, though the source of that information was shaky at best."

Ryan perked up, but Liam quickly dashed those hopes. "I've already been on the phone to the investigating officer. They didn't have Shane as a suspect; they believed her death was a terrible accident."

"Okay," Ryan said. "Let's get searching through staff records where Shane works for a Carly or Carol. I spoke with the mayor, and he thinks we should get the Walkers on television ASAP."

Nikki and Liam looked at each other, the panic in his eyes matching the butterflies swarming in her gut. "With all due respect, Chief Ryan, I don't think that's a good idea. Not yet, anyway."

"Why?"

"Britney would need to be coached extensively," Nikki said. "We can do that, but it will take a day or so to prep her. I'd also like to have a better idea of our suspect so that we can try to control the narrative and get him to make a mistake."

"But the pleas of a parent can do wondrous things, and Doctor Walker is something of a celebrity," Ryan said. "I think it's a good idea. We need to humanize Abby, remind the killer he can still make things right."

"He's not going to do that," Nikki said flatly. "If he was, he would have left Abby with Thea, dead or alive. And there's been no demand for ransom, so Doctor Walker's celebrity status really doesn't come into play. In fact, getting him on television could backfire, especially if the kidnapper is doing this out of revenge." By now, whoever took the girls likely would have seen the news coverage. Thea Walker's face, along with her father's, had been on the news all day. "We don't know the motive. If Doctor Walker says the wrong thing, it could end up costing Abby's life."

Ryan sighed. "I'm stuck between the mayor and your advice."

"Then let me make it easy. The mayor's putting politics first. That's his job, unfortunately. Our job is to find Abby and who did this to her and her sister. My team has the capability to put an end to this, but you have to give us time to do our jobs."

"How about this," Liam interjected. "Give us until tomorrow. Let Agent Hunt and I run down leads and see if we can get a better idea of who the suspect is and his real motives. Then one of us can sit down with the parents and prep them for the media. We can hold a press conference the following day." He looked at Nikki. "What do you think, boss?"

She hated to play this game with Ryan, but Nikki also understood dealing with the mayor was part of Ryan's job, and it couldn't be easy. Liam's idea was good, and it bought them a little time. "I'm okay with that."

Ryan folded her arms across the table. "I'll agree to it, but on one condition: regardless of how much we know by this time tomorrow, we plan to prep the Walkers for a press conference the next day." She rubbed her temples. "The mayor respects your team's accomplishments, so I think I can put him off a day using the reasoning you just laid out. But not beyond that."

"Fine," Nikki agreed. Twenty-four hours wasn't much time to dig up enough information to come up with a profile, especially with as many unanswered questions as they still had. But for Abby's sake, Nikki's team had to get it done.

Chen cleared his throat. "How certain are we that they were taken onto a boat?"

"Right now, I'd say fifty-fifty," Nikki said. "We know the bag was found on land, but we haven't found any video footage of the girls."

"So it was left at Trinity Lutheran's lot to throw us off?" Chen asked.

"It's not very big," Nikki said. "Easy to hide and drop. I just think we have to look seriously at anyone who docked a boat Saturday night. My people recovered several fibers from Thea's body, but it will be a day or so before they're able to determine what they're made from."

"Combined with the timing of the boats that left during the search, I think Nikki's right," Ryan said. "Word was out quickly enough that getting the girls out of here by car, unnoticed, would have been difficult."

Chen nodded, his jaw muscles tight. "Excuse me." He shoved his chair back and slipped out of the room.

Ryan looked down at her notes. "Sergeant Chen takes things to heart. I've no doubt he's blaming himself for not checking the boats sooner."

"I understand," Nikki said. "But we need everyone sharp and focused on the present, not on what we could have done."

Ryan studied her for a moment. "I agree, but I'm not sure what Sergeant Chen thinks of me yet. I'm not sure my going after him would do much good."

"Then I'll go talk to him," Nikki said. "We don't have time to waste."

Nikki found Chen in the break room, staring out of the window onto Fourth Street. "You doing okay?"

"Not really." His voice caught, and he cleared his throat. He moved to sit on the cracked leather loveseat Nikki had fallen asleep on earlier. Chen rested his head in his hands, looking more like an academy recruit instead of a seasoned sergeant. She hated to be harsh, but if he couldn't handle the intensity, then Ryan needed to replace him.

Nikki wasn't sure how to respond. She'd only just met Chen, and she didn't want to say something that diminished his feelings. "I think everyone in law enforcement has these moments over their career," she said. "It's a lot harder to deal with an investigation when there are children at risk."

Chen turned around. "Agent, do you really think Abby could still be alive?"

"Absolutely," Nikki said. "Right now, we don't know what the kidnapper intended to do with the girls."

"Was Thea assaulted?" he said.

"I haven't spoken to the medical examiner about that yet," Nikki said. "But if this person intended to take both girls, whatever their reasoning, Thea's death may buy Abby more time."

"That's an awful way to put it," Chen said.

"I know, but that's the truth."

Chen seemed to be fighting an internal war, but he finally nodded. "You're right. I can't sit in here feeling sorry for myself with that baby out there. I'm going over to the marina." He hesitated. "You want to ride along?"

Nikki wanted to be the one to follow up on Shane's supposed girlfriend, but she could tell that Chen needed a partner, and she knew the team could handle it. It would be a tedious task searching through personnel records.

"I'll follow you to the marina."

Nikki wished she'd grabbed her sunglasses. The hot sun glinted off the fiberglass boats and water, making her eyes sting. Minus the temperature, the day was stunning. A handful of boats dotted the St. Croix, most of them sailing. She counted at least fifty boats docked, and more out on the water. They had their work cut out for them, especially since the marina's security was so lax. Nikki marveled at the extravagance of some of the cabin boats, many of them as expensive as a car or house. How had the marina gotten away with such lax security for so long?

She knew the answer. It was the Midwest, beautiful downtown Stillwater, where bad things don't happen. People just couldn't accept that there were bad apples everywhere, even in the most picturesque setting.

Nikki walked to the end of the dock to get a better view of the river. She was certain the girls hadn't gone into the water. What—or who—could have caused them to go near the marina? She'd thought about it on the short drive over, and Nikki was certain the girls had to have been taken away by boat. The Stillwater police had acted quickly and efficiently. Thea and Abby were by the docks, their mother having directed them to stay put. People packed the river walk and Lowell Park in anticipation of the fireworks. Not only would the kidnapper have to get the girls' attention without anyone else noticing, but if he'd gone anywhere other than the river, someone would have noticed. The cyber guys had spent hours poring over CCTV footage from businesses across the river, hoping to see the girls walk past. They'd come up empty.

"It had to be a boat," she said as Chen joined her at the edge of the dock.

"I think so, too," he said. "I went back over the reports from Saturday night. My guys did their job. We didn't miss anything."

"I know." She fanned herself. "Let's see what the marina owner has to say."

Chen pointed to the man in the Packers hat arguing with two older men fishing off the dock. "That's him."

"I don't care how many times you done it before." The man

wagged his finger. "The dock is full. You can't be casting round here. Go."

One of the men laughed and said something rude, but the marina owner had spotted Chen and Nikki. "You were supposed to be here fifteen minutes ago." He stalked back inside. They followed him; a bell over the door announced their entry. Behind the counter that ran the length of the small building, the river glistened in the summer sun.

"My apologies on our late arrival," Chen snapped. "Missing children cases tend to run on their own schedule." He hooked his thumb over his shoulder. "This is Agent Hunt with the FBI. Agent Hunt, Doug Martin, the marina owner."

Martin nodded gruffly at them, his wrinkled cheeks pink. "Not sure how much I can help you all out. I can't just turn over a bunch of personal information without a warrant."

Nikki sensed Chen getting ready to lay into the man, and she stepped in before things could get any worse. "We have a warrant for a full list of slip owners and rentals, along with the names of all employees."

Chen thrust the warrant at Martin, who didn't bother to read it. "Only two employees. Myself and my son, who's usually here on the weekends. He's out of state right now, or he'd be in here instead of me."

"What about security video?" Nikki asked. "I know the city's in the process of replacing and adding several new ones, but do you have any that overlook the water and the slips?"

Martin shook his head. "Only one we have is in here." He pointed to the corner. "It picks up whoever walks in, but I have to tell you, that's not a lot of people nowadays. Most rentals are done online."

"I understand," Nikki said. "Can you think of any boat owners who have caused problems in the past?"

"What sort of problems?" Martin demanded. "I thought you

all found a girl's purse in the church parking lot. Why are you asking about the boaters?"

"We're looking into all angles," Chen said. "What about people who might have rented a slip but are no longer allowed? Is anyone banned? Or stopped paying their bill?"

Martin opened the laptop sitting on the counter and awkwardly typed, his sausage fingers slamming the keyboard. "Yeah, there are a few who were banned because they'd come in drunk and caused a lot of problems on the docks. And of course, Pirate Pete." Martin snickered.

"Pirate Pete?" Nikki echoed.

"Pete Fisher," Martin clarified. "Lost an eye from a shrapnel shard in Afghanistan. Used to rent a slip because being on the water brought him peace, but he's got real bad PTSD, and he had a couple of flashback episodes on the dock, scared the shit out of kids. They called him Pirate Pete. He stopped coming around a year or so ago, and I'm not sure what he's up to right now."

"He's local?" Chen asked, writing the name in a small notebook he'd retrieved from his uniform pocket.

"Assume so," Martin said. "But Pete wouldn't hurt anyone. He wouldn't hurt little kids at least."

Nikki guessed that Fisher's PTSD would have kept him far away from the fireworks, but she'd have someone check him out.

"How late is the marina open?" Chen asked.

"Office closes at six p.m., but anyone who owns or rents a boat slip can access their property at any time."

"And I assume you don't have security video to keep track of who goes out at night?"

"Not my responsibility," Martin said. "Might check with that photography place that takes aerial photos though. I believe they had a helicopter out at some points Saturday. Not sure if they got any that would help, but I'm sure they took lots of the water and riverfront."

Chen looked like he wanted to kick himself, but Miller hadn't mentioned the aerial photography either. Nikki had assumed the helicopters flying around Saturday were reporters and police. She doubted the photographer took close enough shots to be of use to them, but they had to check it out.

"Do you know who took the photos?" Nikki asked. "Were they hired by the city?"

Martin shrugged. "Maybe, but there's a group of amateur photographers who hire a pilot to fly around and take photos at certain times of the year, like when the fall colors come in." He scratched the gray scruff on his chin. "I can't remember the name of the group, but a guy named Hank Wall started it. He's the one you want to talk to, and, no, I don't have his number."

They thanked him for his time, and Nikki went outside to make a phone call while Martin gathered up the records the warrant required.

Hank Wall Photography was easy enough to find online, but her call went to voicemail. She left a message, asking for Wall to call back as soon as possible. Pete Fisher was harder to find, as the name turned out to be fairly common. The fastest way to get his information would be from the Minnesota Veterans Bureau, and she fired off a text to Liam to follow up on Fisher. Chen soon joined her, carrying a sizeable stack of paper.

"Don't worry about Pirate Pete," he told her. "He's got bad PTSD. I can't see him around fireworks, and as harsh as it sounds, I don't think he could stay sober long enough to kidnap anyone. I'll have a patrol officer track him down to make sure."

"I figured as much." Nikki started the Jeep with her remote, hoping to cool off the inside a degree or two. "Let me know what you find out. You need any help on that list?"

Chen shook his head. "Nah, I've got a couple of officers willing to help. I'll let you know if we find anything." He cleared his throat, his free hand in his uniform pocket. "Listen, thanks for not judging me back there. I know you've seen a lot worse."

"It's all terrible," Nikki said. "And you're welcome. I know a good cop when I see one."

Nikki yawned as she turned in to Rory's driveway. Light streamed from the outbuilding where Rory kept his construction tools and recreational vehicles. He and Mark were constantly tinkering with something, and tonight appeared to be no different. Nikki parked in her usual spot in the garage and headed across the grass. Twilight stretched across the western horizon, trillions of stars already bright in the clear sky. Classic rock music came from the speakers Rory had put in last year. Nikki walked around Mark's big truck, smiling when she heard Lacey's voice.

"I got grease on me."

"That means you put in a good day's work," Mark said.

"Mommy!" Lacey raced across the concrete floor, black streaks on her T-shirt and cheeks. "We're workin' on the boat."

Rory and Mark both loved to fish, especially trolling for larger fish along the outer edges of Minnesota's many lakes. But with Nikki and Lacey in the picture, Rory wanted more room than his regular fishing boat offered, so he and Mark had gone in on a cabin boat. The brothers had been raised to be frugal, and even though they could both afford to buy their own houseboats, they'd elected to buy an older model they could tinker with and "modify." Nikki could only imagine how fast the thing would go after those two were done with it, and she suspected they'd wind up putting more money into their modifications than they would have if they'd just bought a newer one.

"I see that." Nikki looked at the pile of discarded carpet and worn-out leather cushions. "You really are gutting her."

Rory grinned. "Yep. This sucker's going to be so sweet when we get it done."

"You think that will happen before the water freezes?" Nikki teased.

Rory and Mark both shot her looks. "Maybe," Rory said. "But she's got to be ready, right, Lace?"

"Yep, and I'm going to learn how to drive her."

Nikki would never understand men's need to refer to anything with a motor as a female, but she was excited to take the boat out some weekend, whether they fished or not. She just wanted to relax and enjoy the summer.

But not until Abby Walker was found.

"Uncle Mark's gonna teach me to weld. It's a skill he learned when he was at Oak Park."

Lacey didn't know Mark, whom she adored, had spent twenty years in prison for the murders of Nikki's parents—a crime Nikki had helped clear him of when she returned to Stillwater.

"Not before we get you eye protection that fits," Rory said.

Nikki walked over to the carpet and knelt down. The steel-colored material had a tighter weave than regular carpet, and while it smelled like old fish and oil, it wasn't moldy. Courtney would test Thea's clothes for particulates, but Nikki wasn't sure about mold transferring. She was more interested in the different types of carpeting used for cabin boats. "How do you keep the carpet from getting moldy?" she asked. "Water gets into the boat no matter what."

"It's water-resistant carpeting, so the fibers are unaffected by moisture," Rory said. "But carpet's gross. We're putting in woven vinyl."

"What's the difference, other than the obvious?"

"Easier to clean, doesn't feel wet, and doesn't trap odors, like fish."

Nikki thought about the fibers Courtney had found with

Thea's body. Her parents hadn't been wealthy enough to own a boat, but she'd been inside plenty of them growing up on the lakes. She couldn't remember ever seeing anything like the vinyl Rory had propped against the wall. "When did this stuff come out?"

"Woven vinyl?" Rory thought about it for a few seconds. "Around 2010, 2011. I remember because one of my first clients had it in his boat, and I'd never seen anything like it."

Nikki's tiny flame of hope burnt out. "That's too much time."

"What are you talking about?"

"Fibers." She emphasized the word with a nod toward Lacey. "They look different under a microscope. If the woven vinyl was a newer thing, less people have it. But if it's been around that long, there's no point. What about marine carpet?"

"What about it?" Mark asked. "It's been around forever."

"But it's different than regular carpet, right? At a microscopic level?"

"I'd think so, since it's different material and tighter weave." His eyebrows knitted together, but Nikki shook her head. She didn't want Lacey to associate Thea and Abby with Rory's boat.

"You guys eat yet?"

"Bought Italian in," Rory said. "Yours is in the microwave."

"Lacey, you want to come in with me and keep me company while I eat?"

Her daughter bit her lower lip, looking between Rory and Nikki. "Can I stay out here and keep helping?"

"Of course." She motioned to the two men. Nikki needed to keep working on the case anyway, and she didn't want to push Lacey aside while she did so. "Lord knows they need supervision."

. . .

With Lacey still occupied outside, Nikki sat down at the kitchen table and checked her email. She took out her notebook, flipping blindly through the pages as though some unseen piece of information might pop out at her. Nikki mentally walked through the last twenty-four hours, jotting down a few things she wanted to follow up on tomorrow.

Her stomach growled with hunger, but she didn't feel like eating. Had Abby eaten since yesterday? Was she even still alive?

She wasn't sure if they'd been taken by a stranger or if Shane and Britney were hiding things and somehow caught up in this. All she knew was that they needed to find the teenager who dropped the pink purse, and she just needed to keep going.

Nikki looked down at the legal pad she'd been taking notes in since last night. They looked more like a mind map for a brainstorming session than actual leads. Nikki found a couple of aspirin in her bag and swallowed them dry.

"Make a list of everything you know and you don't know" had been one of the first things Nikki had learned when she entered the academy years ago. Lists helped a cop feel more in control, even when things weren't going their way. She divided her page in half and started filling in the columns. The left side filled quickly with all the things Nikki still didn't know, but everything circled back to whether or not the girls left with a stranger.

Nikki believed Britney when she said that Thea was responsible, mostly because she'd dealt with type 1 diabetes her whole life and had been forced to be much more aware of her health at a young age. Both the Walkers and Alyssa said Thea was the cautious one, the one who listened to her mother's worries the most. Neither could she recall the girls playing with any kids other than Lacey for the short period of time Britney had been recording.

Britney was a stay-at-home mom, but she'd started taking

some online courses at Shane's urging to help her feel more independent, which meant Alyssa often took the girls to the park and other outings. By her own admission, Britney didn't like going to public places, so Alyssa did much of that. By the time the girls were taken, Britney had been dealing with the public crowd and her kids by herself for more than three hours, which had to be tough for her. Nikki didn't blame her for getting a drink or telling the girls to go sit down; they were the sort of things parents did every day, and 99.9 percent of the time nothing bad happened.

Shane Walker had no known enemies, no medical malpractice suits ongoing, and no other financial strains. Nikki had texted Trooper James, asking for Bridget Hyland's file, but right now Shane's involvement seemed like a stretch, as did Britney's former church. Thea hadn't been sexually assaulted, but was that because she'd died before the kidnapper could do anything? Was Abby being subjected to those horrors instead?

What about Rodney? Liam hadn't been able to find anything concrete about the accusation, and the guy's record was clean, plus the owner of the beer garden had confirmed that Rodney worked until two a.m. when everything had finally been closed down and cleaned up.

Her phone vibrated on the wood coffee table. Nikki recognized the Thief River Falls area code but not the number. "Agent Hunt."

"My name is Silas Hatch, from the FSZ chapter in Thief River Falls." He spoke softly, as though he were weak, and Nikki remembered that Silas had been much older than Britney when she'd been forced to marry him. "I understand you are investigating a case involving a former member of our church. Trooper James suggested I speak with you."

"Yes," Nikki answered, trying to think of the best place to start without immediately offending him. "It's my understanding that Britney was your wife in the eyes of the church?"

Silas hesitated. "I was her priesthood head, but I'm not sure why that's relevant. No one from our church has had contact with Britney."

Nikki knew from her research that the term "priesthood head" meant the man who essentially owned the woman, whether he was her father or husband. She knew Silas wasn't about to admit he'd "married" Britney when she was fifteen and under the age of consent. Nikki ran into the kitchen and grabbed her old digital recorder out of the drawer and asked Silas if he minded her recording the conversation to make sure she didn't miss anything.

"Whatever you feel is appropriate," Silas said. "I have nothing to hide."

Nikki hit record and put the phone on speaker. "Did you know why Britney left?"

"She was unhappy here," he said. "And she'd lost her faith."

"Forgive me if I'm wrong"—Nikki tried to think of a way to phrase her question so that Silas didn't feel like he was being judged—"but your religion believes multiple wives are the key to the everlasting kingdom, so to speak."

"Yes," Silas answered. "A man must have at least three wives to reach the celestial heavens."

Given everything she'd read about the Utah sects sneaking women around to hide them and break their will, Nikki had her doubts. "As her priesthood head"—she made sure to emphasize the words, a hint of disdain in her tone—"you didn't know she was planning to leave, then?"

He sighed. "If I had, I certainly would have done everything in my power to convince her to stay." Nikki wanted to gauge how angry Silas was, but he didn't seem angry at all.

"Let's back up a bit. Is it true that your family and Britney's were some of the first to leave the compound in Utah and set up a new church in Thief River Falls?"

"Correct," Silas said. "My older brother and Britney's father were elders who questioned the leader about his moral choices and were excommunicated for it. The families banded together and moved in hopes of starting a new church that operated with both God's law and societal law."

"You're talking about scores of underaged girls being spiritually wedded to much older men and forced to have children in order for those men to get into the celestial heaven?"

"Yes, sadly. My oldest brother was within the prophet's inner circle. He saw some terrible things and heard even worse. He actually tried to help the investigation after we were kicked out of the church."

"I understand her father has passed away and her brother Hyrum is in charge?"

"The council is in charge." Silas's voice had taken on a sharp edge. "Hyrum inherited his father's seat on the council. Why do you ask?"

"Britney is fearful he may want her to return. She and her husband are worried that someone from your group may have found out where she was living and decided to take her daughter as a punishment."

"Agent Hunt, I can assure you that until this morning, no one in our community knew Britney remained in the state, much less that she had a child."

Nikki was careful not to reveal that Thea had been Silas's biological child. "Thank you for getting in touch with me. Is it alright to call you at this number if I have follow-up questions?"

"Of course, but may I ask you for a favor in return?"

"I'll do my best."

"We try very hard to be good citizens in the community, as we're aware of the state's restrictions on our marriages, which means we don't completely isolate our young people. But I would appreciate it if you were able to leave Britney's connection to the church here out of the media."

Nikki promised she'd do everything in her power to keep

the information private. She ended the call feeling even more confused—not about the Fundamentalist Saints of Zion and their lifestyle, but about Britney herself. Silas likely hadn't taken the girls, and with no motive or real suspect, they were back to square one.

THIRTEEN

Nikki managed to fall asleep sometime after midnight. Vivid dreams woke her up shortly after four a.m., the long T-shirt she'd worn to bed soaked in sweat. She eased out of the bed, careful not to wake Rory. Goosebumps broke out over her arms as soon as she left the warmth of the blankets. Rory and Lacey both ran hot and liked to sleep in the cold. Shivering, Nikki slipped on a lightweight cardigan she'd hung on the bathroom doorknob and went into the kitchen. She made a pot of strong coffee and sat down at the kitchen table to check her messages. Miller would have called her if they'd had a major break in the case, but Nikki also hoped Courtney had been able to finish up with the forensics. Blanchard had recovered several fibers from the tape used to cover Thea's mouth, along with a few taken from the inside of her mouth, likely distributed after she'd worked the tape off in a desperate attempt to stay alive. The fibers likely wouldn't help them in court, because the science was less reliable than the experts used to believe. Still, Courtney could determine if they were from marine carpeting from someone's boat. The lividity marks on Thea's body showed she had been facedown when she died, her hands and feet restrained with heavy twine—a material extremely difficult to fingerprint.

Courtney had emailed her to say they were still working on the fiber evidence, and she hoped to have more information for Nikki today. Blanchard had sent Thea's clothes and shoes to the lab to test for DNA and fingerprints, and Nikki had asked Courtney to prioritize those things on the off-chance the DNA profile would give them a hit in CODIS, the national DNA registry.

Before she left, Nikki peeked into Lacey's room. Her small, six-year-old daughter somehow managed to take up most of the space in her bed, her arms and legs stretched out like a cat's. She'd come in with Rory not long after Nikki's call with Silas with even more grease on her clothes and hands. Even her shoes had gunk on them.

Nikki scooped her daughter up and took her to the bathroom before she made too much mess in the house. As usual, Lacey chattered on about her day and all the things she'd done with Rory and Uncle Mark, barely taking time for a breath. Nikki relished the time with Lacey, even though she kept seeing Britney's video of her daughters playing with her. Rory's mother had kept Lacey away from the news during the day, and she'd been too preoccupied with the boat to ask too many questions about Nikki's middle of the night call. By the time her head hit the fluffy pillows, Lacey was out, and Nikki breathed a sigh of relief she didn't have to discuss Thea and Abby with her. Nikki had been so tired last night she doubted she would have been able to control her emotions if Lacey had asked about the girls.

Careful not to wake her, Nikki closed the door and went back to the kitchen to write a quick note for Rory. He would be up before six a.m. and drop Lacey at his parents' before heading to his latest construction project. At times like these, she often wondered if Rory had realized what he was getting into before they started dating. Lacey's father had been murdered by a serial killer who'd tormented Nikki for years, and Rory had stepped up to the plate to help take care of Lacey. He never showed any frustration with Nikki's always-changing schedule, and she knew how lucky she'd gotten with Rory. Once this case was over, she would do something special to make sure he understood how much she appreciated him. Knowing that he and his family were there for Lacey had been a crucial part of Nikki returning to work after Tyler's murder. If she hadn't had the support system with the Todds, Nikki wasn't sure what she would have done.

She signed the note with a hastily scribbled heart and hurried out the door. She didn't want to make the head of orthopedics wait when she'd come in early to meet with Nikki.

Nikki called Trooper James on her way to the hospital and filled her in on her conversation with Silas last night.

"That sort of jives with what we've been told," James said. "I still have my reservations about this place, but I've read a lot about what happened with the fundamentalists in Utah and Arizona, and I can tell you we haven't experienced any sort of intimidation or threats, and the ranch is always open to visitors, although there's usually a guard who checks you in. I did notice people were tight-lipped about Britney at first, but it struck me as more out of respect for Silas than anything else."

Nikki agreed with her assessment after talking with Silas the night before. She just didn't see the motive for anyone from the fundamentalist group to take the girls now, especially since Thea's body had been left behind. Thea had been Silas's flesh and blood, not Abby. Nikki was certain she would have been the victim if the church group had taken Abby. It had to be someone closer to the Walkers. "Any chance you could stop by today, tell Silas you spoke with me, and ask if you could talk to a few more people to verify things and get a better idea of what Britney was like before she left the ranch?"

"I'm in court this morning, but I can head over after lunch," James said. "No sign of the other little girl?"

"Not yet." Nikki prayed Abby hadn't already run out of time.

While Minneapolis and St. Paul were known as the Twin Cities because of their proximity to each other, they were two different urban areas. Downtown Minneapolis consisted of the University of Minnesota and its hospital, so the area was always busy, even during the summer. Unlike the state's rural areas, the urban centers were a melting pot of different cultures. The university and the job sector brought people from all over the world. Beautiful, brightly colored hijabs mixed in with baseball hats and scrubs, not to mention the food.

While Minneapolis was more for the trend-setters and night owls, St. Paul had a more refined feeling to it. The state's incredible science center was in St. Paul, along with the children's museum and the Mississippi National River and Recreation Area. Plenty of immigrants called St. Paul home as well, but the city always struck Nikki as more laidback and family oriented than Minneapolis.

Smaller and more confined, Regions Hospital was much easier to navigate than the university hospital. Nikki checked in at the main entrance and asked for directions to the orthopedic floor.

Dr. Zhang was waiting for Nikki when she stepped off the elevator, and for a moment, Nikki was tongue-tied. Zhang was one of the most stunning women Nikki had ever seen. She normally tried not to focus on such things, but it was impossible with Zhang. She had glossy, black hair and delicate features, but she was taller than Nikki's 5'7" by at least two inches, and the doctor wore sneakers. They exchanged pleasantries as Zhang led Nikki to her office at the opposite end of the floor.

"Please, have a seat." Her dark blue eyes followed Nikki as she sat down in the leather chair in front of the doctor's immaculate desk.

"Thank you for seeing me at such short notice," Nikki said.

"Of course." Dr. Zhang's distinctly Irish accent threw Nikki off. "Although I'm not sure how much help I will actually be."

"You're Irish," Nikki said, embarrassed by her surprise. "I'm sorry, that's probably offensive. I just assumed you were Asian American."

Dr. Zhang smiled. "It's all right. It happens every time I meet someone. My father is Asian American, but he was living in Dublin, Ireland when he met my mother. They moved to the states when I was a teenager."

"What a fascinating childhood," Nikki said. "Were your parents doctors?"

"My mother is a nurse, retired," Zhang said. "She worked right here at Regions and after listening to her talk about how underappreciated nurses were, I made up my mind to become a doctor. I spent most of my orthopedic residency here and have been fortunate to remain here since."

Nikki had done her homework on Zhang's accomplishments. On paper, she was every bit as qualified as Shane Walker.

"How long have you been the Director of Orthopedics here?"

"Three years in May," she said. "Frankly, when the position opened, I expected Doctor Walker to try for it, but I guess he's busy with his medical center and the sports teams."

Nikki caught the note of derision in Zhang's voice. "Have the two of you butted heads in the past?"

Zhang's smile didn't reach her eyes this time. "He was an attending physician when I started here as a second-year resident. At twenty-eight, I should have been out of his orbit, but I wasn't."

"I'm sorry, I'm not quite following you," Nikki said.

"Shane Walker likes younger women," Zhang said. "I thought someone would have mentioned this? I thought that's what you wanted to talk to me about? Even though he's married, he told me that I was so beautiful he'd make an exception."

Nikki recoiled in disgust. "How long ago was this?"

"Eight years ago," Zhang said. "I turned him down and reported him to Human Resources, who did nothing about it. He was a rising star by then, and the hospital brass saw him as a marketing opportunity. Once he started working with the Vikings, he really became untouchable."

"That was before he opened his Twin Lakes facility, right?"

She nodded. "He used the Vikings deal to leverage more money from Regions. He had offers from Abbott Northwestern to head their ortho department and teach, but he stayed here. He stepped down from full-time orthopedic shifts after Twin Lakes opened, but he does at least two trauma shifts here a month, and he comes back to check on patients. They all just love him."

Nikki couldn't help but wonder if Zhang had some professional jealousy about Shane's success. "Does it bother you that he's so well respected?"

"As a surgeon, no. He's excellent, and he's good with patients. As a person, yes. I personally witnessed him flirting with new interns, and there are rumors he was caught having sex with one of them in an on-call room, but she didn't want to say anything, and again, he's untouchable." Zhang sighed. "I'm sure I don't have to tell you that women in medicine have to work twice as hard as men when it comes to competing for top positions. It's getting better as some of the old guard retires, but it's still an issue. And in my opinion, he's using his position of power over these women, even if they instigated the flirting. It's unprofessional and flat-out wrong. There's no time for that crap in medicine, as far as I'm concerned. This isn't *Grey's Anatomy*."

"Believe me, I get it," Nikki told her. "Did any of these women ever file a complaint?"

"Not that I know of," Zhang said. "I always thought that was part of the reason he went after younger ones."

"His wife is significantly younger than him."

"Poor Britney." Zhang shook her head. "I met her at a few functions several years ago. She's very sweet, but she seemed completely out of her element. I always got the impression that she was more in awe of Shane than in love with him."

"Do you believe he's still unfaithful?"

"I think that's why he continues to work as an on-call trauma surgeon," Zhang said flatly. "He's smart enough not to mess around with anyone who works for him. But the hospital is always getting new nurses, aides, you know how it goes."

"And the board is aware?"

"I've told them on more than one occasion," she said. "They don't care because Walker's affiliation with the hospital is so important for publicity. I've thought about trying to put together a formal complaint, gather witnesses and all of that, but I don't think it will matter. And I didn't get into medicine to fight others. My focus is on the orthopedic surgery program and our patients. I don't have time for the rest of it. If his actions start affecting patient care, that's a different story, and he knows I'm watching."

Nikki liked Dr. Zhang immensely. She knew what it was like to be a female in a male-dominated job and how difficult it was to walk the line of being seen as capable and professional while fending off chauvinistic pigs. "What about Shane and Britney's relationship? How was he toward her?"

Zhang considered the question. "Patient, protective. He didn't want her being asked questions about her childhood. It was rough, and that's part of the reason she was so painfully shy and nervous in social situations."

"What about his daughters?" Nikki asked. "Did he talk about them much?"

"He doesn't wear a wedding ring here, much less talk about his children. I wasn't even aware he had any until months after I started here, and I worked with him almost daily at the time."

"Do you know if any of these women caused trouble for Doctor Walker? Maybe wanting more of a relationship, or threatening to report him, that sort of thing?"

"I don't," Zhang said. "But I can say that when he propositioned me years ago, Doctor Walker was very open about wanting a sexual relationship, on his terms, with no attachments."

"One last question. Is there anyone who might know who Walker's latest conquest is?"

"I'm sure some of the nurses have an idea. The good ones see everything. But don't expect any information that goes against Walker. They love him and they know the board does as well. I, on the other hand, don't feel the same sort of loyalty. I'll see what I can find out. A name would be helpful."

"Carly, or Carol, who works at Regions," Nikki said. "And that may not be the right name."

"Give me a day and I'll get back to you."

Nikki thanked Dr. Zhang for her time and handed her a business card. "My cell is on that, so if you think of anything else, call no matter the time."

Nikki stayed at the hospital for another half an hour, trying to talk to as many personnel as possible. She didn't meet anyone with the name she was looking for. As Zhang predicted, blank stares made up most of the answers, although a couple of older nurses tried to shame Nikki for asking such things about the doctor, especially now. Before she left, Nikki stopped at the unit's front desk and talked to the young woman in charge of checking visitor badges. Nikki had noticed the woman's interest in her questions.

"Hi, Lauren," she said, reading the badge clipped to the woman's shirt. "I'm Special Agent Nikki Hunt with the FBI."

"I know who you are," the girl said. "Why aren't you out looking for Doctor Walker's kids?"

"We have a large contingent out searching," she told the girl. "I'm here trying to find out if there was anyone who might have had it in for Doctor Walker, any staff he had issues with, along with any patients."

"No one has it in for Doctor Walker," Lauren said in a low whisper. "Everyone loves him. He's generous, smart, and takes time with his patients."

Nikki smiled and leaned against the rounded counter. Lauren was an attractive young woman, and her spot at the unit's entrance meant that Walker couldn't access his patients without walking by. "That's what I hear. Have you worked here long?"

"Just this summer," she said. "I'm a nursing student."

"That's wonderful. Have you had the opportunity to spend much time with Doctor Walker?"

Lauren looked confused. "Why would I spend time with him? He's super busy. I'm not sure I've ever seen him standing still."

Nikki handed her a business card. "If you think of anything, call me."

FOURTEEN

Dr. Blanchard was the Chief Medical Examiner for both Washington and Ramsey Counties, along with sixteen smaller counties in the state, which meant her schedule was always full. In addition to Blanchard and her autopsy techs, the office staffed ten full-time death investigators, along with the chief death investigator. On a normal death call, if such a thing existed, the death investigators were dispatched to work the scene and bring in the body. If homicide was suspected, Blanchard or her chief death investigator worked the scene. While all of Blanchard's staff were excellent and easy to work with, Nikki was grateful she'd been able to take care of Thea. She'd worked enough cases with Blanchard to know she wouldn't miss anything, even if that meant long hours in the autopsy suite. Her dedication doubled when the victim was a child.

Since the medical examiner's office was next to the east parking ramp at Regions, Nikki decided to walk over. The humidity hadn't kicked in yet this morning, even though the temperature had risen since she'd gone inside the hospital to meet Dr. Zhang. Buildings blocked most of the meager breeze, and by the time Nikki arrived, sweat dampened the back of her neck. She found a clip in her bag and swept her curls into an acceptable knot.

"Good morning, Agent Hunt." The front desk adminis-trator greeted her. Alma was the face of the office and had been since long before Nikki came back to the area. She knew most cops by their names, and more importantly, how to put them in their place if they came in demanding miracles. "Doctor Blan-chard said to tell you she'll be in autopsy suite A."

Nikki had selfishly been hoping to go over things in Blan-chard's office. She hoped meeting in the autopsy suite meant the medical examiner had found something. She stopped in the locker room to slip on scrubs and booties before locking up her things.

She tried not to grimace at the distinctive odor of formalde-hyde and decay. "Sorry I'm late." Nikki pulled on latex gloves. "I had a meeting with the head of orthopedics at Regions." Her gaze drifted to the small body lying on the steel table. Blanchard had removed all of Thea's clothes and sent them to the lab for Courtney to run tests. A blue paper sheet covered Thea's body up to her chin.

Blanchard motioned for Nikki to join her next to the autopsy table.

"Official cause of death is heatstroke, and it happened pretty quickly," Blanchard said. "High temp Saturday was ninety-five degrees, and it was around eighty-six when the fire-works started. Within the first five minutes of closing the doors of a vehicle, inside temp can increase by seventy-five percent," Blanchard reminded her. "That's an interior temperature of more than one hundred and forty degrees."

Nikki was shocked. She had expected suffocation after seeing the marks on Thea's body at the orchard. She thought of the boats at the dock during the first couple hours the girls were missing. "Would a cabin boat that's been sitting in the sun all day be as hot?"

"During daylight, it would be even hotter," Blanchard said. "Sun sets around nine p.m., so the interior was likely nearly as hot when the fireworks started. That's why there are no heat artefacts on her body."

"In layman's terms?"

"Burns, essentially. Kids who are left in cars during the day almost always have a thermal burn somewhere, unless they were in shade."

Nikki nodded. So they were right to have focused on the docks.

"You mentioned it happened quickly?"

Blanchard nodded. "Kids are more susceptible to heat stress as the body fights to bring its temperature down, but sweating isn't effective in a hot car—or vehicle—in cooling the body down. The body sweats until it's totally dehydrated, and things get worse from there. Kids can't regulate their body temperature as well as adults, so they're even more susceptible." She walked around the table. "Thea had a full stomach, so she likely ate within an hour or two of dying."

Nikki mentally ran through Britney's information. "Abby and Thea shared a funnel cake around eight p.m. Please tell me you were able to get something off her body for Courtney to test."

"Oh yes," Blanchard said. "This little girl fought to free herself. She's got a couple of splinters beneath her nails, which are shredded. Courtney recovered several fibers from her fingernails, mouth and clothes. She should be able to figure out what they're from at least."

Nikki made a mental note to call Courtney and ask her to rush the fiber evidence. If they could find the crime scene, they would have a better shot at finding Abby.

"She was out of rigor already when we found her," Nikki said. "That's why you think she died within an hour or two?"

"Thea may not have gone through rigor," Blanchard said.

"It's not uncommon for frail people or children, because they don't have the muscle mass needed to cause rigor. She's a normal height and weight for her age, but she's also a type 1 diabetic. I think she died within a couple of hours of being taken because of the heat, her age, and the lack of insulin."

Nikki's thoughts jumped to little Abby, hopefully still alive. "I'm guessing they were kept together, given the space limitations of a cabin boat or car. So how did Abby not suffer the same fate? Or has her body just been left somewhere else?"

"That's your department, not mine," Blanchard said. "But water intake also plays a part in this. Thea's stomach contents contained fruit juice, which can be dehydrating if they're loaded with carbs and added sugar. If Abby was drinking more water, in combination with better general health than her sister, there's a chance she survived, but she probably needed some kind of medical intervention. IV fluids at the very least."

Nikki perked up. "Meaning someone with a medical background?"

"Not necessarily," Blanchard said. "Before you arrived I googled 'how to put in an IV,' and there are some pretty damn good YouTube videos out there. Anyone can learn, especially if they're not worried about causing the patient pain like you normally are in a hospital setting."

"Christ," Nikki said. "The criminals in this country have better training than half the police thanks to budget issues. Any idea when the tox results and other tests will be back?"

"Courtney said they're her top priority, so I'm hoping in the next day or two."

Nikki asked Blanchard to keep her updated on any results, eager to shed the paper gown and get out of the autopsy suite. She tossed the items in the bin, trying not to think of Thea's pale face lifeless on the autopsy table.

"We're coming, Abby," Nikki whispered to herself as she headed back into the heat. "Just hold on."

Back in the Jeep, Nikki turned the air con on high and fanned herself with her notebook while she checked in with Miller.

"Miller," the sheriff answered gruffly.

"Have you had a chance to read Blanchard's autopsy report?"

"Just looking at it now." Miller's voice shook. "That child suffered, and we're no closer to finding her sister."

"We know Thea was kept in a confined space directly affected by temperature, and that leaves us with a vehicle, or a boat. Given how extensive Saturday night's search was, combined with the traffic, I think a boat is more likely."

"I'll let Chen know to keep hounding the marinas," Miller said. "But until we can physically put Thea in a boat, we'll never get a warrant for either of the marinas."

"Courtney took fibers from under Thea's nails, her mouth and her clothes. She's working to identify them, but it may be another day or so. It's a complicated process. Where are we with the witnesses who saw the boy holding Thea's bag by the church?"

"They're sitting with the sketch artist now," Miller said. "From their description, whoever picked it up and took the insulin likely isn't the killer. He saw a purse and hoped to find money, find drugs of some sort instead. My guess is a junkie. But he may have seen who dropped the purse in the church parking lot. That's who we're looking for."

"Agreed," Nikki said. "Especially if the person the witnesses saw was a teenager. I just don't see someone young and inexperienced being able to pull off a kidnapping like this without calling attention to himself, especially given the quick response of the Stillwater PD."

"Chief Ryan and I thought the same thing," Miller answered. "How'd the interview with Regions' head of orthopedics go?"

"Well, Shane Walker's got a thing for young women working in the hospital," she told him. "The head of orthopedics believes that's part of the reason he still takes shifts at Regions since he's got his own private practice. And I also got a call from Silas Hatch last night. I don't think he's our man. But Trooper James is stopping by the church compound later today for another round of interviews and to keep an eye out for Abby. I'm going to talk to the guy who threatened Shane Walker after the football player got injured, and then I'm heading to the Walkers' to have another chat with Shane."

"I'll let Ryan and Chen know," Miller said. "Ryan wants a task force briefing at the end of the day."

Nikki could practically hear him rolling his eyes. "See you then."

Nikki tried not to make a face at the heavy odor of burning rubber as she followed Jack Buck's manager to his office. Despite air conditioning, the inside of the factory felt like an oven and smelled like one burning off a year's worth of spills.

"You know, Jack got a bad rap over the stuff with Walker," the manager told Nikki. "He's a good guy."

"I believe you," Nikki said. "But I still have to speak with him."

The manager stopped in front of a closed door with faded lettering and turned to glare at Nikki. "There's a big difference between running your mouth about a sports team and taking little girls."

"I'm well aware." Nikki kept her tone even. "Is Jack waiting for us in your office?"

"Yeah." He opened the steel door. "Jack, that FBI lady's here."

Jack Buck reminded Nikki of *Seinfeld*'s George Costanza, with a bit of Kramer's frenetic energy mixed in. He was standing in his manager's small office, pacing. "I didn't do this. I was in the north woods fishing all weekend."

"Do you have receipts for a hotel or gas, anything like that?"

Buck flushed. "I don't keep receipts. I use my bank card. The transactions will show in my account."

"What hotel did you stay at?" Nikki asked.

"I didn't," Buck said. "It's summer. I set up a tent and camped all weekend."

"You catch any fish?"

Buck grinned. "Caught my limit every day. Got a freezer full of fish, too."

"Mr. Buck, we'll get your alibi confirmed as soon as possible," Nikki told him. "We will need a warrant to check your bank records, but that shouldn't be an issue, should it?"

"I don't have anything to hide."

"Good." Nikki shifted her tactics a bit. "You do understand that your threats against Doctor Walker's family a couple of years ago are why we're here, correct?"

Buck scowled. "Look, I threatened his family. I didn't know if he was married or had kids. I just ran off at the mouth, and I paid for it."

Nikki believed him. While their investigation had opened up a lot more questions of Shane Walker and Britney, everyone who knew the couple said they were very private. A lot of staff at the hospital didn't even realize Walker had children. That had bothered Nikki initially, but as she'd learned how high-profile Dr. Walker had become, she understood the need to keep his personal life private. She left cards with Buck and his manager. She'd debated speaking with the Vikings' medical staff, but many were still out on vacation. And Chief Schultz had talked at length with the organization, and the file he'd given Nikki contained full transcripts of all the interviews he'd done.

. . .

Liam didn't answer his phone, so Nikki stopped by the FBI's offices in Brooklyn Park, a picturesque suburb on the north side of Minneapolis, before heading back to Washington County. Her unit was located on the top floor, with a lovely view of the campus, which consisted of a large lake surrounded by trees and a walking path.

Nikki bypassed her boss's closed door. Agent Hernandez, the Bureau chief, was on vacation for another week.

Until Nikki's arrival six years ago, the field office had consisted of a handful of investigators stretched thin, with counterintelligence agents doing double duty as crime investigators. That meant the office often had to kick major crimes over to the state's Bureau of Criminal Apprehension. FBI brass had balked at putting more resources into violent crime because the BCA had experience and a very capable forensics lab. Since the Twin Cities were home to several Fortune 500 companies, including Target, US Bancorp, and Cargill, a major global food corporation, the FBI's primary focus had shifted to counterterrorism and cybercrime after the September 11th attacks. But with the BCA getting more and more dumped on them because Hernandez didn't have agents trained to hunt killers and rapists, he started campaigning to create a dedicated violent crime investigation team.

Hernandez had recruited Nikki from her coveted job at Quantico to run his new violent crime division because of her track record and her profiling skills. Nikki had recruited Liam not long after her arrival, and it had been the two of them until the last couple of years. Her unit's success enabled Hernandez to hire two new investigators. She and Liam both felt that bringing in eager, green agents ready to be trained in profiling and investigation was a necessity, and they were both supposed to be in charge of training them. Unfortunately, the string of upheavals in Nikki's personal life meant Liam had shouldered much of the training workload.

His desk at the head of the bullpen area was empty, but Kendall and Jim sat at their desks, poring over files.

"How's it going?" Nikki asked. She'd spent the summer trying to get to know the junior agents better, but Liam was still their immediate supervisor. Nikki always felt like she'd walked into a room unannounced whenever she spoke to the duo.

"Good." Kendall spoke for both agents. "We're still trying to track down a Carly or Carol at Regions."

"Good." Nikki noticed Liam's organized desk. He carried his laptop with him, but he hadn't turned on his work computer. "Where's Agent Wilson?"

The agents shrugged. "He stopped in for a few minutes, got an update and said he was heading out to chase more leads."

Nikki checked her watch. "How long was he here?"

"Five minutes, tops," Jim said. "He said he'd be working at the Washington County Sheriff's after he was done with the leads."

"Did he say what the leads were?" Nikki asked.

They shook their heads.

Nikki didn't want to undermine Liam's authority, nor did she want the junior agents to suspect that Liam hadn't communicated his plans with his superior. She thanked Kendall and Jim for their efforts and left the bullpen without going into her office.

Outside, Nikki tried Liam's cell, but it went straight to voicemail. She left a message and then texted him. Nikki called Caitlin next, but the call also went to voicemail. It wasn't like Liam to ignore her calls. Was he having problems from his concussion and didn't want Nikki to know? She hadn't noticed any signs he was struggling, but Liam was good at hiding how bad he actually felt.

Maybe Liam had his phone on vibrate and didn't realize she'd called.

She'd just started the Jeep when Miller's call came. "Someone spot Abby?" Nikki asked immediately.

"No." Miller's voice was tight. "We've got the sketch back. Where's Liam?"

"Running down a lead." Nikki didn't like the edge in Miller's voice. "Why?"

"Because the sketch matches someone. I'm texting it to you now."

Her phone dinged with the notification. Nikki opened the image, her excitement morphing into confusion and anger. The witnesses had definitely gotten a good look at the teenager, right down to the slope of his shoulders.

"It's Zach," she managed to say. Nikki felt sick. How could this have happened? Surely Liam didn't know anything about it, or he would have told Nikki. She thought about the task force meeting yesterday. "Yesterday, when I mentioned the eyewitness, Liam physically jerked. I didn't think much of it then, but after seeing the sketch, I think he knew right then and there that the witnesses were describing him. Maybe he wants to protect Caitlin... she and Zach have been through a lot..."

"That's not good enough," Miller said.

"Thea was already dead," Nikki said, automatically coming to the defense of her partner.

"Abby's not," Miller shot back. "Why hasn't Liam said anything about this? How can he try to protect Zach when there is a little girl out there—"

"I don't know," Nikki cut him off. "But you're jumping to conclusions. And if Liam did know, then I'm sure there's a good explanation." Nikki hoped her bluff turned out to be true. Liam could be in serious hot water, especially if Abby wasn't found alive, and soon.

"There'd better be," Miller fumed. "I'll charge his ass with obstruction."

Nikki hoped it didn't come to that. The three of them

worked well together, and Miller charging Liam would definitely throw a wrench in things. "Let's just take this one step at a time. Is the sketch public?"

"Going on the twelve o'clock news in twenty minutes."

"Okay," Nikki said. "Then I've got twenty minutes to find out what the hell Liam is thinking."

FIFTEEN

Liam didn't answer his phone. Nikki wasn't about to sit around waiting for him to call. She'd driven straight to Caitlin's place. She lived at Stillwater Mills, a luxury condo complex in downtown, just blocks from the river and the senior living apartments where Rodney lived with his grandmother.

What the hell had Liam been thinking? Nikki was confident the sketch was accurate, because she'd seen Zach shortly after the fireworks, wearing the same clothes the witness had described. Had he found the purse along the way? Or was he somehow involved in the kidnappings?

Nikki ran through Saturday night's events in her head. Zach had walked past her after the fireworks, around the same time that the search for the girls started. He could have picked the purse up anywhere between the river and the church parking lot where it had been found, or he could have taken it from Thea. Would he have done something like that? She knew he'd been having a hard time lately. Had he taken the purse for money? Technically, she couldn't rule Zach out as being involved, but it didn't make logistical sense, especially if Nikki had seen him without the purse around the same time the police started looking for Thea. Despite the crowd, the SPD moved quickly, and several people immediately volunteered to help search.

Zach would have been spotted, she was certain.

Nikki couldn't see fourteen-year-old Zach inflicting any sort of harm on anyone, especially after what he'd endured. But he could know something, and Liam's actions made Nikki worry that the teenager knew something that could get him in trouble.

She turned into the parking area for Stillwater Mills and cursed. Liam's silver Prius was parked behind Caitlin's SUV. Whatever empathy Nikki had evaporated.

"You're kidding me," she shouted, whipping into the nearest open spot. She slammed on her brakes. Nikki killed the engine and grabbed her bag. How could Liam keep this from her? He knew better. Nikki trusted him more than anyone else, because that's what partners did. Covering up for Zach was not like Liam.

Caitlin, on the other hand, was a pushy investigative reporter. Nikki had hated her at first because she'd been working to free Mark, when Nikki still believed Mark had killed her parents. Their relationship had grown from mutual dislike to tolerance before Caitlin's stubbornness had saved Nikki and Lacey from the Frost Killer, cementing their friendship. That didn't change the fact that Caitlin excelled at getting information and had more sources than Nikki could count. When Liam had started dating her, Nikki worried she would put him in a precarious position, but that hadn't happened until now.

Nikki had been to Caitlin's swanky apartment a few times, so the doorman recognized Nikki and allowed her access to the elevator. She tried to think of the best way to handle the situation, but Nikki had a feeling her temper would win over rational thought.

More than anything, she was hurt that Liam hadn't trusted her. And if Caitlin was behind it, they were going to have an even bigger problem. As much as she felt for her friend, Abby's life took precedence.

Caitlin answered the door before Nikki had a chance to bang on it. "Hi. I guess you're here to see Liam. Come in."

"And your son." Nikki struggled to keep the anger out of her voice. "Did you ask Liam not to tell me?"

"What?" Caitlin tucked her blonde hair behind her ear. "I didn't ask him to do anything. What's wrong with Zach?" The fear in her voice sounded genuine.

"Nothing." Liam joined her, his complexion almost as red as his hair.

"Don't lie to her," Nikki snapped.

Liam's jaw worked, the veins in his neck tight. "I thought I could talk to Zach and clear this up."

"Where is he?" Nikki demanded. "Do you realize how much trouble you could be in?"

"He's at his grandparents'."

"Would one of you two please tell me why you're talking in code about my son?" Caitlin demanded.

Nikki showed her the sketch. "A witness saw this boy with the felt purse one of the missing girls had Saturday night. It contained insulin, which is gone."

Caitlin paled beneath her summer tan. "What? Are you saying you think Zach might have been involved in all of this? After everything he's endured?"

"I'm saying someone saw him with the purse and Liam knew it and said nothing." She glared at her partner before turning her attention back to Caitlin. "What time did Zach get home Saturday night?"

Caitlin hedged. "He was supposed to be home by eleven, and he didn't come in until almost one a.m. But Zach would never do this, not to mention he's only fourteen and doesn't have access to a vehicle to transport those girls."

"Zach had nothing to do with this," Liam said firmly.

"He probably didn't, but you deliberately withheld information in a missing children case—"

His eyes narrowed. "We've both let our personal lives cloud our judgment."

Nikki took a deep breath. He wasn't wrong, and she knew the main reason for her anger was worry for Liam, not the case. "This could cause serious issues for you if Miller chooses to pursue it."

"I'll make sure he doesn't."

Caitlin was still staring at the sketch, her hands shaking. "What happened to the insulin?"

"We don't know," Nikki said.

"What is it?" Liam asked.

"Nothing." Caitlin reached for her cell phone. "He's just not answering his phone and he's been talking about... leaving."

"What do you mean, leaving?" Nikki asked.

"He tried to take his own life two months ago." Caitlin started bawling. "What if he took the insulin to really do it this time?"

Caitlin called Zach's paternal grandparents at home and on their cells, but both went to voicemail. "Shit," she said. "They're grocery shopping, and neither one of them ever hear their phones. He's supposed to be at their house."

"What about GPS on Zach's phone?" Nikki asked. "It should tell us where he is."

Liam shook his head. "He turns it off." He glared at Caitlin.

"Before you start," Caitlin cut in. "I'm not exactly an experienced mom, you know? Zach didn't know I was his real mother until eighteen months ago. He's been through hell, and I don't know how to help him."

"You have to put your foot down," Liam snapped. "At least about the GPS so you know where he is. You pay for that phone, right? If he doesn't leave it on, take it from him."

"I can't do that," Caitlin said. "He'd never forgive me, and you know that. Is that what you want?"

Liam rolled his eyes, and Nikki spoke before they could continue arguing. "Caitlin, I understand how hard it's been for you and Zach, and I'm not here to question your parenting skills. But we need to find Zach, for his own good."

Zach's paternal grandparents lived about thirty minutes north of Stillwater. Caitlin begged to go with them, but Liam had refused. "Let us find him and explain. The two of you will just fight. Keep trying to reach his grandparents."

Neither spoke for the first few minutes. Nikki tried to get her thoughts in order, but she couldn't get past Liam not trusting her.

"Why didn't you tell me once you heard about the sketch?" she finally asked.

Liam stared straight ahead as he spoke. "Plausible deniability."

"What?"

"If you knew I thought he might be the kid in the sketch, you'd be in the same position as I am with Miller right now."

"No, I wouldn't," she snapped. "If I'd known, I'd have talked to Zach myself. What if he saw something that could have saved Thea?"

"I don't think he did, but it's not like I've been sitting on my ass or hiding him. He's refused my calls and Caitlin's. He left a note this morning saying he had a ride to his grandparents'. Caitlin got an alert that her card had been used at a rideshare service. The charge was high enough that he likely did go to his grandparents', and I was about to head there when you showed up. He's not even supposed to be there this week, which is probably why they aren't paying attention to their cellphones. He probably showed up after they left to run their errands."

"When did he start getting into trouble?" Nikki's hands clenched the wheel as she tried to keep the frustration out of her voice.

"He's been hanging out with older kids who've got driver's licenses and cars," Liam said. "And before you say anything, I already ran their plates and checked their alibis for Saturday. Both kids are on vacations out of state."

Nikki didn't appreciate the tone in his voice, but she focused on the matter at hand. "But he was at Lumberjack Days. I saw him myself." Had Zach acquired the pink bag when he walked past Nikki that night? If she had stopped him about the vaping, would the night have unfolded differently? She couldn't see Thea or Abby willingly leaving with Zach that night, especially if he'd looked the way he had when Nikki saw him.

But he'd had his hands on the purse.

Had he found it? Or had he seen something?

"He was supposed to be home after the fireworks, but he didn't get home until almost one a.m."

"What was he doing during that time?" Nikki demanded.

"He said he was out walking. I believe him, Nik. He doesn't have access to a vehicle or a boat right now. He hasn't even got his learning permit."

She briefly took her eyes off the road to glare at him. "Don't 'Nik' me. Yes, we've both let personal stuff interfere, but two little girls were taken, and one is dead. We might have a chance to save the other if we act fast enough, and if Zach knows anything, we need to hear it." Nikki was sure Zach wasn't the killer—he didn't have motive or real opportunity. But he was a witness; they didn't know how or why he'd found that bag and taken it.

"I'm sure he doesn't," Liam told her. "We called him after the ride service charge came in, but he didn't answer."

"Before the sketch? You already suspected—"

"He walks downtown at night," Liam said. "Some nights he walks and walks and walks. I've followed him a few times to keep an eye on him."

Nikki couldn't believe what she was hearing. "He's vaping," Nikki said. "Is he also using drugs?"

"His grandfather caught him puffing a couple of times," Liam said. "He swears he doesn't do it anymore. Kid is so messed up, and I don't know how to help him."

"I'm sorry it's so hard for you right now, but you can't lie to me like this. I would never think Zach would do something or treat him like a criminal. We could have figured this out together."

Liam snorted. "Because we always work as a team, don't we?"

"I thought so," she snapped back.

"What about—"

"I know what you're going to say." Nikki cut him off. Her ex-husband had been a casualty of Nikki's search for the Frost Killer. "And just because I handled that situation poorly doesn't mean you should do the same. I had some leeway because my daughter was kidnapped. As much as you care about Zach, this is different."

"I'm aware."

Nikki sighed. They weren't going to get anywhere arguing. "Has he told you anything?" she asked.

"I told you, I didn't have a chance to speak to him. I knew when I heard the witness description that it might be him. I wasn't one hundred percent sure."

"Why didn't you tell me then?" Nikki demanded. "You already knew he came home late, and you knew he walked that area. Did you ask him about it when he got home?"

"I haven't seen him," Liam said again. "I didn't think you needed to know about his walking around because the area was crawling with cops, and we didn't miss the girls." He sighed and rubbed his temples. "Caitlin's been through hell with him, and I didn't want to make it worse. I know he's innocent, but I didn't realize what a good look the witness got at him, or I would have said something. You know if I thought for one second—"

"That's why you're too close. You can't see the situation as clear as I can, and that's why you should have stepped back." Nikki didn't want to argue with Liam. He was a good cop and a good person, and she needed him to be in the right headspace. "It's what I should have done after Frost talked to Lacey at the mall, Liam. If I had swallowed my pride and ego, her father might still be alive. I'll never know, and it will haunt me until the day I die. I just don't want that for you or Caitlin."

"Neither do I, and I know you're more worried than angry," Liam said. "He needs to get out of Stillwater and Minnesota altogether for a while. I found a place in Illinois that specializes in the kind of deep trauma therapy he needs, but it's an in-patient program. Caitlin wanted to see how the summer went before making a decision."

"You know I'll do everything I can to help Zach get the help he needs," Nikki said. "But we have to find out what he knows." She pulled off onto the shoulder as an ambulance rushed past them.

The hairs on the back of Nikki's neck stood as she watched the ambulance speed down the road ahead of them. "How close are we to Zach's grandparents'?"

"Five, ten minutes," Liam said.

"I have a bad feeling." She hoped her imagination was just getting the best of her. "If he tried to take his own life once and he's got that insulin..."

Liam had turned white. "Drive faster."

Nikki did as he asked, barely keeping all four tires on the road as she navigated the curves.

"Next drive on the left." Liam sat on the edge of his seat, trying to see through the thick grove of trees. "Oh God, Nik."

"I see them." She skidded to a stop behind the ambulance and grabbed her badge. "Let me handle this."

Liam was already out of the vehicle and heading toward the house. "Zach!"

Nikki jogged to keep up with his long strides. She could hear voices from inside the house, including a woman crying. An SUV had been left running in front of the house, the back hatch open. Judging from the bags, Nikki guessed Zach's grandparents must have come home and found him. She just prayed they hadn't been too late.

SIXTEEN

Abby woke up on the same stinky mattress she'd been lying on when the man brought her back from the bath. Hot tears streamed down her cheeks as she remembered the things he'd done.

Not to her but to the other girl. Whatever he'd been doing must have hurt, because she'd screamed and cried all night while Abby drifted in and out of a weird dream. She and Thea were running down a long dock, like the one by the river but much bigger. They were happy and skipping and giggling, and suddenly the man appeared.

In her dream, Thea shoved Abby behind her. But dream Thea was different than real Thea. Dream Thea was bigger and smelled different. She looked different, too. The man approached, dream Thea whispered for Abby to stay behind her, no matter what. Abby obeyed, but the man rushed at them, grabbing her sister and tossing her into the water.

The other girl's screams had pulled her out of that dream, but another bad one had come after it, and then another. Abby tried to force herself to stay awake, but her eyelids were too heavy, until now.

Slowly, she sat up in bed, pushing the dreams out of her mind. Thea would tell her to suck it up and not cry. Crying was for babies, and Abby was pretty sure she wasn't a baby anymore, especially after all this. She'd begged the man to tell her what he'd meant when he said her sister was at peace, but he'd told her to stop asking questions or she'd be punished.

Deep down, she knew what "at peace" meant, because she'd heard her mommy talking about it after something bad happened in the city last summer. That meant the person had died.

Thea was dead. She had to be, or she wouldn't have allowed that man to touch her.

The door handle turned. Abby's stomach turned into a giant rock, her bladder weakening as the door slowly opened. Dream Thea stood there, staring at her with the same dark eyes.

Abby blinked. "Who are you?" she whispered.

"No one," the other girl said. "Come out to the kitchen and eat."

SEVENTEEN

Liam rode with Zach in the ambulance while Nikki followed in the Jeep. She filled Miller in during the drive to the hospital. "I don't think Zach had anything to do with what happened to the girls." She explained what Liam had said about Zach's issues and his habit of walking at all hours of the night.

"I doubt he did, either," Miller said. "But I've got the mayor and the Stillwater police chief on my ass. If he found the purse, he could have seen something. Any idea how long he's been down?"

Nikki was still shaken by the sight of Zach. He'd looked lifeless on the gurney, despite the heartbeat the paramedics had been able to find. "They thought his heart stopped at first, but his pulse was really weak and uneven. They gave him something to counter the effect of the insulin, but I don't know if it will be enough."

Years ago, before she'd moved back to Minnesota, one of Nikki's colleagues at Quantico worked a homicide that involved the wife using her insulin to kill her non-diabetic husband. She didn't remember all of the details, but the medical examiner had explained the insulin found in his system had been enough to send an elephant into a diabetic coma—far more units than one insulin pen contained.

"I'll take care of the media and inevitable shitstorm that's coming after the sketch hits the news. Keep me updated on Zach."

By the time Nikki arrived at the hospital, Zach had been stabilized in the emergency room and transferred to the pediatric ICU. She hurried off the elevator and showed her badge to the nurse at the charge desk, who directed her to the ICU family waiting area. Unlike the rest of the hospital, the family area wasn't bathed in fluorescent lighting. Instead, cozy lamps and furniture attempted to create an inviting environment for the parents terrified of losing their sick child.

She stopped in the doorway. A doctor in blue scrubs was speaking with Caitlin, Liam and Zach's grandparents. Nikki turned to leave, but Liam caught sight of her.

"This is my supervisor and lead agent, Nikki Hunt," Liam said.

"She's family, so you can continue." Caitlin's voice shook.

The doctor nodded, clearly more concerned with Zach's condition than Nikki's presence. "The insulin pen contained 3 ml of insulin, or about 300 units per ml, designed to work more quickly than human insulin," the doctor said. "We have seen insulin death in non-diabetic patients after as little as 20 units, but doses of 400 units or more are usually the ones that cause fatality. Too much insulin makes you hypoglycemic. Right now, his blood glucose is 54. Anything lower than a blood glucose of 50 can trigger seizures and coma, so we are giving him medicine to counteract the insulin. He's still unconscious, but as long as we can get his blood glucose up, he should start coming around in a while."

"Will he have brain damage?" Caitlin asked.

"Possibly," the doctor said. "We normally see permanent damage when the number drops below 50, but he's close enough so there could be impairment. We really won't know that until he wakes up. Would you like to see him?"

Caitlin nodded. Zach's grandparents also stood. "We share custody," Caitlin said. "We all want to see him."

"Normally it's only two people, but given the situation, I'll allow it, but only for a few minutes."

Caitlin grabbed Liam's hand. "Will you wait outside the room? I feel better knowing you're close by."

"Of course." He looked at Nikki, and she nodded.

"I'll wait, but if he becomes alert, we need to talk to him. And by 'we,' I mean me. You need to steer clear of anything involving Zach other than being there for him and Caitlin. Understood?"

She hated to sound harsh, but Liam's decision could have consequences on the case and his career. As long as he used his head from this point on, Nikki hoped Miller would be satisfied with only chewing Liam's ass out instead of filing a complaint.

"I got it," he said.

While she waited, Nikki went over everything they'd learned. Britney had been drinking and didn't want to admit it, Shane hadn't been suspected in his former wife's death, the FSZ had been cooperative with the state troopers, and there had been no sign of Abby. And if the FSZ were involved, it made no sense to keep Abby or to kill Thea. They could have dropped Abby off somewhere. It just didn't add up in Nikki's mind.

Rodney had an alibi and so did Buck. Liam was right—Zach couldn't drive, didn't have a boat, didn't know much about the apple orchard and didn't have access to a vehicle to steal, either.

The girls didn't have life insurance policies, so no one stood to gain financially from their deaths. She needed to find Shane Walker's girlfriend. And the owners of every boat on that dock.

Several more minutes passed before Caitlin and Zach's grandparents returned, all of them red-eyed and sniffling.

"He wants to talk to you." Caitlin sniffled. "He won't tell anyone else what he knows. I guess he doesn't trust me to keep him safe."

"It's not that," Liam said. "Nikki saved his life. I think Zach wants to tell his story himself, that's all."

Nikki shut the door behind her. Fortunately, the pediatric ICU didn't have shared rooms, so they could talk in private. He was still pale and clammy-looking, oxygen flowing into his nose via cannulas. His heart rate was low, but steady, and his blood pressure had improved since the paramedics first took it.

"Zach?"

He partially opened his eyes. "Agent Hunt?"

"Yes, it's Nikki." She sat on the edge of the bed and took the boy's hand. "How are you feeling?"

"Awful," Zach answered. "But I'm alive, I guess."

"Did you really want to take your own life?" Nikki said. "I know you've been through unimaginable pain and some days it seems like it won't get better, but it can. Sometimes it takes a while to find the right therapy or program that really clicks, but it's out there."

"Caitlin says dying lets the bastard win," Zach said, referring to the serial predator who'd raped and kidnapped him. "I say it stops the memories. Sometimes I can still smell him." Tears pooled in his eyes.

"There are other ways to stop the memories," she said. "Not completely, but you can learn to control them. And believe it or not, you can learn to accept yourself as a good person worth love. It's hard work, and it's really unfair that after you've already endured so much, healing comes down to how much you put into it, but that's how it works."

"That's not the only reason," he said, looking at the pulse monitor on his index finger.

"Would you like to tell me what the other reason is, then?" Nikki asked, trying not to prod him too much.

"You haven't asked me how I got the insulin." He looked sheepish.

"I know how you got it and whose it is," Nikki said. "Can you tell me what happened Saturday night?"

"I didn't do anything to those little girls."

"I believe you, but I need to know what happened."

"I didn't want to go home, so I walked around downtown. Liam tell you I do that a lot at night?"

Nikki nodded.

Zach cracked a small smile. "Liam thinks I don't know when he follows me, but I do. Anyway, I walk by that church a lot. I found the pen and took it thinking I'd sell it, until I realized it was insulin. I wasn't going to do anything with it, but then I saw the news about those two little girls."

"You wouldn't have been in trouble for taking the pen," Nikki said.

"It's not that." Zach hesitated, and when Nikki didn't say anything, he took a deep breath. "I saw those girls on the dock before the fireworks started. They were holding hands, walking along behind someone. I didn't know they were in trouble, and I didn't know the purse I'd found was hers, either. I saw it on the news today, and it was just one more thing I'd screwed up. If I'd been paying attention, I could have told someone about the girls before it was too late. But I was feeling sorry for myself—"

"I'm going to stop you there," Nikki said gently. "You did not screw up, and trying to deal with pain isn't feeling sorry for yourself. You're fourteen years old, Zach. No one blames you for not paying attention. Most people wouldn't even remember seeing the girls, much less put two and two together."

He didn't look convinced. "I thought the taller one had a pink bag. I guess that's why I decided to pick up the one I saw."

"You saw them on the dock before the fireworks started?" Nikki clarified.

Zach nodded. "I went to the end of the dock to watch. People weren't supposed to do that, but no one paid any attention."

Nikki rummaged in her bag for the printout of downtown Stillwater. "The fireworks were set off by the river, at Lowell. You were walking that direction before the fireworks and the girls were walking away?" The spot Britney had showed police had been near enough to the dock that someone could have called over to the girls to join him without anyone noticing, as she'd suspected, but the boats that left during the search had been the ones anchored closer to Lowell, not farther away. Had Thea and Abby been in one of those boats the entire time people were searching?

"Can you describe the man they were with?"

"It wasn't a man," Zach said. "It was a girl. Or at least, they looked like a girl. It was dark, and they were wearing a black hat, but I remember seeing long blonde hair and thinking about the way she walked. She had a nice butt." He flushed. "I'm pretty sure it was a girl."

Nikki's mind had already jumped to Shane Walker's rumored affairs. "Was she white or black or another race?"

"White," he said. "Her skin was pale."

"Okay, good," Nikki said, her heart pumping. "Tall? Short? What color shoes?"

"Taller than me, slim build," he said. "White Adidas. Looked new. I remember thinking they were cool."

"Okay, and the girls didn't look scared or nervous walking behind this person?"

"No," Zach said. "One was smiling."

"Did you say anything to them?"

Zach shook his head. "I should have."

"You acted like a normal person would in that situation. You had no way of knowing what was going on. I would have done the same thing," Nikki said. "You did nothing wrong besides taking the insulin and using it."

"Liam said there's a sketch," Zach said. "Of me."

"Yes, a witness saw you pick up the bag. That doesn't mean everyone thinks you killed Thea. It just means you might know something, and you did. You filled in a big gap that might help us find out who did this, and maybe find Abby alive."

EIGHTEEN

Nikki found Liam outside the family area. He leaned against the wall, hands in his pockets, nodding as Miller spoke to him in low tones, his jaw tight, undoubtedly chewing Liam out.

"You're damn lucky I don't go to your superior, and I'm not talking about Nikki. I'm talking about the unit chief," Miller fumed.

"I know," Liam agreed. "If I'd had a chance to speak with Zach, I would have said something. But I hadn't seen him."

"You still should have told us." Nikki finally joined the conversation. "Just like I should have stepped off the case back when Frost talked to Lacey in the mall." Nikki still felt the terror of that day, and the anger when she'd found out the serial killer known as Frost, a man she'd chased for years, had approached her daughter. Instead of backing off, she dug her heels in and refused to step back. If she had kept clear, maybe Lacey's dad might still be alive. "It's impossible for you to see objectively, even if you aren't Zach's parent. You know him, you've spent the last year and a half acting as a father figure and helping him recover from the terrible things that have happened to him. You. Are. Too. Close." She emphasized the last few words.

Liam's pale cheeks turned pink. "I know. But please let me help find Abby."

"You aren't going back out on my investigation," Miller said, fire in his dark eyes. "I will not allow you to jeopardize putting Thea's killer behind bars when we catch him. You've already done enough damage."

Liam's pained expression made it clear he expected Nikki to back him up, but Miller had pulled rank on them for the first time since they'd started working together. Technically, it was his call. And Nikki thought he'd made the right one. "Miller's right. I think we're still okay from a legal standpoint, but we need you in the background." Which really sucks, she wanted to add. They needed every investigator they had on the case.

"You're going to bench me?" Liam stared at Nikki. "You didn't bench yourself."

"We've discussed this." She wasn't going to back down. "My mistakes involved my family—these victims are different. As hard as it is, Miller's right. And doesn't Caitlin need you here?" Nikki glanced into the family room where Caitlin sat with her former in-laws. She had a good relationship with them, but Nikki knew having Liam by her side would keep Caitlin from getting into her own head and blaming herself.

"I can work from here," Liam said. "Even if it's all computer work. Please. You need my help."

Miller looked at Nikki, who shrugged. "This is your investigation, and I'll follow your lead. We'll respect whatever decision you make."

Miller sighed. "As long as you don't have anything to do with Zach's role in this. Only reason I'm not completely kicking you out is because I know how good you are with a computer. But that's it. Can you stick to office work?"

"Yes, thank you." Liam reached for Miller's hand. The

sheriff glared at him but shook it. Liam looked at Nikki. "What did Zach say?"

"Zach watched the fireworks from the middle dock in the marina." The dock adjacent to Lowell Park was shaped like a reverse "L," with the fireworks off the southeast part of the floating dock. "Zach walked out to the end of the southeast part and sat there to watch the fireworks." Nikki quickly found an aerial photo of the Stillwater Marina. "While he was sitting there, the girls walked past with someone. They turned left—north—and went all the way to the end. He never saw them after that." Nikki reminded them that she'd seen Zach walking away from the river, roughly ten to fifteen minutes after the fireworks ended.

"He get a look at the guy?" Miller asked.

"He's almost certain it was a woman." Nikki recapped Zach's description. "Obviously that's not ironclad, but given what we know about Shane Walker, it adds up. Zach said the person was white, very pale, wearing new white Adidas. The girls didn't appear to be afraid. He never saw them again, but he remembered seeing Thea's purse. That's why he picked it up. I showed him photos of Alyssa and Britney, and he confirmed it wasn't them."

"Why didn't he call and tell me?" Liam demanded. "I left him several messages. So did his mother."

"He heard about Thea this morning and recognized her on the news. That's why he took the insulin. He blames himself."

"Christ." Miller shook his head. "Kid's been through enough. He see if they actually got in a boat?"

"No." Nikki pointed to the marina photo she'd saved to her phone's camera roll. "They walked north toward the end, and he didn't pay much attention after that. We know there were boats that left and Chen's trying to account for them, but those boats were close to where Zach was sitting at the end of the south dock, next to Lowell Park."

"Meaning this person convinced the girls to walk away from the fireworks?" Liam asked. "How?"

A familiar form strode past the family area's open door. "Why the hell is Shane Walker here?" Nikki didn't give the others a chance to answer. "Call Kendall and see if she's tracked down Walker's mistress Carly or Carol at Regions yet."

Nikki raced down the corridor, trying to catch up with Shane's long strides. "Doctor Walker, I didn't realize you were on call at this hospital as well."

He spun around to face her. "Where is he?"

"I'm sorry?" She played dumb.

"The kid who took Thea's insulin." Shane's voice shook with anger. "Did he take my daughters? If you're trying to protect the little bastard—"

"Doctor Walker," Nikki cut him off. "I'm not sure what you were told, or by whom, but Zach isn't a suspect in the kidnapping. He's a witness."

"He didn't go to the police," Shane snapped. "You don't think I know who his mother is, and who she's dating?"

Nikki wondered how many loyal supporters Shane Walker had throughout the hospital system. He didn't work at Lakeview in Stillwater, but he definitely knew someone who did.

"Did Carly tell you about Zach, or another young female?" Nikki knew she was taking a risk, but she hoped to catch him off guard.

Shane snorted. "I know what you're trying to do, and I'm not falling for that."

"Well, Zach believes he saw the girls walking with a blonde female, likely in her early twenties. Definitely wasn't Alyssa."

Shane stared at her for a moment. "What are you getting at, Agent?"

"Anyone outside of your marriage that you might have had any sort of physical relationship with is now a suspect."

He narrowed his eyes. "I assure you, that isn't the case."

He hadn't denied the affairs, only the idea one of the women might have been involved. Was he that naïve, or had he already contacted the other women in his life? "How can you be so sure? Look, we aren't the morality police. But unless you're entering deep relationships with these women, how do you know what they're capable of?"

"What's their motive?" Shane challenged. "I haven't received a call for any ransom money."

"Money isn't the motive," Nikki said. "This could be about revenge or a way to eliminate your ties to your family." Shane started shaking his head again. Nikki continued. "Listen, I understand why you're focused on Zach, but I promise you, he isn't responsible. He'll be able to sit with a sketch artist and give a description of the suspect. You may recognize her."

"I'm not waiting for that."

Nikki heard footsteps coming fast behind her, along with the scent of Liam's cologne. She put a hand out to stop him. "Stay. Out. Of. This."

"He's not bothering Zach," Liam hissed.

"Doctor Walker." Nikki kept her voice firm. "I can't allow you access to the witness. It could compromise the entire case. A good defense attorney would rip us to shreds if they found out you had contact with a witness, and that risks allowing Thea's killer to go free."

Shane's gaze honed in on Liam. "You're the one who didn't say anything, right?"

"Agent Wilson isn't a suspect, nor is Zach," Nikki said, trying to defuse the situation.

"I didn't handle things correctly," Liam admitted, his face almost as red as his hair. "But I assure you, I haven't seen Zach since Saturday evening, before the fireworks. I haven't had time to question him."

"You aren't going to question him," Shane said. "If you think I'm going to allow that, you're crazy."

"I'm handling all communication with Zach," Nikki said. "Doctor Walker, you need to leave before the situation worsens."

He looked over her head at Liam. "Mark my words. If anything happens to Abby, I'm coming after you."

Liam stepped out of the doctor's path as he marched back to the elevator. He didn't speak until the doors closed. "How in the hell did he find all of this out so quickly?"

"He's a much-loved specialist with a network of colleagues. We can't worry about that right now. We need to get him to tell us the names of all the women he's slept with over the last year. Right now, that's our best lead."

Her thoughts raced as they walked back to the room where Miller had remained, studying a map of downtown. His face looked ashen. "Nikki, we missed it."

"What do you mean?"

"It didn't dawn on me until I heard Zach's story," he said. "The connecting dock. I'd completely forgotten about it."

"Connecting dock?" she asked.

"Technically, there are two marinas," Miller said. "Stillwater Marina and West Marine, but they operate as one. That's why the connecting dock was put in." Miller pointed to his wrinkled map of downtown. "Here's Lowell. The marina next to it is owned by West Marine, but they were having trouble keeping up with costs, so they started working with the city marina next door. This connecting dock"—he tapped on the map—"was placed at the beginning of this summer season. You and Chen spoke to the guy at Stillwater Marina, and Chen's following up on West Marine today, but we aren't going to be able to get a search warrant for a list of slip owners and renters unless we can put Thea in a boat. All this time, we've been focused on the wrong area of the docks."

"Courtney's working on the physical evidence." Nikki was still focused on the connecting dock. "You're telling me they could have walked all the way to far north end? Across from the Zephyr Theater?"

Miller nodded. "Zach mentioned the person's shoes," Miller said. "What about height?"

"He said taller than him, so around five foot ten, slim build," Nikki answered.

"And white Adidas are made for both men and women." Miller scowled. "That's basically a needle in a haystack."

"Yeah, well, Shane Walker might have an alibi, but he's also known to have sexual relationships with younger women who work at the hospital," Nikki reminded him.

"Just a tad unethical," Miller grumbled. "You think one of these girls got pissed off and did something to the girls? Seems like a lot, even for a jilted lover."

Nikki shrugged. "At this point, anything's possible, especially after Zach's description. The person the girls left with could very well be female."

Miller rubbed his temples. "I've got to call Chen. He's working on getting warrants for the marina, but he's looking at the wrong end of the dock."

"You think the kidnapper hid them on a boat?" Liam asked.

"Thea died of heat exhaustion, and if the boat was closed up and not running, depending on how long they were inside, it's possible. It was still eighty-five degrees at ten p.m.," Nikki answered. "I think whoever took them left them on the boat and then walked in the opposite direction to get rid of the purse."

"But they didn't take the insulin," Liam said. "Zach did. So either this person didn't care about Thea being diabetic because he was going to kill her anyway, or he didn't know."

"We keep saying 'he,' but remember, it could have been a woman," Nikki said. "The girls weren't afraid, so either they knew the person, or it was someone they didn't feel threatened by. It's still not enough to get a warrant for the marinas' customer list or any kind of search."

"Courtney's got the forensic evidence," Liam said. "She'll come through. I hope." His eyes widened as he stared at his phone. "I had Kendall get the Walkers' financials. Shane Walker wrote a check for $50,000 last month to Carly Thompson. It was cashed immediately. Kendall followed up and confirmed Carly works at Regions."

Bingo.

NINETEEN

After several minutes of deliberation, Nikki, Miller and Liam agreed to keep the discovery of the $50,000 between them until they had Shane Walker backed into a corner. She'd called Dr. Zhang at Regions on the way over and asked her to check the employee logs for Carly Thompson, along with any security videos they could find of her leaving. Nikki wanted to have as much information as possible before they approached Shane Walker.

Half-dizzy from the heat, Nikki knocked on the Walkers' door and waited. Alyssa's car was in the driveway, and Nikki hoped she'd have a chance to speak with the girl away from the Walkers. She was certain that Alyssa knew more than she'd let on about the Walkers' private lives, and she might be able to help them come up with the names of Shane's mistresses if he didn't cooperate.

Alyssa answered the door, her cheeks flushed. "Agent Hunt. Did you find Abby?"

"No. I have a few more questions for the Walkers." Nikki peered over the girl's shoulder. The house's layout provided a clear view of Shane Walker's office. Unlike Nikki's first visit, when the office appeared immaculate, Shane's desk had files strewn across it. Cardboard storage boxes sat on both chairs, papers sticking out of them in all directions.

Alyssa followed her gaze and glanced behind her toward Shane's office. "Doctor Walker must have been going through files before he left."

"He's not here, then?" Nikki asked. "What about Britney?"

Alyssa shook her head. "He came and picked her up about half an hour ago. I'd stopped by to check in, so I offered to do some dishes and laundry while they were gone."

Judging by her flushing and fidgeting, Alyssa wasn't telling the entire story. "Doctor Walker left his laptop open?" The laptop's yellow barcode tag looked similar to the one she'd noticed on Dr. Zhang's computer in her office. The computer sat on the side of the executive desk, angled toward the door just enough for Nikki to see that it wasn't in screensaver mode, but fully awake. "I can't believe he'd be so careless with a hospital-issued laptop. You know, HIPAA laws and all of that."

Alyssa shrugged, sweat beading on her forehead. "Is there anything else I can help you with? I really want to finish tidying up before Doctor and Mrs. Walker get back."

"It's more humid than the steam room at the gym out here." Nikki fanned her face. "Would you mind us talking inside?"

Alyssa nodded and moved so that Nikki could enter, and then closed the door. They stood awkwardly in the entrance-way, staring at each other.

"You don't have any new leads on Abby?" Alyssa gnawed at her fingernails.

"Is that an engagement ring?" Nikki pointed to the solitary diamond on Alyssa's right hand. She knew some cultures, like Greek Orthodox, wore wedding rings on their right hand instead of the left, but she hadn't noticed the diamond the other day.

"Oh no." Alyssa glanced at her hand. "It was my mom's.

She passed away when I was a kid." Her voice trembled. "Sometimes I wear it to feel closer to her."

Nikki could tell by the emotion in Alyssa's voice she was telling the truth. "I understand. I lost my parents when I was sixteen."

"I read about what happened to them," Alyssa said. "Is that why you became an FBI agent?"

"Partially," Nikki said. "I wanted to understand the type of person who could destroy innocent lives, so I studied psychology. The rest sort of fell into place."

"I wish I could do what you do," Alyssa said. "You're a trained profiler, right? So you can read people?"

"It's not like it's depicted on television," Nikki said. "And profiling isn't a science, it's just another tool. We look for patterns of behavior that we can apply to a current situation. We aren't mind readers."

"But you know when someone's lying?"

"Any experienced law enforcement officer can do that," Nikki said. "But it's funny that you asked, since I know you're lying about Doctor Walker leaving his computer open."

She waited for the argument, but Alyssa almost looked relieved. "I'm sorry. I'm no good at this sort of thing."

"Alyssa, what's going on?" Nikki asked.

The young woman wilted against the wall. "Last week, before the girls went missing, I heard him talking to a woman on the phone. He was really mad, asking her how she could do this to his family."

"How do you know he was talking to a woman?" Nikki asked, thinking of the threats toward Dr. Walker.

"He called her a dumb bitch. I assume he was talking to his latest mistress."

"And that's why you're looking through his laptop?"

"I just can't stand waiting around while Abby's still out there," Alyssa said. "I wanted to get into his email and text messages to find out exactly who he'd been talking to so I could let you guys know. I don't know if it was Carly or some other woman."

"That's not your job," Nikki snapped. "You should have told my partner and me everything so that we could investigate. That computer's issued by Regions Hospital, which means login credentials and verification. If it's like our computers, the user will be able to see every time someone logged into it."

"I'm decent at hacking," Alyssa said. "I just thought if I could get the information and give it to you, then you wouldn't need a warrant."

"That's not how it works. Even if you found something, I would need to get a warrant to see the information for myself."

"Well, I didn't," she said defensively. "He covered his tracks really well."

Nikki sighed and looked down at the floor, trying to quell her irritation with Alyssa. Her gaze was immediately drawn to the white Adidas shoes on Alyssa's feet. They looked brand new, without as much as a speck of dirt on the shoelaces. They were also the exact style Zach had described the person who'd taken the girls as wearing, but Alyssa had brown hair. She could have worn a wig and the hat to cover it, but unless her manager had covered for her, Alyssa hadn't left the restaurant Saturday night until close. And since the popular shoe was made for both men and women, Alyssa's weren't exactly a smoking gun.

Something still didn't sit right about the entire situation. She debated asking Alyssa to come to the police station to talk, but that would scare her. If she expected the Walkers to be home soon, then she wouldn't want to talk here either. "You like the Adidas? I love the look, but they're not cushy enough for me."

Alyssa shrugged. "I'm still breaking them in. I'm a Converse girl, but my dad gave these to me for my birthday." She studied Nikki for a few seconds. "I'm surprised you're not at the press conference," Alyssa said. "Doctor Walker said that's where they were going."

"What press conference?" She and Liam hadn't had a chance to coach the Walkers on what to say to the media, so they hadn't settled on a time for the conference.

"With Chief Ryan," Alyssa answered. "Doctor Walker came in kind of upset and told Britney to get dressed for it." Alyssa checked her watch. "It should be starting in a few minutes. And I need to get ready for my shift at the restaurant."

Nikki managed not to swear as she directed Alyssa not to do any more snooping and to let the police handle things from now on. She found her small notebook in her bag and flipped to a fresh page. She handed the notebook and a pen to Alyssa. "Write down your availability tomorrow. I'd like to talk more."

Alyssa hesitated and then took the notebook, balancing it on her left hand. "I haven't done anything wrong." She handed the items back to Nikki.

Nikki nodded. "I'll be in touch."

She stalked out of the house and called Miller as soon as she got back to the Jeep. "Do you know the Walkers are having a press conference?"

"I thought you and Liam were going to talk to them before they spoke to the media," Miller said, confused.

"Yeah, well, Alyssa just told me that Shane picked up Britney about half an hour ago for the press conference with Chief Ryan." She glanced at her text messages. "Dr. Zhang got back to me. Carly worked a double shift the Saturday the girls disappeared. Zhang had security pull footage from the floor Carly had been assigned to, and they didn't see anything on the video that suggested she left that night. Multiple coworkers confirmed she didn't leave the hospital until her shift was over at two." Nikki debated tracking down Carly Thompson herself, but at this point, she needed to deal with the Walkers. "I'll have one of our junior agents talk to Carly."

"How soon can you get to Stillwater?" Miller asked.

She tore the paper Alyssa's thumb had touched out of her notebook. "I have to drop something off at the lab for prints, and then I'm headed your way."

After dropping the paper off at the lab, Nikki sped through Brooklyn Park's idyllic neighborhood to I-694. During the thirty-five-minute drive to Stillwater, Nikki's imagination conjured up all the ways Chief Ryan may have torpedoed any chance they had at finding Abby alive. She'd pegged Ryan as someone who genuinely wanted to change the system and do the right thing. Had she let her ego get in the way, or had Shane Walker wedged Ryan between a rock and the proverbial hard place?

She also thought about Alyssa during the drive. Nikki was certain the girl was keeping something from them. It may or may not affect the investigation, but given the circumstances, Alyssa needed to come clean. Nikki had been at this job long enough to know that the oddest details often broke an investigation wide open, especially if the investigators were as seasoned as Nikki and Miller. Alyssa's age and beauty made her a perfect target for Shane Walker, and if he'd been dumb enough to mess around with the nanny, she could have seized the opportunity to blackmail him. Alyssa's alibi Saturday night was solid, but that didn't mean she didn't have help. And if Alyssa had enlisted a friend, they could have used her name to gain the girls' trust.

Nikki exited I-694 and cut through the heart of residential Stillwater. As a teenager, Nikki could have walked these streets with her eyes closed and still reached her destination, but the city had changed so much, with more and more residences and commercial buildings pushing west of downtown, that Nikki made sure to follow the GPS. She parked behind the Stillwater police station and opened the video Miller had sent moments ago. Her blood pressure soared as she watched Chief Ryan stride to the podium in her uniform, a tiny hint of satisfaction in her smile.

"Thank you for coming." Chief Ryan opened the leather padfolio she'd brought with her to the podium.

"As you know, Stillwater has experienced a devastating forty-eight hours. Our hearts go out to Doctor and Mrs. Walker for the loss of their daughter, Thea. We will continue to do everything in our power to find Abby and bring her home, alive. We have an eyewitness who saw both girls walking on the Stillwater docks with a woman. He walked right past the trio and has given us a detailed description of the person he saw."

Nikki stared at her phone in disbelief. Zach hadn't given any detailed description of the kidnapper other than the white Adidas shoes and the black hat obscuring their face.

Ryan glanced to her left and nodded. "Now, Doctor Walker and his wife have a statement prepared."

A string of profanities spewed from Nikki. She hadn't sat down with Shane or Britney to walk them through what they should and shouldn't say. What the hell was Ryan doing?

Her phone lit up with more furious texts from Sheriff Miller and Liam, but Nikki ignored them as she watched the Walkers reach the podium. Britney held onto Shane's arm, her slumped shoulders and frightened eyes making her appear even younger than she was, especially next to her graying husband.

"My wife and I are heartbroken at the loss of our sweet Thea. She was full of life and promise, always making plans for what she wanted to be when she grew up." Shane's voice caught in his throat. He paused to collect himself. "I'm speaking to the person who took my children. We understand Thea's death was an accident. Please let Abby go. Just leave her alive where she will be easily found." Shane's jaw muscles worked, and Nikki could tell he was fighting to stay on script.

"No." Shane suddenly shook his head and folded the paper he'd been reading from. He looked directly into the camera. "Thea's death might have been an accident, but it happened because you took her from us. Letting Abby go will help you in court, but you mark my words: I won't rest until you're punished for destroying my family. If it takes every penny I own, Thea and Abby's cases won't go cold, no matter how well you covered your tracks. You will see the inside of a cell or better yet, the business end of—"

Ryan had the sense to put her hand over the microphone, but Shane's lips were easily read. He'd promised the kidnapper that he'd see the inside of a cell, or the business end of Shane's revolver.

Nikki wanted to bang her head on the steering wheel. All Ryan's press conference had done was establish that someone had seen the girls on the dock and that the police had little control over what the parents were doing and saying. If the kidnapper was smart—and given his actions, Nikki assumed he was not only intelligent but experienced—he'd know that Shane Walker's outburst meant the police had little real evidence.

Liam called for a third time.

"What the hell?" Liam exploded. "Does she know anything about real police work? Kent said he knew nothing about this. So much for us all working together. And she's put Zach in danger. If Walker is somehow involved, he or this mistress have got easy access to Zach!"

"I know," Nikki said. "How long are they going to keep him in the hospital?"

"At least for a few days," Liam said. "Caitlyn and I are camping out here, but Miller's sending deputies to guard the room around the clock."

"Good," Nikki said. "As long as the media doesn't publish where Zach is, we should be okay."

"I'm not leaving the hospital until he's home. I don't care

what their visitor policy is," Liam said flatly. "Kendall and Jim are headed to Carly's apartment now. She lives in downtown Minneapolis. Hopefully they can catch her at home, but she's scheduled to work tonight."

Nikki told him what Zhang had learned about Carly. "She wasn't the woman on the dock with the girls. But that doesn't mean she isn't involved."

"So what's your plan?" Liam asked.

"Not sure yet," Nikki said. "But Walker's going to have to explain the $50,000 check."

TWENTY

Nikki held her badge up for the desk sergeant without slowing her stride. Judging from the raised voices coming from Ryan's closed office door, Miller had beaten her to the station. Nikki forced herself to knock instead of barging into Chief Ryan's office. The door was yanked open by Miller.

"Agent Hunt, please join us."

She waited for him to close the door before addressing the chief, who sat at her desk looking surprisingly calm. "Why did you have the Walkers speak? Giving the press conference without consulting either one of us is one thing, but allowing Shane Walker to speak his mind has put Abby in further danger, not to mention Zach. You know, the teenaged witness you basically outed in the press conference."

"He chose to keep his silence," Ryan said. "We might have found the girls in time if he'd said something. At any rate, after you rebuffed him at the hospital, Doctor Walker came to me, mad as a hornet. He demanded the press conference and said if we didn't put it together at that very moment, he'd do it himself." Ryan met Nikki's gaze. "He would have, so I agreed, in the hopes we could control the information."

Miller said something dismissive, but Nikki understood that Ryan was in a tough position.

"Do you know anything about the witness?"

"He's the son of a well-known documentary maker, who happened to be in a relationship with your partner." She narrowed her eyes. "If we don't find Abby in time, I may have to file a complaint against Agent Wilson."

Miller started to speak, but Nikki waved him off. "Do that, and I'll make sure the mayor and the media know that you didn't follow procedure before speaking to the media about a minor who may be a witness in a serious crime. A minor who's also a victim of severe sexual abuse and was responsible for putting away a very bad guy less than two years ago. He's still working through the trauma and learning to trust people again."

Ryan shifted in her chair. "I wasn't aware of that."

"You can't let people like Shane Walker push you around," Miller said. "You're the chief of police. It's your job to make sure you have all the information. You not only put Zach in jeopardy, but you also showed our hand. The kidnapper knows we don't have anything on him."

"How could you say that?" Ryan demanded.

"Because we've done actual police work," Miller snapped. "We didn't lobby for our jobs."

Ryan narrowed her eyes. "I warn you, Sheriff, tread carefully. I'd hate for this to dissolve into bigoted insults. After all, you and I both know what it's like to come up the ranks as a black person. You don't, however, know what it was like to go through the system as a black woman. I had to climb twice as many barriers."

"You wanted to be an administrator," Miller shot back. "I've seen your file. Your time on the street is limited—"

"Kent." They weren't going to get anywhere using this tactic. Ryan had experience, but she'd never worked a case like this. Nikki looked at Ryan. "I don't care what your background is or how you got here. You showed our hand because you allowed Shane to get up there and make threats. The fact that you had no control over his comments—something your expression clearly showed, by the way, the second he went off script—makes us look desperate."

Ryan considered that for a moment. "I think you're giving this person too much credit."

"You're not giving them enough credit," Nikki snapped. "I don't see how the woman Zach saw could have acted alone. Britney might not have realized how long she'd been away from the girls, but an inexperienced criminal doesn't slip away with the girls with law enforcement all over the place. That's the decision of an experienced, confident individual." She glanced at Miller. "You have someone at the hospital?"

He nodded. "Liam says he's staying, but they won't let him stay all night. Only Caitlin can since Zach is a minor. I'll keep a deputy posted, and I've already contacted the Minneapolis police in case we need their assistance." Miller was still visibly upset, his hands trembling. Nikki couldn't blame him, but isolating Ryan right now would be a mistake.

"Kent, could Chief Ryan and I speak privately for a moment?" Nikki had worked with him long enough that she knew Miller wouldn't take her request personally.

"I'm heading to the sheriff's station."

"I'll be there shortly."

She waited for him to close the door, her eyes on Ryan. She'd seen the look of sincere worry when she'd been talking about Zach's background.

"Agent Hunt, if you plan on more lecturing, please don't waste your time."

"I'm not going to lecture you," Nikki said. "That was my plan coming in here, but it seems Kent took care of that. Shane Walker is an intimidating guy with a lot of pull. I believe you have Abby's best interests at heart, and I don't think you're just a pencil-pusher."

"I appreciate that," Ryan said dryly.

"But I do think you have something to prove to the mayor and the city, and maybe a lot more," Nikki said. "I did a little research. I couldn't find the number of black, female police chiefs in this country, but less than ten percent of police chiefs in the US are female. The Department of Justice says black people make up only 4 percent of chiefs in all agencies combined. The mayor went out on a pretty shaky limb appointing you, and this is the kind of case that could make or break your career."

"My only concern is Abby," Ryan said, indignant.

"That's just not possible," Nikki said. "I can compartmentalize with the best of them, but I'm human, and so are you. It's okay to be thinking of all the repercussions of not solving this case. What's not okay is to make a decision and act on it without speaking with the task force, especially when you're working with people as experienced as my team and the sheriff."

"You're right," Ryan said. "When it got back to me that Agent Wilson knew this witness, I didn't handle the situation correctly. My assumption was that you all were trying to protect him, as Doctor Walker intimated."

"Not at all," Nikki said. "But I also know what it's like to become personally embroiled in a case, and I know Liam well enough to know that he didn't do anything malicious."

"But we could have known about the girls on the dock if he'd spoken with Zach earlier," Ryan said.

"That's the thing, Liam hadn't spoken to Zach at all since Saturday night. He'd hoped to talk to him before the witness sketch came out. He told Doctor Walker as much, but apparently, he didn't believe him."

Ryan sighed. "Well, none of us can take back our decisions, so what do we do next?"

"We have to play hardball with Shane Walker. We need to know who he's hiding from us." Nikki went through the various pieces of information, including Shane's own words, relating to his affairs. "My team has discovered a large payment to Carly Thompson. She's a CNA at Regions Hospital and was working the night the girls disappeared." She reminded her of Alyssa's information about Walker arguing with an unknown woman before unlocking her phone and showing Ryan the driver's license photo of Carly Thompson that Liam had sent a few minutes ago. Between the suspect's long, blonde hair and impressive height—almost 6'2"—Nikki was certain Carly wasn't the woman on the pier.

"But after hearing Zach's description, we now know the person who took them is a woman and not Alyssa or Britney." A quick glance at Carly Thompson's driver's license photo showed a full-figured woman with chin-length, dark hair. "Unfortunately, Zach didn't get a good look at their face." She explained Miller's theory about the connecting docks. "We should go through the Zephyr's closed-circuit outdoor cameras, along with any other business that might have captured this person walking with the girls."

Ryan nodded. "I put in that request shortly before Sheriff Miller arrived. We should have information by this evening. But what does that have to do with playing hardball with Doctor Walker?"

"He still paid her a large sum of money less than a month ago," Nikki said. "The nanny overheard him arguing with Carly not long ago. And remember the head of orthopedics at Regions, Doctor Zhang?" Nikki reminded the chief of Zhang's story about Shane's interest in younger women. "Tell him we've learned there are women who will confirm his behavior, and we think one of them could be behind what's going on. He's not going to give me the information, but I think he'll tell you."

She told the chief what she'd learned from Alyssa this afternoon. "We can't give witness names, but we've spoken to more than one woman, that sort of thing."

"He's going to think I'm not on his side," Ryan said.

"Blame me," Nikki said. "Say I told you that we're going to keep pushing for the information, and we'll be ruthless, regardless of his privacy. That's where you come in. If he can provide you with a list of names, we can quietly investigate these women."

Ryan looked unconvinced. "I don't know. If he hasn't given their names to this point, I can't see him doing it now. He doesn't think they're relevant."

"But that's not up for him to decide," Nikki said. "And I'm not bluffing about how far we'll go to get the information. If it turns out to be tied to one of his affairs and he withheld things, he can be charged as accessory after the fact."

"You'd do that to a grieving father?"

"I don't want to," Nikki said. "But we are spinning in circles, and this is the first solid lead we've had."

"Can I think about it?" Ryan asked. Nikki wanted to say no, but that wouldn't have fazed Ryan. She nodded. "Where is your lab with the forensic evidence? If we could prove Thea was actually in a boat, we'd have more chance of securing a search warrant."

"Courtney's on it." Nikki hoped she hadn't grown overconfident in Courtney's ability. "It would be nice to have a list of names from Doctor Walker to cross-reference as soon as Courtney gets the information to us."

Ryan sighed. "All right. I'll talk to Doctor Walker and see what I can do."

"Agent Hunt!"

Nikki turned at the sound of Chen's voice. She'd left the building and was heading towards her car. Chen jogged down the sidewalk, his dark hair plastered to his sweaty forehead. "Sergeant, is there news about Abby?" Nikki asked.

"I wish." He stopped to catch his breath. "I just wanted to let you know I was against the press conference, and for the record, so was Chief Ryan. But Shane Walker was insistent."

"The tone of your voice makes it sound like 'insistent' isn't the right word."

He shook his head. "No, probably not. I know he's a big-time doctor, but it really frustrated me that he refused to listen to us about what was best for Abby right now."

Nikki sensed that Chen had more to say, but she could feel the top of her head burning from the sun. She was waiting to hear back on several leads and had intended to sit in her car to think through her next move. "Is there somewhere we could talk more without melting? Preferably somewhere with food."

"It's only four p.m.," Chen said. "A lot of the good restaurants don't open until at least five. There's No Neck Tony's on Myrtle Street. It's kind of a dive bar with great cocktails and Giovanni's pizza. They aren't too busy this time of day."

Nikki grinned. "As long as they serve something other than alcohol and have air conditioning, I'm game."

No Neck Tony's had the classic dark interior of a dive bar, but the bay window facing Myrtle Street allowed for plenty of light in the small establishment. Like the rest of downtown Stillwater, No Neck's was housed in an old building dating back to the early days of the town, and the décor made sure to highlight that, with enlarged photos of historic Stillwater on their walls.

A few people sat at the rounded bar, but Chen ushered Nikki to a small table near the window. There were only a handful of tables in the place, with the pool table and Skee-Ball taking up a fair amount of floor.

Nikki stopped at the pull-tab machine, which looked

exactly like the old cigarette vending machines that used to be in every bar in the country. Instead of cigarettes, the machine dispensed various types of tickets or cards with break-open tabs. They weren't a money-maker for the bar by any means, but No Neck Tony's donated their proceeds to youth hockey teams. Nikki found a few dollar bills and bought a handful of tickets.

"These always make me think of an old college friend," she said as she sat down across from Chen. "She was from Illinois, and they had these games there, but she called them instant Bingo cards, and she always bought a round of drinks if she won, even though the prize never covered the cost of the drinks."

"They look like lottery tickets to me, without the scratch-off. You want to order pizza?"

"Absolutely, and I'll eat anything except Hawaiian and anchovies." She shuddered, still able to recall the briny taste of the anchovies her father had convinced her to try when she was a kid. She'd almost vomited, and he'd howled with laughter.

Chen went to the bar to order while Nikki pulled off the tabs.

"Not a winner," she said when he returned with two red, plastic glasses of water. "You moonlight as a server?"

He grinned. "I'm in here a lot."

Awkward silence fell between them. Nikki was too tired and jittery from coffee to let it last very long. "Can you tell me exactly what happened with Shane this afternoon?"

Chen sipped his water. "I'd just come back from following up on a possible sighting of Abby that turned out to be a false tip. Ryan was in the middle of telling me about the kid who'd taken the insulin when Shane burst into her office. I guess he bulldozed past Dee at the front and thought it was perfectly okay to open the chief's door without knocking." Chen shook his head. "I know his daughter's missing and all, but the entitlement is something else."

"He's a WASP," Nikki said.

"Pardon?"

"White, Anglo-Saxon Protestant," Nikki said. "Used when we were kids learning history. Basically the old-world version of the aggression we see in some white males today."

"I guess," Chen said. "I feel shitty speaking ill of the man, but it just rubbed me wrong. I know what it's like to lose someone and wait for news." He took another drink.

She sensed that Chen wanted to share something, but he wasn't quite ready. "Me too. When my daughter was taken by the serial killer I was hunting, I thought I'd crawl out of my skin sitting and waiting. Worst days of my life. I hope that wasn't your experience."

"My little sister, Marie." His eyes watered. "She was eight years younger than me. She would have been twenty-seven this year."

"What happened to her?"

"The summer between my junior and senior year of high school, I was supposed to pick her up from school, but I hung out with a girl instead. Marie never came home. Her body was found a week later. If I'd just done my job, she would be alive." Chen took another long drink. "Just like Thea."

"Surely, the rational side of you knows that's not true," Nikki said. "Someone chose to steal her and take her life. That is no one's fault but theirs. It's the same with Thea and Abby."

"Maybe, but Marie only got into that position because I screwed up." The muscle in his jaw twitched. "Blinded by stupidity. I won't let that happen again."

"You were a teenager," Nikki said. "Barely more than a child. How many other brothers have done similar things, being a normal teenaged boy, and their younger siblings came home? You cannot take on the blame for everything. Trust me, I speak from experience. The guilt will slowly choke you to death if you allow it to."

The cop in her wanted to ask when Chen's sister had been taken, where her body had been found, and if there were similarities between her death and Thea's, but she kept those questions to herself. Chen had no doubt already gone over all those scenarios.

"They arrested a drifter for killing her," Chen said, reading her expression. "He's out on parole, but he's in his seventies and lives up north, near the Canadian border. I don't think he did this."

"Probably not," Nikki agreed. "Listen, I hope I'm not overstepping, but I can tell you're a good cop who cares deeply about his job, and the people in this city need you to stay that way." She leaned forward, resting her elbows on the table. "You've got to find the balance between caring and emotional involvement, or you will burn out."

"I know," he said. "That's why I became a cop, you know? I wanted to make sure what happened to her didn't happen to other little kids."

"We still have a chance to help Abby," Nikki reminded him. "That's the best way to honor Thea and your sister."

He nodded and cleared his throat. "Back to Shane Walker. Something about that guy seems off. Maybe it's just the way he acted today."

"His alibi is airtight," Nikki said. "But he does have a history of affairs." She explained her conversation with Ryan from earlier. "Zach likely saw a young woman. Shane Walker has a reputation for going through them."

Chen's eyebrows knotted together. "Blows my mind to think of a woman doing that to innocent children. I know, I'm naïve."

"We know Thea died from the heat, so maybe the intention was to scare Shane or punish him, and everything went wrong. That would make leaving her body where it was sure to be found make sense, especially since the medical examiner confirmed Thea wasn't sexually assaulted." Nikki chewed on a piece of ice. "But I don't see anyone pulling this alone."

"She could have died before there was time to assault her." Chen shuddered. "Small bit of grace, I guess."

"I know what you mean," Nikki said. "If she's done this to get back at Shane, she may not have an accomplice. I'm praying Miller gets some closed-circuit video of her on the north side of the docks. Zach said she was walking in that direction with the girls. His statement's also enough to get a warrant for a list of slip rentals from both arenas. We'll be able to cross-reference that with Shane Walker's girlfriends, assuming Ryan can get the information out of him."

"He prefers them younger?"

"As far as I know. Nursing students, CNAs, temps."

"How many girls that age own a boat?" Chen said. "We need last names, too. It might be registered under her parents."

"Good point," Nikki said. Her team had already checked public records. Carly Thompson wasn't a registered boat owner. "If we don't get any matches from cross-referencing the marina list, we may have to do a little digging and find out if any of the slip owners have stepdaughters or girlfriends with a daughter in her early twenties. But that's going to take time."

"Well, between myself and the patrol officers, we know just about everyone who's around the marinas, if not by name, then by face. Hopefully that'll make the process easier." He waved to someone behind Nikki. "Hey, man, what's up?"

The volunteer Britney had run to for help Saturday shook Chen's hand. "Working on the A/C across the street." He nodded politely at Nikki. "Any news on the other little girl?"

"Not yet." Nikki glanced at the name emblazoned on his white T-shirt, Merrill's Service. "I bet this heat is keeping your guys busy."

"I wish." Merrill grinned. "It's just me, and I'm swamped."

"Is that why you told me I could wait?" Chen asked dryly.

"I told you to wait 'cause you always come last, buddy." He clapped Chen on the shoulder. "Nah, I knew you wouldn't be home until this was over. Hope you fed those fish of yours."

"I did." Chen looked at Nikki. "Bobby's been a pain in my ass for a long time."

"That's what friends do," Merrill said.

"Hey, Bobby," the bartender called. "That pizza you ordered is ready. Since when do you get pineapples on pizza?"

"Lost a damn bet." He pulled several bills out of his wallet. "I better get back. Hope you guys find that little one soon. I'm praying for her."

Their pizza came out a few minutes after Merrill had left. "Hope you don't mind, but I just got a couple of personal pizzas and asked them to box them up. Chief doesn't care for long lunches, no matter what time of day they happen. And I feel like a cad just sitting here while Abby's still out there."

Nikki's phone vibrated on the table. "Yeah, me too." Nikki's heart jumped into her throat as she read the text message from Courtney. "I've got some information to run down."

TWENTY-ONE

Nikki had learned early on in her career that surprising a person of interest at work was the best way to get the truth quickly. No one wanted the police milling around their job, and most people readily complied so they didn't cause a scene.

After making sure Alyssa had showed up for her shift, Nikki found a place near the trendy restaurant in Eden Prairie and strode inside, trying not to let her adrenaline get the best of her. She wasn't sure exactly what role Alyssa had played in all of this, and she wasn't leaving without speaking to the Walkers' babysitter.

Fortunately, Alyssa had been assigned hosting duties for this shift. Her eyes widened at the sight of Nikki walking towards the hostess stand. "What are you doing here?"

"We need to talk."

"I've told you everything—"

"No, you haven't," Nikki shot back. She kept her voice low and stern. "Either you tell your boss you need to speak to me, or I will take you to the sheriff's station."

Alyssa's face flushed red. "You know who I am," she said

flatly. "I knew that's why you wanted me to hold that notebook. You got my print."

"Yep, and right now, you look like the best suspect. Did you take Thea and Abby to get revenge on Doctor Walker because of your mother's death?"

Nikki was still reeling from the news. Alyssa's fingerprints had come back registered to Alyssa Hyland. She was the step-daughter who'd accused Shane of murdering her mother for the insurance money. Given her age when her mother died, Alyssa's father had likely influenced her to believe Shane had murdered her mother for the insurance money, because the Thief River Falls police hadn't found any reason to consider Shane Walker a suspect.

Alyssa nodded and walked to the bar to speak with the woman Nikki presumed was the manager. The older woman looked irritated and pointed to her watch but nodded.

"I have five minutes," Alyssa said. "Let's talk outside."

Outside in the oppressive heat, Nikki didn't waste any time. "Does Shane know who you are?"

Alyssa ignored the question. Her alibi for Saturday night was ironclad, but that didn't mean she wasn't involved in what-ever had happened to Thea and Abby. Nikki needed answers. "Just let me explain."

"You should have explained this when we first spoke. You certainly could have told me yesterday when I caught you snooping in Walker's office." Nikki kept her tone stern, watching Alyssa's face for any sort of reaction. "Will your prints match the ones we got off Thea's shoes?"

"They won't." Alyssa looked horrified. "Look, I get how it seems, but I swear on my mother's grave I didn't do anything to those babies. I love them both."

"Then why don't you explain it to me?" Nikki demanded.

Alyssa leaned against the brick exterior. "When Shane and my mom got together, they had to wait for my parents' divorce to be finalized before they could get married," she said. "Dad always believed Mom had cheated with Shane, and he never got over her. After she died, he became obsessed with Shane Walker. Growing up, when my dad wasn't drunk and causing trouble, he was investigating Walker. He followed his career, kept tabs on him. Blew all of our money, too. Shady private investigators, booze and casinos got most of it." Her eyes started to water. "Liver failure killed him last year, and I kind of went crazy. I decided to find Shane."

"What was your plan?" Nikki asked.

"Money for college," Alyssa confessed. "I got some scholarships, but Dad's funeral obliterated my savings. I figured I'd show Shane what Dad had worked on, bluff that I had proof, and get some money. Thanks to Dad's obsession, I knew where Doctor Walker worked, so I showed up at his clinic, Two Rivers. I remember hearing Dad's voice in my head when I pulled into the parking lot. The place is massive, Shane's some kind of local hero, and my parents are dead. By the time I got the nerve to go inside, I was furious all over again."

Nikki could imagine Walker's surprise at the girl's appearance. He'd probably been blindsided, but if Alyssa had accused him of killing her mother and extorted him for money, then why give her a job? If he saw her as a threat, why would he expose his children to her?

"I thought I could go into his fancy orthopedic clinic and make a scene, but he didn't give me the chance."

Nikki waited.

"He recognized me, and the look of sheer joy in his face completely threw me off my game." Alyssa laughed through her building tears. "We went into his office, and I told him everything my father had done since Mom was killed and how lousy our lives had been." Her chin trembled. "I wanted to be angry, you know? But then Doctor Walker told me about my college fund."

"You didn't know about it?"

She shook her head. "I guess he contacted Dad a couple of years after the accident and wanted to help me out financially. He showed me the letter Dad wrote back. He was so angry, told Doctor Walker to stay away from me. Anyway, Doctor Walker has been putting money into a college savings plan for me since then. He gave me full access to the account that very day and said he'd like me to spend it on college, but he wasn't going to stipulate."

Nikki couldn't hide her surprise. It didn't sound like blackmail but a pseudo-family reunion. "You didn't think it was all a way to make you leave him alone?"

"At first, yes," she said. "But then he showed me photos of his daughters, and he still had my school photo with him. He'd kept it after all these years. I just felt like he wouldn't have done that if he was guilty."

Walker keeping Alyssa in his family's life was the sticking point for Nikki. "How did you end up working for the Walkers, then?"

She half-smiled. "He found out I was living in a hotel and offered me the position. His only stipulation was not to tell Britney because she didn't need reminders of her old life in Thief River Falls, where I grew up." Alyssa wiped tears off her face. "I spent all these years hating him. But now, after all of this, I know he didn't hurt Mom. He just doesn't have it in him. He'd rather kill himself than hurt the girls, too."

"What about Carly and the affairs?" Nikki asked. "Why would you tell us that if you don't think he's involved?"

Alyssa checked her watch. "My five minutes is almost up. Oh, he's got issues with keeping it in his pants, and I did hear them arguing. All of that was true. I thought she might be involved." She glanced behind her. "Listen, I have to go back inside, but I'll be at the Walkers' tonight if you have more questions."

"Am I supposed to pretend I don't know who you are?"

"Not with Doctor Walker," she said. "We've actually had conversations about when and how we were going to tell Britney before the girls were taken. I want her to know, and so does he. But please don't tell her now. I don't think she can handle anything else right now."

Nikki agreed that she wouldn't say anything to Britney as long as Alyssa's story checked out. "You realize I'll have to confirm everything you said about your father?"

She nodded. "It won't be too hard. Most people in Thief River Falls knew him as 'the conspiracy guy.'" She turned to head back inside and then hesitated. "Abby might still be alive, so whatever you need to clear me from your suspect list, do it. Then bring her back to us, Agent Hunt."

* * *

A Guns N' Roses song blared in Nikki's ears. She peeled her face off the old leather couch in the break room at the sheriff's station and reached for her phone.

"This is Agent Hunt."

"Finally," Courtney huffed. "I've called three times."

Nikki needed a few seconds to acclimate. After she'd left Alyssa's work, she'd rushed to the sheriff's office to fill Miller in on the new development. Several database searches and phone calls later, she'd crossed Alyssa off the suspect list. Everything she'd said checked out, right down to her father's cause of death. Liam had called to update her on the Carly situation: Kendall and Jim had split up, with Kendall interviewing Carly about the deposit while Jim kept tabs on her for the evening. The young woman freely admitted to the affair and the blackmail, tearfully stating she was a single mom struggling to make ends meet. Her story appeared to check out, but they would keep eyes on her anyway.

Fighting a yawn, Nikki double-checked the time on her phone. "At two a.m.? Tell me it's good."

"Thea was definitely in a boat before she died."

Nikki sat up so fast it made her dizzy. "You're sure?"

"Positive. Marine carpeting has a true rubber back, and we found microscopic pieces of the rubber under Thea's fingernails."

"Not on the fiber itself?"

"No, but that's a good thing, because a couple of fibers are going to be challenged hard in court," Courtney said. "They are made of propylene yarn, which is consistent with marine carpeting, but the defense can say she could have picked those up anywhere. Finding the rubber under Thea's fingernails is much stronger evidence, especially since having the rubber under her nails means the carpet she was lying on had to have holes, or chunks of missing carpet fibers. That's the only way she could have gotten them."

"So a renovation?" Nikki asked, thinking of Rory and Mark's project.

"Or an old boat that's rough inside," Courtney said. "We're running tests on the rubber to figure out the manufacturer and hopefully narrow down our options, but that's going to take some time."

"What about Thea's purse?"

"I finished lifting it this morning and ran it through AFIS." AFIS was the national fingerprint database, and at times, could deliver a smoking gun in a case. But only if the perpetrator had prints on file. "I don't have a suspect, but the print matched two other unsolved cases in Green Bay, Wisconsin, and Mason City, Iowa. Check your email."

Nikki put her phone on speaker and grabbed her work laptop from the other end of the couch.

"Green Bay, Wisconsin, 2020." A gap-toothed girl around five or six grinned at her, blue eyes shining with mirth. "Crystal

Johnson, disappeared from Fourth of July celebrations in down-town Green Bay. Found six weeks later."

Nikki's stomach churned as she read the girl's autopsy. Crystal had been tortured for weeks before her body had been left in the woods near a popular Green Bay farmers' market. "Thea was in an orchard, and Crystal left near a farmers' market. Maybe there's an agricultural connection?" She skimmed the lead detective's notes. "Suspects included the summer help at the farmers' market, but none of these names have come up in our investigation. Where was the print taken from?"

"Her shorts, which were the same ones she wore the night she was taken," Courtney answered. "They were polyester, with a nice high thread count."

Nikki moved on to Gretchen Meyer from Mason City, Iowa. She'd disappeared in 2017, during the fireworks at the close of a Memorial Day celebration. "Found two months later, about forty miles across the state line, near a busy truck stop."

"Guy saw her body from the road," Courtney said. "This doesn't help the age connection, but all three bodies were placed in locations where they'd be found quickly. The only difference is that Thea died before she was assaulted and tortured like Crystal and Gretchen."

"But he's still got a pattern," Nikki said. "He uses big social events with a lot of moving parts so he can blend in easier."

"And both Crystal and Gretchen died within twenty-four hours of their bodies being found," Courtney reminded her.

"He clearly wanted them to be found," Nikki agreed. "He must be confident in his abilities, because those girls' bodies contained a lot of evidence."

"Makes you wonder how many more there are," Courtney said. "But if he keeps some of them for that long, maybe we still have a good shot at finding Abby."

Nikki prayed her friend was right and told her to call with

any new information. On her way to Miller's office, she stopped at the bathroom to splash water on her face and rinse the dryness out of her mouth.

Miller's door was partially open, and she could see him asleep in the recliner, case files in his lap. Nikki knocked on the door. "Kent?"

"Yeah?"

"Courtney can put Thea in a boat shortly before she died. She also matched the print to two other murders."

Miller finally opened his eyes. "Time to get a warrant."

"Rentals lists from both marinas, hot off my printer." Miller looked expectantly at Chief Ryan. "Did Shane Walker cooperate?"

"With conditions." Ryan sighed and slid a pair of reading glasses on. "He doesn't want anyone but me having the names. I promised I would do the cross-reference myself and if nothing matched, toss the list." She made eye contact with everyone in the room. "If those names get out, it's on me."

Nikki rolled her eyes. As touched as she'd been by Walker's care for Alyssa, she was also disgusted by his cavalier attitude with young women. According to Carly, the doctor hadn't been fazed at her demand for $50,000, which gave her the courage to ask for more last week. Walker threatened legal action that time, so Carly had decided to back off.

Miller handed out the printed names. "I made copies for all of us. You cross-reference that, and we'll go through looking for any other name that's come up in the investigation."

Chen nodded as he read through the names. "I doubt any one with criminal convictions is allowed to rent a slip, but I'll run the names through the offender database and see if we get a hit."

"Nikki, have you heard back from the Green Bay or Mason

City police?" Miller asked. "We need to get our hands on a suspect list, ASAP."

She'd already filled them in on Courtney's breakthrough. "Not yet, but it's only a little past eight. If I don't hear anything in the next hour, I'll call them both again."

"Did you receive my email with the CCTV footage north of the marinas?" Ryan asked.

"Already sent it to our tech department," Nikki said. "We need to print these out, but these are the images they managed to enlarge." She turned her tablet so everyone could see the grainy, black and white photos of a tall, long-legged person with cut-off shorts, a dark T-shirt and a black cap walking north past the old Zephyr Theater, hands in their pockets. "They do a good job of keeping their head down until a few blocks later."

Nikki clicked on the next photo. "It's not great, but it's enough to see the face." They'd glanced up to check the pedestrian light, revealing a young, fresh face with pale skin and delicate features. The girl was thin, her clothes baggy. "I've got it online and running on the local news stations during the morning show breaks."

"That's definitely not Alyssa, right?" Miller asked.

"Nope. It's not Carly, either."

"Chief, you see any familiar names on the list of women Walker gave you?" Chen asked. "Any names match our suspects or the list of boat slip renters?"

"So far, I don't see any matches, but I'll run the names and see if I can get anything more."

He nodded. "Agent Hunt, you mind emailing me those photos from the CCTV? I want to make sure every patrol officer on the street has them."

Chen continued to skim his list of slip renters. "I recognize a couple of these names. One of them has a stepdaughter the right age for Walker and the girl on the closed circuit, other has a niece."

"Go talk to them, now," Ryan ordered.

Chen practically raced out of the door. The three of them spent the next hour going through the list and comparing names, although Ryan was mostly silent. Every time she made any movement, Nikki's head jerked up, hoping to see she'd found some connection, but Ryan just shook her head.

A Green Bay number flashed on Nikki's screen. "This is Agent Hunt. Thank you for returning my call."

"No problem," a gruff voice said. "I'd also like to know why you're circulating an image of one of my missing persons as a suspect in these cases?"

TWENTY-TWO

Abby sat at the uneven table while the older girl made peanut butter and jelly sandwiches. She'd cowered in the single bedroom, listening to the bad man complain about his stomach before finally revving his big truck and spraying dust as he left. Heart pounding, Abby had run to the small window and tried to open it, but it was locked. She tried the bedroom door, but it was locked, too. Maybe if she could break the window, Abby could slip out unnoticed. She searched the room for something strong enough to break the glass, but found nothing. Exhausted and scared, Abby sank to the floor and started to cry. After a few minutes, the older girl came in and told her it was going to be okay.

"You're not allergic to peanuts, are you?"

Abby shook her head. She'd asked for food, and the girl told her they were only allowed to get the peanut butter and jelly when the man wasn't at home. She couldn't stop thinking about the second night the man had tried to take her into the shower. He'd stripped her clothes and then his own. She'd cowered in the corner, terrified. Why did he want to be naked with her?

Even though she didn't understand it, Abby knew something bad was about to happen to her.

The man moved to turn on the shower, and Abby's heart tried to jump out of her chest. But then he'd grabbed his stomach and started going out about how much it hurt. He'd grabbed Abby by the arms and dumped her outside the door. "Go play with my daughter."

Abby had cowered in the single bed next to the older girl, terrified to sleep. He'd come in the middle of the night and grabbed the other girl, dragging her out of the room. Her screaming had invaded Abby's dreams again. She studied the dark bruises on the girl's thin arms. The bad man had done that, Abby was certain.

"What's your name?" Abby asked.

"Doesn't matter." The girl moved gingerly, as though her entire body hurt.

"Of course it does," Abby said. "How else will people know what to call you?"

She didn't answer, instead setting a paper plate with the sandwich and apple slices on the table in front of Abby. "He doesn't want people to call me anything."

Abby didn't say anything at first. She picked at the sandwich, forcing herself to take a few bites even though she felt too disgusted to eat. She watched the older girl move around the dingy kitchen, scrubbing the counters even though they were already clean. From her seat at the small table, Abby could see the kitchen led to a front room that had a big television, a couple of gaming consoles, and a stack of games. This place was so bare and sad, kind of like the girl. "Why?" she finally said.

"Why what?"

"Why doesn't he want people to call you anything? Doesn't he like the name he gave you?"

The girl finally stopped moving, her eyes locking with Abby's. "He didn't name me. He isn't my father."

"Then why are you here?"

Her dark eyes met Abby's. "Why do you think?"

"Because he took you like he took me and Thea."

"Smart girl."

Abby peeked down the hall and lowered her voice to a whisper. "Where is he now?"

"At the bottom of a cliff, hopefully," the girl grumbled.

"He's a bad man." Abby thought about the night he'd taken her into the shower. "What was he going to do to me?"

Her new friend stopped scrubbing the counter. She came back to the table and sat down across from Abby. Her stern expression reminded Abby of her mommy when she was upset with something she or her sister had done.

"You don't want to know," the girl finally answered. She pulled a plastic bag out of her pocket and studied the crushed, red powder. "I need to grind up more laxatives, but he'll catch on soon."

Abby didn't know what a laxative was, but she was certain the girl had something to do with the bad man's stomach problems. Part of her wanted to giggle at the panicked expression on his face when he'd thrown her out of the bathroom. She'd heard him on the toilet before he screamed at her to leave, and the older girl had led Abby back to their room with a sly smile on her tired-looking face.

"Your name is Abby, right?"

"Yes." Abby squirmed, trying to work up the courage to ask her next question. "How come you don't leave? We could leave now."

"Sweet pea, he's got cameras mounted everywhere." She held up her arm and pointed to the big watch on her wrist. "He can track me with this."

But he isn't here now, Abby wanted to say, her eyes on the watch. She was pretty sure her friend Alyssa had the same watch. It kept track of how many steps she took and her heart rate and a whole bunch of other things Abby didn't understand. It also had a phone... "Your watch is a phone!" Abby couldn't contain her excitement. "I've seen my friend use hers to send messages—"

"He doesn't pay for that plan. Believe me, I've tried."

Tears of frustration rolled down Abby's face. "I want to go home. I want my mommy." She gulped, trying to stop the big sobs that wanted to come out of her chest. When she could talk again, she asked another question. "How long have you been here?" Abby asked.

"With him?" The girl shrugged. "Long enough. He leaves me alone unless he makes me look for new girls like you and your sister."

Abby's eyes welled at the thought of Thea. Deep down, she knew that she'd never see her big sister again because of what the bad man had done to her. She started to cry again.

Rough fingers touched her knees. The older girl crouched in front of Abby, her eyes frighteningly serious. "I'm going to do everything I can to protect you, but that means you have to do what I say, when I say it, okay?"

Abby nodded. "What are you going to do?"

"I don't know, but people are looking for you and your sister," she said. "It's on the news. The FBI is looking for you and so are the police. It's only a matter of time before they figure things out... at least, I hope so. Point is, we stick together, and you do as I say, and we might be able to get out of here soon. But that's our secret, right? He'll kill us both if he finds out." The girl's pretty eyes looked dead serious. "Unless I kill him first."

Abby knew what that word meant. It was a terrible, awful sin. Mama had told them that certain sins couldn't be forgiven, and Abby was certain that killing was one of them. But Mama also talked about an eye for an eye, and Thea had explained that meant bad people get what they deserved sometimes. Abby was positive her mama would feel the same way about the bad, smelly man who'd taken her away.

"Okay," she said to the girl. "But what's your name?"

"Tori."

TWENTY-THREE

Nikki put the call on speaker. "Detective Johnson, I'm with Chief Ryan from the Stillwater PD and Sheriff Miller, the Washington County Sheriff. Can you repeat what you just asked me?" The mood of the room had shifted. A flurry of adrenaline swept through Nikki. They were getting close.

Johnson cleared his throat. "I asked why you're circulating a missing girl from Green Bay as a suspect in your kidnappings?"

Ryan's dark eyes looked over the rim of her glasses, while Miller unlocked his phone to record the call.

"This girl was seen walking north on the docks with our victims Saturday. The image was taken from CCTV at a cross-walk. You're certain it's your missing person?" Nikki asked.

"Positive. Tori Snyder disappeared during a Memorial Day parade five years ago. If you look closely, there's a birthmark on her cheek, down by her jaw. Almost looks like a peninsula."

Nikki enlarged the photo on her tablet. "I didn't even notice that."

"She also has a mole on her collarbone, almost dead center. It's right above her shirt collar in the photo."

"Tori disappeared during a major event, just like Thea and Abby," Nikki said. "Did you have any suspects?"

"None that were viable," Johnson said. "We had a bunch of volunteer firefighters out that night, because of fireworks, along with volunteer police officers to help control the crowd."

Nikki drummed her fingers on the table, remembering the few times she'd been to Green Bay. It wasn't as big as she'd expected, especially with a football team as popular as the Packers. She didn't know much about the city or its layout. "So did Stillwater. How close to Lake Michigan were the fireworks?"

"They were set off on the lake front, downtown."

"You have a marina there?" Miller asked.

"We have two marinas downtown, by the old Grassy Island Lighthouse. Why?"

Nikki told him about the fiber evidence Courtney had found, along with Thea's cause of death. "We think the girls were taken to a boat and locked in until the kidnapper could escape in the boat without anyone noticing. Thea died from heat exhaustion."

"And you don't have any leads on the other little girl?" Johnson asked.

"No," Nikki admitted. "Until you called, our working theory is that a jilted girlfriend took the girls to punish Doctor Walker, and things got out of control. But your information changes that." She rubbed her temples, wishing she could catch the stray thought racing in her mind. She'd been convinced that someone who either knew the girls or knew enough about them to gain their trust had kidnapped Abby and Thea. Much of the circumstantial evidence pointed to a connection to Walker, and stranger abductions were so rare that many agents referred to them as unicorns. Why hadn't Nikki kept that possibility on her list? She knew better than to rely on statistical evidence alone. What else had she missed?

The video Britney had taken on the jungle gym kept flashing in her head like a neon sign with a couple of letters out.

"You said you didn't have any good suspects," Miller said. "Anyone in particular stand out?"

While Johnson answered the questions, Nikki found the video Britney had taken that day. She played it on mute, using her phone to look frame by frame, her mouth going dry. "She was *right* there."

"I didn't catch that," Johnson said. "Say again?"

Miller and Ryan looked at her quizzically. She showed the paused video to Miller. "Look, under that maple tree, drinking soda." Her heart rate accelerated as she played the video again. Lacey could have been chosen instead of Thea and Abby.

Tori leaned against the tree trunk, arms folded across her chest. She watched the kids playing on the jungle gym intently. Without any context, she looked like a brooding teenager stuck watching her younger sibling play.

"That's the red flag," Nikki murmured. "She's a teenager doing nothing, without a phone."

She started to say more, but the words died in her throat. A painful knot formed in her chest as though she'd been struck. Bile brewed in her stomach. He'd been under their noses the entire time.

"Nicole."

Miller's sharp voice snapped Nikki out of her shock. "What is it?"

"Volunteer."

"What?" Miller asked.

Nikki tapped her laptop screen, trying not to shake from frustration. "See the muscular guy there, with the hairy arms? He's wearing a 'volunteer' shirt and hat, and he's making sure you can't see his face."

The three of them watched in silent horror as Bobby Merrill leaned in and said something to Tori. On autopilot, she walked to the jungle gym where the kids were playing. "You see him, Kent?"

"Yes." Miller's voice sounded hollow.

Ryan rolled her chair around to peer over Miller's shoulder. "Wasn't he one of the initial volunteers?"

"Yes," Nikki said. "He also picked up a Hawaiian pizza from No Neck's while Chen and I were there." She remembered Chen looking a little surprised when he heard the order, but she'd dismissed it. The pizza must have been for Abby.

"She's still alive." Nikki pushed away from the table. She explained her theory to the others. "He picked that pizza up yesterday, for Abby, because she likes pineapple pizza." Nikki had missed it then, but she wasn't going to miss anything else. "Detective Johnson, does the name Bobby Merrill sound familiar to you?"

"Merrill?" Johnson echoed. "Seems like that name might have been on the list of volunteers." Nikki heard the sound of shuffling papers. "Yeah, he was volunteer security for the fireworks that night. Helped with the search for Tori. Why?"

"I'm emailing you a video right now. Let me know when you receive."

They sat in silence, Ryan's manicured nails tapping against the table.

"Got it," Johnson said. "Let me get it going..."

"Look at the maple tree on the right side of your screen."

"That's Tori," Johnson exclaimed. "When was this taken?"

"Saturday, during the festival," Nikki answered. "The barrel-chested guy who leans in and talks to her is Bobby Merrill."

Johnson's sharp intake of breath let them know he'd watched until the end. "She's completely under his control. Do you know where this guy lives? How soon can you move on him?"

Nikki looked at Miller, who nodded. "As soon as we can get geared up. I'll call you as soon as I can."

She hung up the phone and looked at Miller. "Is Bobby Merrill's name on the slip rental list? The section Chen has?"

Miller searched his master list. "There's a K.R. Merrill, slip twenty-one." He glanced up at the map of the marinas they'd taped onto the wall. "That's the north end, damn it."

Nikki typed the name into Google and came up with an obituary from several years ago. "Kathy Richard Merrill's only child is Robert Merrill. She was an avid boater and known to spend nights on the water in her cabin cruiser. The obit picture is actually of her on the boat."

She enlarged the photo as much as possible. "No name on the boat, though. But my team might be able to figure out the model—"

"No need." Miller closed his laptop. "The boat's registered to Bobby Merrill. *The Sweet Marie.*"

Chen's strange reaction when he saw the list flashed through Nikki's mind. "Between that and the pizza order yesterday, Chen must have started putting things together when he saw the list," she told them. "Chen thinks Merrill killed his sister years ago, and he may be right." Nikki looked at the chief. "Where did Chen go? We have to stop him before he does something that ruins his life."

Ryan called dispatch and asked for Chen's location. "Chen's black and white is parked at 977 Norell Ave North," Chief Ryan said.

"That's north Washington County." Nikki pulled up the address on Google Earth. "Looks like an old farmhouse, surrounded by fields and woods. Some kind of metal barn or shed on the property." She ran the address through the system. "It's still in Merrill's mother's name, too." She chided herself for telling Chen to follow his leads on his own.

"Let's go," Miller said.

"I'm going with you," Chief Ryan said, rising from her chair.

"It's better if you stay here," Nikki said. "Shane Walker trusts you, and we need someone to coordinate from here."

"Agent Hunt, I just don't—"

"Chief, with all due respect, I don't have time for what you don't understand right now. And before you try to pull jurisdiction, I'll remind you that we now have a missing child from Wisconsin involved. That makes this my investigation."

"Then it will be your mess to clean up if you're wrong," she replied.

"I know," Nikki said. "But I'm not."

TWENTY-FOUR

She and Miller loaded the tactical gear in the back of her Jeep. Sweat stung her eyes, the humidity almost unbearable. The hot breeze from a few hours ago had stopped, leaving the air deadly calm. She pointed to the dark line of clouds to the northwest. "Let's hope we can move faster than that storm."

"You sure you don't want to call for backup?" Miller asked as Nikki put the Jeep into gear. "This guy could be holed up with guns." She gripped the wheel, trying to slow the adrenaline racing through her. The media had been watching the case like a hawk. If they called in SWAT or any kind of significant backup, Nikki was certain Merrill would find out before they could get in position. He'd been doing this long enough that he likely had an escape plan. They couldn't let him leave the area.

"I don't want to pour gas on the situation and put Chen in danger," Nikki said. "Can you have Reynolds and a few other deputies waiting down the road, ready to go if we need them?"

Miller nodded and called Reynolds, giving him directions. "Okay," he said after he'd finished the call. "How did you put all of this together so quickly?"

"Pineapples," Nikki said.

"I'm sorry?"

Nikki told him about running into Merrill at No Neck Tony's. "Bartender made a point to ask why he was getting pineapples on pizza. Saturday night, Britney said Abby's a 'quirky little girl who loves pineapple pizza and bugs.'"

Miller stared at her.

"It gets worse," Nikki said. "Chen's little sister Marie was murdered when she was eight, he was sixteen. While you were getting your gear, I did a little research. A drifter was charged with her murder, but guess who found the body?"

"Bobby Merrill." Miller spit the words out.

"Chen blamed himself for his sister's death for decades, and turns out, the wolf in sheep's clothing was right next to him all along." Nikki thought about her parents' real killer, who'd gone on to have a prosperous life for two decades before justice finally caught up with him. He'd been someone close to her, staying right by her side during the initial investigation, playing the concerned boyfriend as she sobbed over her murdered parents. "When I found out who really killed my parents, I almost killed him out of anger and a need for revenge. The thought of Lacey is the only thing that kept me from pulling the trigger." She cleared her throat. "I know how hard that was, how much I wanted to strangle him with my bare hands and watch him die. Chen's got to feel just as betrayed by Merrill."

"I hope we aren't too late," Miller said. "If Chen figures this out and kills Merrill before we find Abby, we may never find her alive."

Northeastern Washington County always reminded Nikki of the big north woods, despite the spattering of rural homes and cornfields. Known as the unincorporated community of Scandia, it was named after the Swedish settlers who first settled the area. In its height, the community stretched to west of Big Marine Lake, and several original buildings, including a schoolhouse dating back to the late 1800s, had been preserved to celebrate the area's heritage. As thick as the trees were, she knew logging had taken many of them out, and for once, she was grateful for natural resources being squandered. Less woods to contend with was always a good thing when it came to law enforcement.

Miller opened a battered map of Washington County that he carried everywhere. "Merrill's address is off St. Croix Trail, near the intersection of 240th Street and the Washington and Chisago county borders, by Cedar Bend."

The history nerd in Nikki remembered learning about the Cedar Bend, the part of the river that curved east. The scenic byway followed the St. Croix River and had been established in the 1850s as a route for troops moving between Point Douglas, Minnesota, and Superior, Wisconsin. An 1825 treaty had established an imaginary line across the bend in the hopes to end bloodshed, keeping the Sioux south of the line and the Ojibwa north of it. "North or south of the bend?"

"North," Miller answered. "His property has woods on the north and south sides, cornfields to the west and the road to the east. Reynolds is set up a mile from the property. Chisago's supposed to fortify their side." He glanced at Nikki. "The SWAT leader has been told to ready the team but to stay put for now."

"Let's hope we don't have to call them," Nikki said. "Let's get a good look at the actual property and see if we can locate Chen and hopefully any sort of security traps."

They'd located the property online before leaving the sheriff station, so they knew Merrill owned ten acres and lived in the dilapidated farmhouse with a sizeable clearing. It wouldn't be the first time a predator like Merrill had booby-trapped his yard.

As Nikki crested the hill, she saw Deputy Reynolds pacing next to his patrol vehicle. Her heart kicked into high gear. As much as she trusted Miller, she wished Liam had been able to join them. In situations similar, Nikki would draw the bad guy out while Liam prowled the perimeter out of sight, ready to intercept a running suspect.

But Liam wasn't here, and that had been his own doing. She couldn't think about it right now.

She parked the Jeep behind his cruiser, Miller's feet hitting the gravel before she'd shifted to park. Nikki eyed the north-western sky. The storm had started to move in, although it was still a few miles away. Angry thunderclouds loomed in the distance.

"Any sign of them?" Miller asked.

"No, sir," Reynolds answered. "The SPD cruiser is there, in the clearing in front of the house." He paced next to his car. "I know Danny Chen. He's a good cop. We can't let him do this alone."

"He's not." Miller instructed Reynolds to stay in position and be ready to intercept if Merrill tried to run. "Going by the satellite images, the only way Merrill can leave the property in a vehicle is his driveway. Chicago deputies are watching the county line and have set up a roadblock on the main road. But since his property is adjacent to the river, there's plenty of woods and wetland to hide in."

Nikki pulled her thick hair into a ponytail before putting on the hot Kevlar. She double-checked her pistol, made sure she had an extra magazine of ammo, along with her knife slipped into her left boot. It had saved her life more than once. "Any-thing else we should know?" she asked Reynolds.

"Property is surrounded by an electric fence, and I'm assuming it's live. Two-story farmhouse, metal storage shed. I didn't notice anything else suspicious in the yard, but I'd keep an eye out." Reynolds unlocked his phone and showed them the photos he'd taken. The front yard was mostly weeds growing up to Nikki's waist, so they had to assume anything—or anyone—could be hiding. "I don't think we should approach from the front."

"Agreed." Miller pointed to the cornfield across the road. "We sneak through there, then we can take cover at this outdoor shed." He tapped the map. "Reynolds, can you draw him out front without being seen? Create a distraction?"

"Absolutely." Reynolds wiped the sweat off his brow. "I've been saving some M-150 firecrackers to prank my lady. If I set those off behind Chen's vehicle, anyone in that house is going to come running."

Thanks to Rory and Mark, Nikki knew the M-150s were the short, red firecrackers that popped off loudly on the ground with some sparks instead of shooting into the sky. To the untrained ear, they sounded like gunshots, and they scared the hell out of everyone within earshot.

"Once that happens, we cross the yard to the house. Nikki and I will hopefully be able to figure out how many people are inside, including Chen." Miller looked at the deputy. "Cell phones on silent, but watch your text messages. Don't want to use the radios once we're close to the house. What do you think, Nikki?"

Nikki tried to muster the words to agree, but the idea of walking through the cornfield, as she'd done the night her parents had been murdered, made her weak at the knees. It hadn't been as hot, but the corn had been even taller, close to harvesting. She'd darted into the cornfield in a blind panic, heading for the neighbors. To this day, she wasn't sure how she'd navigated the field to the closest house. Nikki pushed the memory out of her head and nodded at Miller.

They jogged across the road in silence. Sweat stung Nikki's

eyes, the bulletproof vest feeling like an iron corset. Her heart hammered against her chest as they approached the cornfield. This far into the summer, the corn topped five feet. She hesitated at the edge.

"You want to try another way?" Miller asked.

"No," Nikki said. "This is the best way, and the field isn't all that big. Like you said, we walk straight north and hit the other side." She took a deep breath and stepped into the field, making sure to crouch low enough for the corn to hide her. She tried to ignore the heat and the smell of mildewed corn, an issue farmers fought all season long. A few feet into the field and the stalks closed behind them, swallowing them up. Nikki led the way without looking behind her. The rule of thumb for planting corn was 8–10 inches, but these had been planted closer together, leaving little room for sunlight or people to move through without wrestling with the stalks. Merrill had likely done so to provide more protection from the outside world. The house wasn't even visible from the road.

Gnats and various insects seemed to form a halo around Nikki's head. She kept her mouth shut and waved her hand in front of her face as she slipped between the stalks. Spotted-winged stink bugs feasted off the plants. Nikki shuddered and kept walking. She could watch an autopsy of a child, but bugs were another story. God only knew how many spiders... no, she couldn't go there, or she'd start thinking about all the creepy-crawlies that were probably taking a ride on her shoes.

It only took a few minutes to work through the field, but the plants' height and proximity made airflow next to nothing. Nikki was soaked in sweat and her face felt like she'd stuck it into the oven. Finally, light began to peek out between the stalks. In the time it took to cross the field, the sky grew darker, the storm clouds creeping in front of the sun. Miller pushed through the plants to stand next to Nikki. Only a few rows of corn separated them from the yard, but any further and they'd likely be spotted.

He crouched next to her, and they watched the house for a few minutes. Nikki listened, hoping to hear Chen and Merrill, but there was only eerie silence.

Every damned bug in the cornfield seemed to converge on them. Nikki hissed as gnats hovered near her eyes and nose. Between the smothering heat and the bugs, she wasn't going to last much longer.

Thunder growled in the distance.

They could see the second floor of the house on the other side of the shed. Both windows were covered by blinds or curtains, giving up nothing about the activity inside the house. Nikki's best estimate was that they had to have been separated by less than one hundred yards. The house looked like every other old, white farmhouse, including the one she'd grown up in, but without any of the TLC her parents had always provided. Blinds covered all the windows.

"What do you think?" Miller's voice was barely audible. "It's damn quiet. Chen might be in trouble."

Nikki went over the plan one more time in her head. She was a fast runner, and no one seemed to be around. She scanned the trees and top of the house for a shooter one more time. "Text Reynolds. I'm ready."

Time seemed to stand still as they waited for Reynolds' distraction. Nikki tried not to think about all of the things that could go wrong. In less than a minute, the fireworks started going off in rapid succession. Nikki crept forward, keeping her gun ready. No time to waste.

She took a deep breath and sprinted across the yard to the shed, trying to stay as low as possible. She made it to the shed and listened, her heart racing. The fireworks had stopped, and the area remained silent. She signaled Miller to follow, and he joined her, both panting from the heat. They moved in unison

around the side of the metal building until Nikki had a full view
of the house. She scanned the front yard. The air reeked of gun
powder, and the charred remains of the fireworks were a few
feet behind Chen's cruiser. Nikki saw no sign of Chen, Merrill,
or the girls.

"Something's wrong," Nikki said. "There's no way he didn't
hear that from inside the house."

"No sign of Chen, either."

The silence was deafening, save for the low rumble of
approaching thunder. Lightning flashed through the clouds.
Nikki hoped it stayed up there.

"No one in the downstairs window," she whispered,
picturing Merrill hiding behind the blinds with a sniper rifle.
"At least not that I can see. Cover me."

Gun ready, she stalked toward the house, careful to stay low
and use the unkempt grounds to her advantage. Old, plastic
furniture and a barbeque that had seen better days sat on the
cracked patio. The sliding glass door on the patio was open.
Nikki glanced back at Miller, who nodded.

Her body tight against the rotting wood siding, Nikki
inched along toward the door, careful to avoid the window overlooking the patio. Sweat ran into her eyes, but she could feel the
cold air seeping out of the house. When she reached the door,
she paused and listened for any sign she wasn't alone. She
retrieved her phone from her back pocket and turned on the
camera to face her. The sight of her red face didn't deter Nikki.
She slowly eased the phone in front of the door, her eyes on her
phone.

She saw only a small, dingy kitchen. Without looking back,
Nikki signaled for Miller. He joined her seconds later. The sky
darkened further. Unkempt bushes lashed at the windows from
the increasing wind.

They snuck inside, past the uneven table and mismatched
chairs. Despite its small size and poor lighting, the kitchen was

clean to the point of being sterile. Nikki's heart thundered against her chest; her breathing sounded like she'd been running a marathon. She paused and listened for movement upstairs, but the only sound came from the growing storm.

Until the gunshot.

TWENTY-FIVE

Nikki and Miller raced outside, Miller radioing Reynolds for backup. The deputy jogged out of the woods, sweating and red-faced.

"You hear what direction that shot game from?" Miller shouted.

"North, I think," Reynolds said. "Sounded close."

Nikki double checked her ammo while Miller radioed for backup. The still air unnerved her. She scanned the horizon for funnel clouds. It was only a matter of time before the weather became dangerous.

"Better grab the first aid kit." She stopped in mid-stride, the hair on the back of her neck rising. She turned to the cornfield, following its curved path to the side of the house. A few feet from the field's edge, the stalks moved as someone slowly cut a path.

"Take cover," she hissed. The men obeyed, and Nikki joined them on the other side of the patrol car. "West side of the field. Someone's walking through." On her hands and knees, she peered under the police car and waited to see men's boots emerge.

Instead, Nikki saw bare legs and feet. Two pairs of them. All three eased around the car, their gaze on the two girls standing at the edge of the field. She couldn't believe what she was seeing.

Nikki holstered her gun and pulled her FBI badge out of her pocket. "I pray to God this isn't a trap." With Reynolds and Miller covering her, Nikki walked toward the girls, her hands in the air. "Are you okay?" The older girl pushed Abby behind her. "Tori, right? My name is Nikki. I'm a special agent with the FBI. We're here to help you." She eyed the girl's T-shirt, stained with fresh blood. "Is that yours? Do you need help?"

"It's not mine." Tori's flat monotone made her sound almost robotic. She'd probably become that way after years of torment from Merrill. "He found the crushed laxatives when he got home." A smile played on Tori's mouth. "He wasn't very happy with me."

"Is that Merrill's blood?"

Tori nodded. "He was coming for me when there was a loud bang on the front door. A man kept shouting that he knew what Merrill had done. He told me not to move while he handled things. I started to do what I was told, but then I saw the police car. He must have realized I knew, because he started coming at me again." She pulled something out of her back pocket. It was an impressive shiv, made out of metal with jagged edges. It was also coated in sticky blood.

"Where did you get that?"

"I made it. Kept it hidden for the right time." Tori looked at the shiv and smiled. "He never saw it coming." Her smile vanished. "Didn't kill him, but it gave me enough time to take Abby and run. The other cop saw us, said to hide in the field, so we did. Not long after that, we heard a gunshot. He ran out the back door and into the woods. The other cop followed him, but he's hurt worse than him."

Tori's matter-of-fact delivery made Nikki wonder if she

would ever recover from what she'd experienced. How long had Merrill made her help him in his sick endeavors? "Which direction?"

Tori pointed northwest, toward the storm and the wetland area. Lightning struck again, followed closely by thunder. Abby burrowed into Tori's side. "How long ago?"

"Like minutes before you crossed the yard, like I said."

The girls had been watching the entire time, with Tori no doubt sizing them up before she revealed herself and Abby. "Can you stay with Deputy Reynolds while the sheriff and I look for Sergeant Chen and Merrill?"

Tori's expression twisted. "As long as you promise to put a bullet in his head."

Nikki's heart hurt for the girl, but they didn't have any time to waste. She introduced Reynolds just as the wail of approaching sirens came within earshot.

"Called it in with a different code," Reynolds told her. "Trying to keep the media out of here. You guys go; I got this."

"Call Chief Ryan and let her know the girls are safe and get an ambulance out here. Have her round up the Walkers."

"You okay with that?" Nikki asked the two girls.

Tori stared at her with blank eyes. How old had she been when Merrill grew tired of her and decided to use her as bait?

Nikki and Miller moved into the forest just as the clouds unleashed. She didn't mind the cool rain as it washed over them. It made the Kevlar feel less like a hot, weighted blanket. "How big is this area?" She should have studied the map.

"Maybe a couple of square miles, probably closer to 1.5," Miller said. "That's like seven hundred football fields." Miller had been Stillwater High's star running back in high school and liked to use football fields as measurements so his deputies had a better sense of how much land they were covering. "I'd say more than half is woods, but the rest are wetlands."

"You can say swamp," Nikki grumbled. The wetlands were probably more like a marsh, but Nikki didn't really understand all of the technical differences, only that the wetlands were vital to Minnesota wildlife. "Good thing we're already soaked."

They slipped through the woods in silence. Nikki kept her eyes on the trees in case Merrill had climbed up one of the massive trees to hide. Less than a hundred feet in front of them, lightning exploded, splitting a scrawny birch tree down the middle.

"Jesus," Miller called. "Maybe we should take cover for a few minutes until the worst passes."

"It already has," Nikki said. "It's moving east at a fast rate, and we're headed west. If we keep walking, we'll get out of it."

Miller looked skeptical, but agreed. "Reynolds is communicating with the Chisago County guys in case he makes it across the wetlands into their area."

They trudged on, and within minutes, the storm had moved far enough east the wind stopped howling and the rain slowed to a trickle. The forest seemed to come alive then, with birds calling back to one another. A pair of crows perched on a low-hanging branch, watching them.

The storm had broken through much of the humidity, but it was still hot, and they were drenched. Her feet were soggy inside her even wetter sneakers.

"I just got a text from Ryan," Miller called. "Chen's phone is on. According to the app, it's about fifty feet ahead, which looks to be where the forest ends and the wetlands really start."

They both crouched as low as possible and eased forward. Without speaking, Miller moved to the left and Nikki to the right, ready to face an attack from all angles. Leopard frogs hopped along the edge of the marsh. She didn't want to think about all the species of snake that called the wetlands home. Hopefully snapping turtles weren't also living here.

"Chen." Miller rushed forward through a break in the trees.

Nikki's heart sank at the sight of the sergeant face down in the marsh, his blood staining the water. Miller checked for his pulse, and Chen groaned, lifting his head out of the watery weeds. "Shoulder," he gasped as Miller helped him roll over. "I think my leg is broken, too. Be careful, there's a hole here somewhere."

Miller radioed for help and started assessing Chen. "Straight through," Miller said.

Chen didn't have a bullet inside him, but Nikki was more worried about infection. At least thirty minutes had passed since the gunshots, and Chen had been lying face down in animal muck and marsh water. He needed antibiotics.

"Tori and Abby are in the field," Chen managed to say.

"We found them. They're safe," Nikki said. "Where did Merrill go?"

"He ran through the wetlands," Chen said. "I know where he's headed. His family owned most of this land until his mother died. He's got another cabin boat... it's anchored across from the little island in the middle of the river. He's wounded, too. Go west." Chen grimaced in pain. He needed a hospital.

Nikki looked at Miller and he nodded. She knew he couldn't leave the sergeant, but they'd lost a lot of time. Merrill could have crossed the river into Wisconsin by now. They didn't have time to wait for backup.

She waded into the marsh, oblivious to the angry, honking geese warning her to stay away. She tried not to think about the snakes as she slogged through the murky, knee-high water. Chen said to head west, toward the river, and she could see it now, through a gap in the willow trees.

Nikki tried to run through the water, but throngs of weeds slowed her down. Her feet finally hit mostly dry land, and

Nikki scurried behind a hulking willow tree, its long-hanging branches skimming the ground. She caught her breath and scanned the river.

Less than thirty feet in front of her, the St. Croix River flowed at an alarming rate. Last week's torrential rain caused the river to swell, and today's storm had only made the water angry, the current moving dangerously fast. Nikki didn't know how that worked, but she knew dangerous water when she saw it. Surely Merrill wouldn't be so stupid as to go out on this.

Then she saw the fishing boat, overturned, its rusting aluminum hull bobbing in the water.

"Bastard."

Had Merrill really drowned? Or had he used the boat to trick them? She should have grabbed the binoculars out of the Jeep.

Movement came from behind her and Nikki turned, expecting Miller. Before she could react, a red-faced, sweating and wild-eyed Merrill charged at her. He rammed his shoulder into her side and pinned her down to the ground, her head hitting the wet earth hard, her gun still clutched in her right hand. She gasped, trying to catch her breath after the impact. Merrill sat back on his knees, breathing almost as hard as Nikki. Blood stained his right side, running down his jeans and soaking his shoe.

"That little bitch stabbed me." Merrill pressed his dirty hand to the wound and winced. His eyes burned with hate for Nikki as he pulled a hunting knife from the sheath that hung on his belt. "Guess I will have to take my revenge on you." He trailed the tip of the knife along her jaw, down to her pulsing carotid artery.

"Chen's alive," Nikki said. "He knows the truth, so does Sheriff Miller and probably every cop in the area by now. You won't make it out of Washington County."

"You'd be surprised at how resourceful I can be, Agent

Hunt." He rolled his eyes. "Why in the hell did you have to show up? I had a good thing going." He pressed the tip of the knife into her neck.

"You killed his little sister, didn't you?"

Merrill snickered. "I have to tell you, I think he should have figured it out a lot earlier. I was right next to him the whole time. He tell you I discovered her body?"

"You were his friend." Nikki stalled for time, praying that Miller would emerge from the trees.

"That's what made it so easy. And so much fun." The knife still pressed into her neck, but his eyes had a faraway look, and she could feel his body reacting to his memories as he kept Nikki pinned down. Nikki struggled beneath him, her eyes on the river behind them. A familiar, purple Vikings hat stood out against the trees.

Merrill was still lost in his memories, hovering over her, his hot breath on her cheek. Heart pounding, Nikki seized her chance. She jammed two fingers into the bleeding wound on his side with all the strength she could muster. He screamed in pain and jerked upright.

Nikki closed her eyes right before the bullet shattered Merrill's skull. His body stilled and he started to fall on her again, but Nikki thrashed beneath his weight. She braced her hands on his chest and heaved. Merrill fell to the side, his eyes still open in his mangled skull.

She slowly sat up, groaning in pain. Merrill had broken at least one of her ribs, maybe two. But she would live, and so would little Abby. And Tori, whose quick actions might have saved them all. A shout came from the other side of the river.

Liam, in his old Vikings hat, still had the rifle poised to shoot.

"Stand down," she shouted. "Stand down."

EPILOGUE

"Are you sure this is a good idea?" Nikki asked as Rory let Lacey take the wheel.

"We're in open water," he said. "Take her away, Lace." Rory gave the engine a little gas, and Lacey squealed as the boat moved in the water. "Turn the wheel to the left, and we'll go in a circle."

Nikki held onto the side of the boat while Lacey did donuts in the middle of Big Marine Lake. Summer was in its last days, with school starting next week. Rory and Mark had finished the boat, and after a couple of test runs, deemed it worthy for Nikki and Lacey to take a ride.

"Now go to the right," Rory said. "But not so fast. Ease her around."

"Why is it a her?" Lacey asked, her little tongue sticking out of her mouth as she concentrated.

"I don't know," Rory said. "I think it goes back to the old days and the fishermen who spent more time with their ships than their families."

"The boat was the old lady?" Lacey asked.

Rory laughed. "Something like that."

As her daughter laughed and asked Rory countless questions, Nikki thought about the Walkers. Abby had been reunited with her parents, and while she'd been traumatized from the kidnapping, Tori had managed to protect the little girl from being assaulted.

Tori refused treatment at the hospital. Nikki had missed the Walker family reunion, but Reynolds had told them that Abby immediately asked if they could adopt Tori. She clung to Tori's hand even when she crawled into her mother's lap. Britney promised they would take care of Tori until her parents arrived.

Reynolds told Nikki he'd been worried by the lack of reaction from Tori when she heard her parents were on their way, and he'd made sure that a victim's advocate was available.

Nikki had been afraid the trauma would prevent Tori from recognizing or even reacting to her parents, but Reynolds said the moment she'd heard her mother's voice, she'd leapt to her feet and run to her.

She'd still said very little about what happened to her, but she admitted that Merrill forced her to bring other girls to him, and she'd been so abused that she didn't think she had any other choice.

Tori had told Britney that it was Thea's desire to protect Abby that had got her killed. After she'd given the girls to Merrill on his boat, he'd locked them up in the storage well that housed the pop-up table. Abby had cried, telling Merrill her sister needed her medicine or she'd get really sick. Since she hadn't seen his face, Merrill debated releasing Thea, but Thea had spoken up and said she didn't need medicine, her little sister was lying. She'd protected Abby with her life and Tori had vowed to do the same.

Tori had been kept at Merrill's cabin or on the boat, never out of his sight, until she got too old for them, and by then, he'd broken her psychologically. He'd given her an Apple AirTag on Saturday night and told her that if she lost it, he'd kill her. She didn't know what it was, but she'd recognized the familiar logo, and she was so brainwashed and broken that she obeyed. He'd spent years telling her that her parents wouldn't want her back after what she'd done, that he was all she had.

Knowing what he wanted her to do, Tori had asked if she could stop at the cash station and pay cash for a soda to calm her. Merrill gave her five bucks, but he didn't realize that she'd been scrounging for change around the house for months. Instead of soda, Tori purchased the laxative. She kept the tablets under her mattress, knowing Merrill wouldn't pay any attention to her with the little girl in the house. Tori had smashed the pills to a fine powder, which she hid in the floss container she always carried with her. Since Merrill didn't do dentists, Tori had convinced him to let her start flossing a couple of years ago, and she kept it in her pocket at all times. Merrill believed his control over her was so complete that he didn't pay much attention to the meals she prepared or how she mixed his drink.

Reynolds said that Tori couldn't look Britney in the eye while she told her what happened to Thea, but Britney had taken the girl's hand and told her it wasn't her fault, that she and God would never hold Tori responsible. The two families remained in contact, giving Nikki hope for both girls to recover.

It turned out that Merrill had been a volunteer firefighter in at least six different Midwestern states in the last decade, and a child abduction had happened at each one, all of them at summer events. He stuck to urban centers, always on the river or one of the great lakes. He refused to discuss what had happened to the other missing kids, but thanks to his friendship with Chen, the sergeant knew Merrill owned sixty acres in northern Iowa. Within minutes, the K9 found the first grave. Over the course of the next week, the remains of five girls under ten years old were recovered and taken to the state lab for testing and identification. The final grave belonged to a young adolescent woman around Tori's age. They were still working to identify the remains, and Tori had sat with the sketch artist, doing her best to describe the older girl Merrill had used to lure Tori five years ago. She remembered the older girl disappearing after trying to protect Tori from Merrill's advances. According to Tori, Merrill bided his time with each kidnapping. She'd yet to figure out why he'd chosen to keep her instead of one of the other girls he'd kidnapped. Thea and Abby's kidnapping had been the first one he'd forced Tori to help with, and she'd paid attention to every detail. It didn't take her long to realize that Merrill may have finally made his big mistake, because Thea and Abby weren't lost little girls he'd found like the others after Tori. Thea and Abby had been like her, lured away right under her parents' noses. Tori said Merrill watched the news after each new kidnapping, and she'd never seen him worried until then.

Chen had taken a leave of absence, but he'd assured Nikki that he would return. He had good instincts, an essential part of being a good cop. Chief Ryan had assured Nikki that SPD would provide Chen with counseling as part of his return to work, but Nikki had also given him the name of a handful of therapists in the area who specialized in PTSD, including her own. He'd been resistant at first, but hearing that Nikki still saw her therapist twice a month had changed his mind.

She wondered if Shane and Alyssa had told Britney the truth yet. Alyssa had come to the hospital not long after the Walkers, and Nikki could see the love she had for Abby, but she could also see the genuine affection in Shane's eyes. Given Britney's kind nature, she thought the family would be just fine.

By the time Nikki, Chen and Miller emerged from the wetlands, the police swarmed Merrill's property. An SPD officer took Chen to the waiting ambulance while Nikki scanned the sea of officers until she found the red head among them. Liam sat on a wide, decaying tree stump, the rifle on the ground next to him. She took a few seconds to catch her breath.

"I called him in," Miller said. "I had a bad feeling, and I didn't want to tell you about it because you'd have said no, he could damage the case."

"He could have," Nikki said. "But I'm glad you made the call."

She'd headed over to Liam then. He'd eyed her with trepidation, clearly worried she would be more focused on the legal issues stemming from his involvement.

"Before you say anything, I'd do it again," he said. "My orders were to stay on the perimeter and keep an eye out for Merrill or officers in trouble. I did that, and I don't think a judge is going to care. Especially since Merrill's dead."

Nikki had motioned for him to make room on the stump. "I thought he was going to kill me. Then I saw this flash of ginger-red moving along the river." She nudged him in the ribs. "Knew it was you, and I knew you wouldn't miss. How's Zach?"

"Coming home tomorrow," Liam said. "He wants to be homeschooled. That's where it's the worst because teenagers are awful."

"Is Caitlin going to homeschool him?"

Liam snorted. "Yeah, right. His grandmother's going to do it. She was a teacher. Hopefully between that and more counseling, he'll get better."

"He will. He's got a great support system."

Lacey's screech brought Nikki back to the present. "Mom, you see that big old fish jump?"

"I sure did," Nikki said. "I bet you can't catch it, even with the best worms."

Lacey swiveled in Rory's lap and gave her a death stare. "Watch me."

A LETTER FROM STACY

I want to say a huge thank you for choosing to read *Her Last Tear*. If you did enjoy it, and want to keep up to date with all my latest releases, including the next Nikki Hunt thriller, just sign up at the following link. Your email address will never be shared and you can unsubscribe at any time.

www.bookouture.com/stacy-green

I started writing this book last August, and it had its challenges from the very beginning. My father had a health issue that required a rehab stint, and then, the Saturday after Thanksgiving, he fell and hit his head on his way back from the bathroom. Initially, we thought we'd dodged a bullet, but the blood thinner he took caused a brain bleed. Even then, we thought he was going to be out of the woods, but the seizures started, and it took weeks to get things under control. The Wednesday before Christmas, due to an imposing storm, the hospital pushed for his release to a nursing facility. I met him there Wednesday, and he seemed to understand what was going on. He'd been in the hospital with seizures and unable to swallow, so he had a feeding tube. The nursing home administrator assured me they could handle it. But that night, he tried to get up, because he was unsupervised, pulling his tube out. He was taken to the hospital where it was fixed and then brought back to the nursing home. When I saw him Thursday, he kept saying his "belly hurt so bad." Every time I expressed my concern, the nursing administrator said it was because he pulled the tube out. He was septic by the next day and spent more than a week in the ICU without getting better.

I had to make the decision to let him go, and it was the hardest thing I've done. He wasn't able to come off the vent, and most of the time wasn't responsive. But when I went to the hospital the last time, I told him how much I loved him and how sorry I was, that I'd failed him, even though I know I did everything I could, and it was a storm of bad circumstances. A tear rolled out of his eye, and it gave me some peace to know he heard. My husband and I stayed with him in hospice for more than sixteen hours, listening to his ragged breathing and trying to let him know that he wasn't alone.

Dad is the reason I love mystery and detective stuff, as well as history and basketball. I have so many wonderful memories watching the 90s Bulls with him, and one day I know it won't hurt to think about them. As you can imagine, I lost significant writing time, which caused the delay of this book. But thanks to the support of my husband, daughter, friends and Bookouture, I got through the days and started writing again. As tough as this book was to create, I'm proud of the finished product, and it marks a turning point of sorts for Nikki. I'm working on book eight right now, and it's going to be my most twisted yet!

I hope you loved *Her Last Tear* and if you did I would be very grateful if you could write a review. I'd love to hear what you think, and it makes such a difference helping new readers to discover one of my books for the first time.

I love hearing from my readers – you can get in touch on Facebook, Twitter, Instagram or my website.

Thanks,
Stacy

KEEP IN TOUCH WITH STACY

www.stacygreenauthor.com

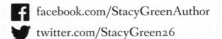 facebook.com/StacyGreenAuthor

twitter.com/StacyGreen26

instagram.com/authorstacygreen

ACKNOWLEDGMENTS

Thank you to the editors at Bookouture for keeping the faith as I struggled through the last year. To Lisa Regan, Maureen Downey and Tessa Russ, thank you for the encouraging words and putting up with the chaos that is my life. John Kelly, thank you for being my sounding board and expert on the lakes and Washington County region. I couldn't have written this book without the help of the Stillwater chief of police, Brian Mueller. His help was vital in making sure the opening scenes were correct from an investigation standpoint. Thank you to Julianne O'Connell from the historic Warden's House for her help nailing down the historical aspects.

And finally, thank you to Rob and Grace for being there through all of this. I simply would not have made it through alone.

Made in United States
North Haven, CT
26 May 2024

52964450R00157